PENGUIN

*Collected Sh*



Edward Morgan Forster was born in Lon Tonbridge School as a day boy, and went on to King's College, Cambridge, in 1897. With King's he had a lifelong connection and was elected to an Honorary Fellowship in 1946. He declared that his life as a whole had not been dramatic, and he was unfailingly modest about his achievements. Interviewed by the B.B.C. on his eightieth birthday, he said: 'I have not written as much as I'd like to . . . I write for two reasons: partly to make money and partly to win the respect of people whom I respect . . . I had better add that I am sure that I am not a great novelist.' Eminent critics and the general public have judged otherwise and in his obituary *The Times* called him 'one of the most esteemed English novelists of his time'.

He wrote six novels, four of which appeared before the First World War, *Where Angels Fear to Tread* (1905), *The Longest Journey* (1907), *A Room with a View* (1908), and *Howards End* (1910). An interval of fourteen years elapsed before his most famous, and perhaps his greatest work, *A Passage to India*, was published. It won both the Prix Femina Vie Heureuse and the James Tait Black Memorial Prize. *Maurice*, his novel on a homosexual theme, finished in 1914, was published posthumously in 1971. He also published two volumes of short stories; two collections of essays; a critical work, *Aspects of the Novel*; *The Hill of Devi*, a fascinating record of two visits Forster made to the Indian State of Dewas Senior; two biographies; two books about Alexandria (where he worked for the Red Cross in the First World War), and, with Eric Crozier, the libretto for Britten's opera *Billy Budd*. He died in June 1970.

E. M. FORSTER

# COLLECTED SHORT STORIES

*

PENGUIN BOOKS

PENGUIN BOOKS

Published by the Penguin Group
Penguin Books Ltd, 80 Strand, London WC2R 0RL, England
Penguin Putnam Inc., 375 Hudson Street, New York, New York 10014, USA
Penguin Books Australia Ltd, 250 Camberwell Road, Camberwell, Victoria 3124, Australia
Penguin Books Canada Ltd, 10 Alcorn Avenue, Toronto, Ontario, Canada M4V 3B2
Penguin Books India (P) Ltd, 11 Community Centre, Panchsheel Park, New Delhi – 110 017, India
Penguin Books (NZ) Ltd, Cnr Rosedale and Airborne Roads, Albany, Auckland, New Zealand
Penguin Books (South Africa) (Pty) Ltd, 24 Sturdee Avenue, Rosebank 2196, South Africa

Penguin Books Ltd, Registered Offices: 80 Strand, London WC2R 0RL, England

www.penguin.com

This collection first published by Sidgwick & Jackson 1947
Published in Penguin Books 1954
Reprinted in Penguin Classics 2002
1



Printed and bound in Great Britain by Antony Rowe Ltd, Chippenham, Wiltshire
Set in Monotype Caslon

# INTRODUCTION

THESE fantasies were written at various dates previous to the first world war, and represent all that I have accomplished in a particular line. Much has happened since: transport has been disorganized, frontiers rectified on the map and in the spirit, there has been a second world war, there are preparations for a third, and Fantasy to-day tends to retreat or to dig herself in or to become apocalyptic out of deference to the atom-bomb. She can be caught in the open here by those who care to catch her. She flits over the scenes of Italian and English holidays, or wings her way with even less justification towards the countries of the future. She or he. For Fantasy, though often female, sometimes resembles a man, and even functions for Hermes who used to do the smaller behests of the gods – messenger, machine-breaker, and conductor of souls to a not-too-terrible hereafter.

The opening item, The Story of a Panic, is the first story I ever wrote and the attendant circumstances remain with me vividly. After I came down from Cambridge – the Cambridge to which I have just returned – I travelled abroad for a year, and I think it was in the May of 1902 that I took a walk near Ravello. I sat down in a valley, a few miles above the town, and suddenly the first chapter of the story rushed into my mind as if it had waited for me there. I received it as an entity and wrote it out as soon as I returned to the hotel. But it seemed unfinished and a few days later I added some more until it was three times as long; as now printed. Of these two processes, the first – that of sitting down on the theme as if it were an anthill – has been rare. I did it again next year in Greece, where the whole of The Road from Colonus hung ready for me in a hollow tree not far from Olympia. And I did it, or rather tried it on, a third time, in Cornwall, at the Gurnard's Head. Here, just in the same way, a story met me, and, since the Panic and Colonus had both been published and admired, I embraced it as a masterpiece. It was about a man who was saved from drowning by some fishermen, and knew not how to reward them. What is your life worth? £5? £5,000? He ended by giving nothing, he lived among them, hated and despised. As the theme swarmed over me, I put my hand into my purse, drew out a golden sovereign – they existed then – and inserted it into a collecting-box of the Royal Lifeboat Institution which had been erected upon the Gurnard's Head for such situations as this. I could well afford it. I was bound to make the money over and again. Calm sea, flat submerged rock whereon my hero was to cling and stagger, village whence his rescuers should sally – I carried off the lot, and only had to improvise his wife, a very understanding woman. The Rock was the title of this ill-fated effort. It was a complete flop. Not an editor would look at it. My inspiration had been genuine but worthless, like so much inspiration, and I have never sat down on a theme since.

One of my novels, *The Longest Journey*, does indeed depend from an encounter with the genius loci, but indirectly, complicatedly, not here to be considered. Directly, the genius loci has only inspired me thrice, and on the third occasion it deprived me of a sovereign. As a rule, I am set going by my own arguments or memories, or by the motion of my pen, and the various methods do not necessarily produce a discordant result. If the reader will compare the first chapter of The Story of a Panic, caught straight off the spot it describes, with the two subsequent chapters, in which I set myself to wonder what would happen afterwards, I do not think he will notice that a fresh hemisphere has swung into action. All a writer's faculties, including the valuable faculty of faking, do conspire together thus for the creative act, and often do contrive an even surface, one putting in a word here, another there.

The other stories call for little comment from their author. The Machine Stops is a reaction to one of the earlier heavens of H. G. Wells. The Eternal Moment, though almost an honest-to-God yarn, is a meditation on Cortina d'Ampezzo. As for The Point of It, it was ill-liked when it came out by my Bloomsbury friends. 'What *is* the point of it?' they queried thinly, nor did I know how to reply.

Original publication was in two volumes. The first was named after *The Celestial Omnibus*, and was dedicated 'To the Memory of the Independent Review'. This was a monthly, controlled by an editorial board of friends who had encouraged me to start writing; another friend, Roger Fry, designed the book-cover and end-paper. The second volume came out many years later. It was called *The*

*Eternal Moment*, and I dedicated it 'To T. E. in the absence of anything else'. T. E. was Lawrence of Arabia.

Now that the stories are gathered together into a single cover, and are sailing farther into a world they never foresaw, should they be dedicated anew? Perhaps, and perhaps to a god. Hermes Psychopompus suggests himself, who came to my mind at the beginning of this introduction. He can anyhow stand in the prow and watch the disintegrating sea.

E. M. FORSTER

Cambridge, 1947

# CONTENTS

# THE STORY OF A PANIC

## I

EUSTACE's career – if career it can be called – certainly dates from that afternoon in the chestnut woods above Ravello. I confess at once that I am a plain, simple man, with no pretensions to literary style. Still, I do flatter myself that I can tell a story without exaggerating, and I have therefore decided to give an unbiassed account of the extraordinary events of eight years ago.

Ravello is a delightful place with a delightful little hotel in which we met some charming people. There were the two Miss Robinsons, who had been there for six weeks with Eustace, their nephew, then a boy of about fourteen. Mr Sandbach had also been there some time. He had held a curacy in the north of England, which he had been compelled to resign on account of ill-health, and while he was recruiting at Ravello he had taken in hand Eustace's education – which was then sadly deficient – and was endeavouring to fit him for one of our great public schools. Then there was Mr Leyland, a would-be artist, and, finally, there was the nice landlady, Signora Scafetti, and the nice English-speaking waiter, Emmanuele – though at the time of which I am speaking Emmanuele was away, visiting a sick father.

To this little circle, I, my wife, and my two daughters made, I venture to think, a not unwelcome addition. But though I liked most of the company well enough, there were two of them to whom I did not take at all. They were the artist, Leyland, and the Miss Robinsons' nephew, Eustace.

Leyland was simply conceited and odious, and, as those qualities will be amply illustrated in my narrative, I need not enlarge upon them here. But Eustace was something besides: he was indescribably repellent.

I am fond of boys as a rule, and was quite disposed to be friendly. I and my daughters offered to take him out – 'No, walking was such a fag.' Then I asked him to come and bathe – 'No, he could not swim.'

'Every English boy should be able to swim,' I said, 'I will teach you myself.'

'There, Eustace dear,' said Miss Robinson; 'here is a chance for you.'

But he said he was afraid of the water! – a boy afraid! – and of course I said no more.

I would not have minded so much if he had been a really studious boy, but he neither played hard nor worked hard. His favourite occupations were lounging on the terrace in an easy chair and loafing along the high road, with his feet shuffling up the dust and his shoulders stooping forward. Naturally enough, his features were pale, his chest contracted, and his muscles undeveloped. His aunts thought him delicate; what he really needed was discipline.

That memorable day we all arranged to go for a picnic up in the chestnut woods – all, that is, except Janet, who stopped behind to finish her water-colour of the Cathedral – not a very successful attempt, I am afraid.

I wander off into these irrelevant details because in my mind I cannot separate them from an account of the day; and it is the same with the conversation during the picnic: all is imprinted on my brain together. After a couple of hours' ascent, we left the donkeys that had carried the Miss Robinsons and my wife, and all proceeded on foot to the head of the valley – Vallone Fontana Caroso is its proper name, I find.

I have visited a good deal of fine scenery before and since, but have found little that has pleased me more. The valley ended in a vast hollow, shaped like a cup, into which radiated ravines from the precipitous hills around. Both the valley and the ravines and the ribs of hill that divided the ravines were covered with leafy chestnut, so that the general appearance was that of a many-fingered green hand, palm upwards, which was clutching convulsively to keep us in its grasp. Far down the valley we could see Ravello and the sea, but that was the only sign of another world.

'Oh, what a perfectly lovely place,' said my daughter Rose. 'What a picture it would make!'

'Yes,' said Mr Sandbach. 'Many a famous European gallery would be proud to have a landscape a tithe as beautiful as this upon its walls.'

'On the contrary,' said Leyland, 'it would make a very poor picture. Indeed, it is not paintable at all.'

'And why is that?' said Rose, with far more deference than he deserved.

'Look, in the first place,' he replied, 'how intolerably straight against the sky is the line of the hill. It would need breaking up and diversifying. And where we are standing the whole thing is out of perspective. Besides, all the colouring is monotonous and crude.'

'I do not know anything about pictures,' I put in, 'and I do not pretend to know: but I know what is beautiful when I see it, and I am thoroughly content with this.'

'Indeed, who could help being contented!' said the elder Miss Robinson; and Mr Sandbach said the same.

'Ah!' said Leyland, 'you all confuse the artistic view of Nature with the photographic.'

Poor Rose had brought her camera with her, so I thought this positively rude. I did not wish any unpleasantness; so I merely turned away and assisted my wife and Miss Mary Robinson to put out the lunch – not a very nice lunch.

'Eustace dear,' said his aunt, 'come and help us here.'

He was in a particularly bad temper that morning. He had, as usual, not wanted to come, and his aunts had nearly allowed him to stop at the hotel to vex Janet. But I, with their permission, spoke to him rather sharply on the subject of exercise; and the result was that he had come, but was even more taciturn and moody than usual.

Obedience was not his strong point. He invariably questioned every command, and only executed it grumbling. I should always insist on prompt and cheerful obedience, if I had a son.

'I'm – coming – Aunt – Mary,' he at last replied, and dawdled to cut a piece of wood to make a whistle, taking care not to arrive till we had finished.

'Well, well, sir!' said I, 'you stroll in at the end and profit by our labours.' He sighed, for he could not endure being chaffed. Miss Mary, very unwisely, insisted on giving him the wing of the chicken, in spite of all my attempts to prevent her. I remember that I had a moment's vexation when I thought that, instead of enjoying the sun, and the air, and the woods, we were all engaged in wrangling over the diet of a spoilt boy.

But, after lunch, he was a little less in evidence. He withdrew to a tree trunk, and began to loosen the bark from his whistle. I was thankful to see him employed, for once in a way. We reclined, and took a *dolce far niente.*

Those sweet chestnuts of the South are puny striplings compared with our robust Northerners. But they clothed the contours of the hills and valleys in a most pleasing way, their veil being only broken by two clearings, in one of which we were sitting.

And because these few trees were cut down, Leyland burst into a petty indictment of the proprietor.

'All the poetry is going from Nature,' he cried, 'her lakes and marshes are drained, her seas banked up, her forests cut down. Everywhere we see the vulgarity of desolation spreading.'

I have had some experience of estates, and answered that cutting was very necessary for the health of the larger trees. Besides, it was unreasonable to expect the proprietor to derive no income from his lands.

'If you take the commercial side of landscape, you may feel

pleasure in the owner's activity. But to me the mere thought that a tree is convertible into cash is disgusting.'

'I see no reason,' I observed politely, 'to despise the gifts of Nature because they are of value.'

It did not stop him. 'It is no matter,' he went on, 'we are all hopelessly steeped in vulgarity. I do not except myself. It is through us, and to our shame, that the Nereids have left the waters and the Oreads the mountains, that the woods no longer give shelter to Pan.'

'Pan!' cried Mr Sandbach, his mellow voice filling the valley as if it had been a great green church, 'Pan is dead. That is why the woods do not shelter him.' And he began to tell the striking story of the mariners who were sailing near the coast at the time of the birth of Christ, and three times heard a loud voice saying: 'The great God Pan is dead.'

'Yes. The great God Pan is dead,' said Leyland. And he abandoned himself to that mock misery in which artistic people are so fond of indulging. His cigar went out, and he had to ask me for a match.

'How very interesting,' said Rose. 'I do wish I knew some ancient history.'

'It is not worth your notice,' said Mr Sandbach. 'Eh, Eustace?'

Eustace was finishing his whistle. He looked up, with the irritable frown in which his aunts allowed him to indulge, and made no reply.

The conversation turned to various topics and then died out. It was a cloudless afternoon in May, and the pale green of the young chestnut leaves made a pretty contrast with the dark blue of the sky. We were all sitting at the edge of the small clearing for the sake of the view, and the shade of the chestnut saplings behind us was manifestly insufficient. All sounds died away – at least that is my account: Miss Robinson says that the clamour of the birds was the first sign of uneasiness that she discerned. All sounds died away, except that, far in the distance, I could hear two boughs of a great chestnut grinding together as the tree swayed. The grinds grew shorter and shorter, and finally that sound stopped also. As I looked over the green fingers of the valley, everything was absolutely motionless and still; and that feeling of suspense which one so often experiences when Nature is in repose began to steal over me.

Suddenly we were all electrified by the excruciating noise of Eustace's whistle. I never heard any instrument give forth so ear-splitting and discordant a sound.

'Eustace dear,' said Miss Mary Robinson, 'you might have thought of your poor Aunt Julia's head.'

Leyland, who had apparently been asleep, sat up.

'It is astonishing how blind a boy is to anything that is elevating or beautiful,' he observed. 'I should not have thought he could have found the wherewithal out here to spoil our pleasure like this.'

Then the terrible silence fell upon us again. I was now standing up and watching a cat's-paw of wind that was running down one of the ridges opposite, turning the light green to dark as it travelled. A fanciful feeling of foreboding came over me; so I turned away, to find to my amazement, that all the others were also on their feet, watching it too.

It is not possible to describe coherently what happened next: but I, for one, am not ashamed to confess that, though the fair blue sky was above me, and the green spring woods beneath me, and the kindest of friends around me, yet I became terribly frightened, more frightened than I ever wish to become again, frightened in a way I never have known either before or after. And in the eyes of the others, too, I saw blank, expressionless fear, while their mouths strove in vain to speak and their hands to gesticulate. Yet, all around us were prosperity, beauty, and peace, and all was motionless, save the cat's-paw of wind, now travelling up the ridge on which we stood.

Who moved first has never been settled. It is enough to say that in one second we were tearing away along the hillside. Leyland was in front, then Mr Sandbach, then my wife. But I only saw for a brief moment; for I ran across the little clearing and through the woods and over the undergrowth and the rocks and down the dry torrent beds into the valley below. The sky might have been black as I ran, and the trees, short grass, and the hillside a level road; for I saw nothing and heard nothing and felt nothing, since all the channels of sense and reason were blocked. It was not the spiritual fear that one has known at other times, but brutal, overmastering, physical fear, stopping up the ears, and dropping clouds before the eyes, and filling the mouth with foul tastes. And it was no ordinary humiliation that survived; for I had been afraid, not as a man, but as a beast.

## II

I CANNOT describe our finish any better than our start; for our fear passed away as it had come, without cause. Suddenly I was able to see, and hear, and cough, and clear my mouth. Looking back, I saw that the others were stopping too; and, in a short time, we were all together, though it was long before we could speak, and longer before we dared to.

No one was seriously injured. My poor wife had sprained her ankle, Leyland had torn one of his nails on a tree trunk, and I myself had scraped and damaged my ear. I never noticed it till I had stopped.

We were all silent, searching one another's faces. Suddenly Miss Mary Robinson gave a terrible shriek. 'Oh, merciful heavens! where is Eustace?' And then she would have fallen if Mr Sandbach had not caught her.

'We must go back, we must go back at once,' said my Rose, who was quite the most collected of the party. 'But I hope – I feel he is safe.'

Such was the cowardice of Leyland, that he objected. But, finding himself in a minority, and being afraid of being left alone, he gave in. Rose and I supported my poor wife, Mr Sandbach and Miss Robinson helped Miss Mary, and we returned slowly and silently, taking forty minutes to ascend the path that we had descended in ten.

Our conversation was naturally disjointed, as no one wished to offer an opinion on what had happened. Rose was the most talkative: she startled us all by saying that she had very nearly stopped where she was.

'Do you mean to say that you weren't – that you didn't feel compelled to go?' said Mr Sandbach.

'Oh, of course, I did feel frightened' – she was the first to use the word – 'but I somehow felt that if I could stop on it would be quite different, that I shouldn't be frightened at all, so to speak.' Rose never did express herself clearly: still, it is greatly to her credit that she, the youngest of us, should have held on so long at that terrible time.

'I should have stopped, I do believe,' she continued, 'if I had not seen mamma go.'

Rose's experience comforted us a little about Eustace. But a feeling of terrible foreboding was on us all as we painfully climbed the chestnut-covered slopes and neared the little clearing. When we reached it our tongues broke loose. There, at the farther side, were the remains of our lunch, and close to them, lying motionless on his back, was Eustace.

With some presence of mind I at once cried out: 'Hey, you young monkey! jump up!' But he made no reply, nor did he answer when his poor aunts spoke to him. And, to my unspeakable horror, I saw one of those green lizards dart out from under his shirt-cuff as we approached.

We stood watching him as he lay there so silently, and my ears began to tingle in expectation of the outbursts of lamentations and tears.

Miss Mary fell on her knees beside him and touched his

hand, which was convulsively entwined in the long grass.

As she did so, he opened his eyes and smiled.

I have often seen that peculiar smile since, both on the possessor's face and on the photographs of him that are beginning to get into the illustrated papers. But, till then, Eustace had always worn a peevish, discontented frown; and we were all unused to this disquieting smile, which always seemed to be without adequate reason.

His aunts showered kisses on him, which he did not reciprocate, and then there was an awkward pause. Eustace seemed so natural and undisturbed; yet, if he had not had astonishing experiences himself, he ought to have been all the more astonished at our extraordinary behaviour. My wife, with ready tact, endeavoured to behave as if nothing had happened.

'Well, Mr Eustace,' she said, sitting down as she spoke, to ease her foot, 'how have you been amusing yourself since we have been away?'

'Thank you, Mrs Tytler, I have been very happy.'

'And where have you been?'

'Here.'

'And lying down all the time, you idle boy?'

'No, not all the time.'

'What were you doing before?'

'Oh; standing or sitting.'

'Stood and sat doing nothing! Don't you know the poem "Satan finds some mischief still for —" '

'Oh, my dear madam, hush! hush!' Mr Sandbach's voice broke in; and my wife, naturally mortified by the interruption, said no more and moved away. I was surprised to see Rose immediately take her place, and, with more freedom than she generally displayed, ran her fingers through the boy's tousled hair.

'Eustace! Eustace!' she said hurriedly, 'tell me everything – every single thing.'

Slowly he sat up – till then he had lain on his back.

'Oh, Rose —,' he whispered, and, my curiosity being aroused, I moved nearer to hear what he was going to say. As I did so, I caught sight of some goat's footmarks in the moist earth beneath the trees.

'Apparently you have had a visit from some goats,' I observed. 'I had no idea they fed up here.'

Eustace laboriously got on to his feet and came to see; and when he saw the footmarks he lay down and rolled on them, as a dog rolls in dirt.

After that there was a grave silence, broken at length by the solemn speech of Mr Sandbach.

'My dear friends,' he said, 'it is best to confess the truth bravely. I know that what I am going to say now is what you are all now feeling. The Evil One has been very near us in bodily form. Time may yet discover some injury that he has wrought among us. But, at present, for myself at all events, I wish to offer up thanks for a merciful deliverance.'

With that he knelt down, and, as the others knelt, I knelt too, though I do not believe in the Devil being allowed to assail us in visible form, as I told Mr Sandbach afterwards. Eustace came too, and knelt quietly enough between his aunts after they had beckoned to him. But when it was over he at once got up, and began hunting for something.

'Why! Someone has cut my whistle in two,' he said. (I had seen Leyland with an open knife in his hand – a superstitious act which I could hardly approve.)

'Well, it doesn't matter,' he continued.

'And why doesn't it matter?' said Mr Sandbach, who has ever since tried to entrap Eustace into an account of that mysterious hour.

'Because I don't want it any more.'

'Why?'

At that he smiled; and, as no one seemed to have anything more to say, I set off as fast as I could through the wood, and hauled up a donkey to carry my poor wife home. Nothing occurred in my absence, except that Rose had again asked Eustace to tell her what had happened; and he, this time, had turned away his head, and had not answered her a single word.

As soon as I returned, we all set off. Eustace walked with difficulty, almost with pain, so that, when we reached the other donkeys, his aunts wished him to mount one of them and ride all the way home. I make it a rule never to interfere between relatives, but I put my foot down at this. As it turned out, I was perfectly right, for the healthy exercise, I suppose, began to thaw Eustace's sluggish mood and loosen his stiffened muscles. He stepped out manfully, for the first time in his life, holding his head up and taking deep draughts of air into his chest. I observed with satisfaction to Miss Mary Robinson that Eustace was at last taking some pride in his personal appearance.

Mr Sandbach sighed, and said that Eustace must be carefully watched, for we none of us understood him yet. Miss Mary Robinson being very much – over much, I think – guided by him, sighed too.

'Come, come, Miss Robinson,' I said, 'there's nothing wrong with Eustace. Our experiences are mysterious, not his. He was astonished at our sudden departure, that's why he was so strange when we returned. He's right enough – improved, if anything.'

'And is the worship of athletics, the cult of insensate activity, to be counted as an improvement?' put in Leyland, fixing a large, sorrowful eye on Eustace, who had stopped to scramble on to a rock to pick some cyclamen. 'The passionate desire to rend from Nature the few beauties that have been still left her – that is to be counted as an improvement too?'

It is mere waste of time to reply to such remarks, especially when they come from an unsuccessful artist suffering from a damaged finger. I changed the conversation by asking what we should say at the hotel. After some discussion, it was agreed that we should say nothing, either there or in our letters home. Importunate truth-telling, which brings only bewilderment and discomfort to the hearers, is, in my opinion, a mistake; and, after a long discussion, I managed to make Mr Sandbach acquiesce in my view.

Eustace did not share in our conversation. He was racing about, like a real boy, in the wood to the right. A strange feeling of shame prevented us from openly mentioning our fright to him. Indeed, it seemed almost reasonable to conclude that it had made but little impression on him. So it disconcerted us when he bounded back with an armful of flowering acanthus, calling out:

'Do you suppose Gennaro'll be there when we get back?'

Gennaro was the stop-gap waiter, a clumsy, impertinent fisher-lad, who had been had up from Minori in the absence of the nice English-speaking Emmanuele. It was to him that we owed our scrappy lunch; and I could not conceive why Eustace desired to see him, unless it was to make mock with him of our behaviour.

'Yes, of course he will be there,' said Miss Robinson. 'Why do you ask, dear?'

'Oh, I thought I'd like to see him.'

'And why?' snapped Mr Sandbach.

'Because, because I do, I do; because, because I do.' He danced away into the darkening wood to the rhythm of his words.

'This is very extraordinary,' said Mr Sandbach. 'Did he like Gennaro before?'

'Gennaro has been here only two days,' said Rose, 'and I know that they haven't spoken to each other a dozen times.'

Each time Eustace returned from the wood his spirits were higher. Once he came whooping down on us as a wild Indian, and another time he made believe to be a dog. The last time he came back with a poor dazed hare, too frightened to move, sitting on his arm. He was getting too uproarious,

I thought; and we were all glad to leave the wood, and start upon the steep staircase path that leads down into Ravello. It was late and turning dark; and we made all the speed we could, Eustace scurrying in front of us like a goat.

Just where the staircase path debouches on the white high road, the next extraordinary incident of this extraordinary day occurred. Three old women were standing by the wayside. They, like ourselves, had come down from the woods, and they were resting their heavy bundles of fuel on the low parapet of the road. Eustace stopped in front of them, and, after a moment's deliberation, stepped forward and – kissed the left-hand one on the cheek!

'My good fellow!' exclaimed Mr Sandbach, 'are you quite crazy?'

Eustace said nothing, but offered the old woman some of his flowers, and then hurried on. I looked back; and the old woman's companions seemed as much astonished at the proceeding as we were. But she herself had put the flowers in her bosom, and was murmuring blessings.

This salutation of the old lady was the first example of Eustace's strange behaviour, and we were both surprised and alarmed. It was useless talking to him, for he either made silly replies, or else bounded away without replying at all.

He made no reference on the way home to Gennaro, and I hoped that that was forgotten. But when we came to the Piazza, in front of the Cathedral, he screamed out: 'Gennaro! Gennaro!' at the top of his voice, and began running up the little alley that led to the hotel. Sure enough, there was Gennaro at the end of it, with his arms and legs sticking out of the nice little English-speaking waiter's dress suit, and a dirty fisherman's cap on his head – for, as the poor landlady truly said, however much she superintended his toilette, he always managed to introduce something incongruous into it before he had done.

Eustace sprang to meet him, and leapt right up into his

arms, and put his own arms round his neck. And this in the presence, not only of us, but also of the landlady, the chambermaid, the facchino, and of two American ladies who were coming for a few days' visit to the little hotel.

I always make a point of behaving pleasantly to Italians, however little they may deserve it; but this habit of promiscuous intimacy was perfectly intolerable, and could only lead to familiarity and mortification for all. Taking Miss Robinson aside, I asked her permission to speak seriously to Eustace on the subject of intercourse with social inferiors. She granted it; but I determined to wait till the absurd boy had calmed down a little from the excitement of the day. Meanwhile, Gennaro, instead of attending to the wants of the two new ladies, carried Eustace into the house, as if it was the most natural thing in the world.

'Ho capito,' I heard him say as he passed me. 'Ho capito' is the Italian for 'I have understood'; but, as Eustace had not spoken to him, I could not see the force of the remark. It served to increase our bewilderment, and, by the time we sat down at the dinner-table, our imaginations and our tongues were alike exhausted.

I omit from this account the various comments that were made, as few of them seem worthy of being recorded. But, for three or four hours, seven of us were pouring forth our bewilderment in a stream of appropriate and inappropriate exclamations. Some traced a connexion between our behaviour in the afternoon and the behaviour of Eustace now. Others saw no connexion at all. Mr Sandbach still held to the possibility of infernal influences, and also said that he ought to have a doctor. Leyland only saw the development of 'that unspeakable Philistine, the boy'. Rose maintained, to my surprise, that everything was excusable; while I began to see that the young gentleman wanted a sound thrashing. The poor Miss Robinsons swayed helplessly about between these diverse opinions; inclining now to careful supervision, now to acquiescence, now to corporal chastisement, now to Eno's Fruit Salt.

Dinner passed off fairly well, though Eustace was terribly fidgety, Gennaro as usual dropping the knives and spoons, and hawking and clearing his throat. He only knew a few words of English, and we were all reduced to Italian for making known our wants. Eustace, who had picked up a little somehow, asked for some oranges. To my annoyance, Gennaro, in his answer, made use of the second person singular – a form only used when addressing those who are both intimates and equals. Eustace had brought it on himself; but an impertinence of this kind was an affront to us all, and I was determined to speak, and to speak at once.

When I heard him clearing the table I went in, and, summoning up my Italian, or rather Neapolitan – the Southern dialects are execrable – I said, 'Gennaro! I heard you address Signor Eustace with "Tu".'

'It is true.'

'You are not right. You must use "Lei" or "Voi" – more polite forms. And remember that, though Signor Eustace is sometimes silly and foolish – this afternoon for example – yet you must always behave respectfully to him; for he is a young English gentleman, and you are a poor Italian fisher-boy.'

I know that speech sounds terribly snobbish, but in Italian one can say things that one would never dream of saying in English. Besides, it is no good speaking delicately to persons of that class. Unless you put things plainly, they take a vicious pleasure in misunderstanding you.

An honest English fisherman would have landed me one in the eye in a minute for such a remark, but the wretched down-trodden Italians have no pride. Gennaro only sighed, and said: 'It is true.'

'Quite so,' I said, and turned to go. To my indignation I heard him add: 'But sometimes it is not important.'

'What do you mean?' I shouted.

He came close up to me with horrid gesticulating fingers.

'Signor Tytler, I wish to say this. If Eustazio asks me to call him "Voi", I will call him "Voi". Otherwise, no.'

With that he seized up a tray of dinner things, and fled from the room with them; and I heard two more wine-glasses go on the courtyard floor.

I was now fairly angry, and strode out to interview Eustace. But he had gone to bed, and the landlady, to whom I also wished to speak, was engaged. After more vague wonderings, obscurely expressed owing to the presence of Janet and the two American ladies, we all went to bed, too, after a harassing and most extraordinary day.

## III

But the day was nothing to the night.

I suppose I had slept for about four hours, when I woke suddenly thinking I heard a noise in the garden. And, immediately, before my eyes were open, cold terrible fear seized me – not fear of something that was happening, like the fear in the wood, but fear of something that might happen.

Our room was on the first floor, looking out on to the garden – or terrace, it was rather a wedge-shaped block of ground covered with roses and vines, and intersected with little asphalt paths. It was bounded on the small side by the house; round the two long sides ran a wall, only three feet above the terrace level, but with a good twenty feet drop over it into the olive yards, for the ground fell very precipitously away.

Trembling all over, I stole to the window. There, pattering up and down the asphalt paths, was something white. I was too much alarmed to see clearly; and in the uncertain light of the stars the thing took all manner of curious shapes. Now it was a great dog, now an enormous white bat, now a mass of quickly travelling cloud. It would bounce like a ball, or take short flights like a bird, or glide slowly like a wraith. It gave no sound – save the pattering sound of what, after all, must be human feet. And at last the obvious explanation forced itself upon my disordered mind; and I realized that Eustace had got out of bed, and that we were in for something more.

I hastily dressed myself, and went down into the dining-room which opened upon the terrace. The door was already unfastened. My terror had almost entirely passed away, but for quite five minutes I struggled with a curious cowardly feeling, which bade me not interfere with the poor strange boy, but leave him to his ghostly patterings, and merely watch him from the window to see he took no harm.

But better impulses prevailed and, opening the door, I called out:

'Eustace! what on earth are you doing? Come in at once.'

He stopped his antics and said: 'I hate my bedroom. I could not stop in it, it is too small.'

'Come! come! I'm tired of affectation. You've never complained of it before.'

'Besides, I can't see anything – no flowers, no leaves, no sky: only a stone wall.' The outlook of Eustace's room certainly was limited; but, as I told him, he had never complained of it before.

'Eustace, you talk like a child. Come in! Prompt obedience, if you please.'

He did not move.

'Very well: I shall carry you in by force,' I added, and made a few steps towards him. But I was soon convinced of the futility of pursuing a boy through a tangle of asphalt paths, and went in instead to call Mr Sandbach and Leyland to my aid.

When I returned with them he was worse than ever. He would not even answer us when we spoke, but began singing and chattering to himself in a most alarming way.

'It's a case for the doctor now,' said Mr Sandbach, gravely tapping his forehead.

He had stopped his running, and was singing, first low, then loud – singing five-finger exercises, scales, hymn tunes, scraps of Wagner – anything that came into his head. His voice – a very untuneful voice – grew stronger and stronger, and he ended with a tremendous shout which boomed like a gun among the mountains, and awoke everyone who was still sleeping in the hotel. My poor wife and the two girls appeared at their respective windows, and the American ladies were heard violently ringing their bell.

'Eustace,' we all cried, 'stop! stop, dear boy, and come into the house.'

He shook his head, and started off again – talking this time. Never have I listened to such an extraordinary speech. At any other time it would have been ludicrous, for here was a boy, with no sense of beauty and a puerile command of words, attempting to tackle themes which the greatest poets have found almost beyond their power. Eustace Robinson, aged fourteen, was standing in his nightshirt saluting, praising, and blessing the great forces and manifestations of Nature.

He spoke first of night and the stars and planets above his head, of the swarms of fireflies below him, of the invisible sea below the fireflies, of the great rocks covered with anemones and shells that were slumbering in the invisible sea. He spoke of the rivers and waterfalls, of the ripening bunches of grapes, of the smoking cone of Vesuvius and the hidden fire-channels that made the smoke, of the myriads of lizards who were lying curled up in the crannies of the sultry earth, of the showers of white rose-leaves that were tangled in his hair. And then he spoke of the rain and the wind by which all things are changed, of the air through which all things live, and of the woods in which all things can be hidden.

Of course, it was all absurdly high faluting: yet I could have kicked Leyland for audibly observing that it was 'a diabolical caricature of all that was most holy and beautiful in life.'

'And then' – Eustace was going on in the pitiable conversational doggerel which was his only mode of expression – 'and then there are men, but I can't make them out so well.' He knelt down by the parapet, and rested his head on his arms.

'Now's the time,' whispered Leyland. I hate stealth, but we darted forward and endeavoured to catch hold of him from behind. He was away in a twinkling, but turned round at once to look at us. As far as I could see in the starlight, he was crying. Leyland rushed at him again, and we tried to corner him among the asphalt paths, but without the slightest approach to success.

We returned, breathless and discomfited, leaving him to his madness in the farther corner of the terrace. But my Rose had an inspiration.

'Papa,' she called from the window, 'if you get Gennaro, he might be able to catch him for you.'

I had no wish to ask a favour of Gennaro, but, as the landlady had by now appeared on the scene, I begged her to summon him from the charcoal-bin in which he slept, and make him try what he could do.

She soon returned, and was shortly followed by Gennaro, attired in a dress coat, without either waistcoat, shirt, or vest, and a ragged pair of what had been trousers, cut short above the knees for purposes of wading. The landlady, who had quite picked up English ways, rebuked him for the incongruous and even indecent appearance which he presented.

'I have a coat and I have trousers. What more do you desire?'

'Never mind, Signora Scafetti,' I put in. 'As there are no ladies here, it is not of the slightest consequence.' Then, turning to Gennaro, I said: 'The aunts of Signor Eustace wish you to fetch him into the house.'

He did not answer.

'Do you hear me? He is not well. I order you to fetch him into the house.'

'Fetch! fetch!' said Signora Scafetti, and shook him roughly by the arm.

'Eustazio is well where he is.'

'Fetch! fetch!' Signora Scafetti screamed, and let loose a flood of Italian, most of which, I am glad to say, I could not follow. I glanced up nervously at the girls' window, but they hardly know as much as I do, and I am thankful to say that none of us caught one word of Gennaro's answer.

The two yelled and shouted at each other for quite ten minutes, at the end of which Gennaro rushed back to his charcoal-bin and Signora Scafetti burst into tears, as well she might, for she greatly valued her English guests.

'He says,' she sobbed, 'that Signor Eustace is well where is is, and that he will not fetch him. I can do no more.'

But I could, for, in my stupid British way, I have got some insight into the Italian character. I followed Mr Gennaro to his place of repose, and found him wriggling down on to a dirty sack.

'I wish you to fetch Signor Eustace to me,' I began.

He hurled at me an unintelligible reply.

'If you fetch him, I will give you this.' And out of my pocket I took a new ten-lira note.

This time he did not answer.

'This note is equal to ten lire in silver,' I continued, for I knew that the poor-class Italian is unable to conceive of a single large sum.

'I know it.'

'That is, two hundred soldi.'

'I do not desire them. Eustazio is my friend.'

I put the note into my pocket.

'Besides, you would not give it me.'

'I am an Englishman. The English always do what they promise.'

'That is true.' It is astonishing how the most dishonest of nations trust us. Indeed, they often trust us more than we trust one another. Gennaro knelt up on his sack. It was too dark to see his face, but I could feel his warm garlicky breath coming out in gasps, and I knew that the eternal avarice of the South had laid hold upon him.

'I could not fetch Eustazio to the house. He might die there.'

'You need not do that,' I replied patiently. 'You need only bring him to me; and I will stand outside in the garden.' And to this, as if it were something quite different, the pitiable youth consented.

'But give me first the ten lire.'

'No' – for I knew the kind of person with whom I had to deal. Once faithless, always faithless.

We returned to the terrace, and Gennaro, without a single word, pattered off towards the pattering that could be heard at the remoter end. Mr Sandbach, Leyland, and myself moved away a little from the house, and stood in the shadow of the white climbing roses, practically invisible.

We heard 'Eustazio' called, followed by absurd cries of pleasure from the poor boy. The pattering ceased, and we heard them talking. Their voices got nearer, and presently I could discern them through the creepers, the grotesque figure of the young man, and the slim little white-robed boy. Gennaro had his arm round Eustace's neck, and Eustace was talking away in his fluent, slip-shod Italian.

'I understand almost everything,' I heard him say. 'The trees, hills, stars, water, I can see all. But isn't it odd! I can't make out men a bit. Do you know what I mean?'

'Ho capito,' said Gennaro gravely, and took his arm off Eustace's shoulder. But I made the new note crackle in my pocket; and he heard it. He stuck his hand out with a jerk; and the unsuspecting Eustace gripped it in his own.

'It is odd!' Eustace went on – they were quite close now – 'It almost seems as if – as if —'

I darted out and caught hold of his arm, and Leyland got hold of the other arm, and Mr Sandbach hung on to his feet. He gave shrill heart-piercing screams; and the white roses, which were falling early that year, descended in showers on him as we dragged him into the house.

As soon as we entered the house he stopped shrieking; but floods of tears silently burst forth and spread over his upturned face.

'Not to my room,' he pleaded. 'It is so small.'

His infinitely dolorous look filled me with strange pity, but what could I do? Besides, his window was the only one that had bars to it.

'Never mind, dear boy,' said kind Mr Sandbach. 'I will bear you company till the morning.'

At this his convulsive struggles began again. 'Oh, please, not that. Anything but that. I will promise to lie still and not to cry more than I can help, if I am left alone.'

So we laid him on the bed, and drew the sheets over him, and left him sobbing bitterly, and saying: 'I nearly saw everything, and now I can see nothing at all.'

We informed the Miss Robinsons of all that had happened, and returned to the dining-room, where we found Signora Scafetti and Gennaro whispering together. Mr Sandbach got pen and paper, and began writing to the English doctor at Naples. I at once drew out the note, and flung it down on the table to Gennaro.

'Here is your pay,' I said sternly, for I was thinking of the Thirty Pieces of Silver.

'Thank you very much, sir,' said Gennaro, and grabbed it.

He was going off, when Leyland, whose interest and indifference were always equally misplaced, asked him what Eustace had meant by saying 'he could not make out men a bit'.

'I cannot say. Signor Eustazio' (I was glad to observe a

little deference at last) 'has a subtle brain. He understands many things.'

'But I heard you say you understood,' Leyland persisted.

'I understand, but I cannot explain. I am a poor Italian fisher-lad. Yet, listen: I will try.' I saw to my alarm that his manner was changing, and tried to stop him. But he sat down on the edge of the table and started off, with some absolutely incoherent remarks.

'It is sad,' he observed at last. 'What has happened is very sad. But what can I do? I am poor. It is not I.'

I turned away in contempt. Leyland went on asking questions. He wanted to know who it was that Eustace had in his mind when he spoke.

'That is easy to say,' Gennaro gravely answered. 'It is you, it is I. It is all in this house, and many outside it. If he wishes for mirth, we discomfort him. If he asks to be alone, we disturb him. He longed for a friend, and found none for fifteen years. Then he found me, and the first night I – I who have been in the woods and understood things too – betray him to you and send him in to die. But what could I do?'

'Gently, gently,' said I.

'Oh, assuredly he will die. He will lie in the small room all night, and in the morning he will be dead. That I know for certain.'

'There, that will do,' said Mr Sandbach. 'I shall be sitting with him.'

'Filomena Giusti sat all night with Caterina, but Caterina was dead in the morning. They would not let her out, though I begged, and prayed, and cursed, and beat the door, and climbed the wall. They were ignorant fools, and thought I wished to carry her away. And in the morning she was dead.'

'What is all this?' I asked Signora Scafetti.

'All kinds of stories will get about,' she replied, 'and he. least of anyone, has reason to repeat them.'

'And I am alive now,' he went on, 'because I had neither parents nor relatives nor friends, so that, when the first night came, I could run through the woods, and climb the rocks, and plunge into the water, until I had accomplished my desire!'

We heard a cry from Eustace's room – a faint but steady sound, like the sound of wind in a distant wood heard by one standing in tranquillity.

'That,' said Gennaro, 'was the last noise of Caterina. I was hanging on to her window then, and it blew out past me.'

And, lifting up his hand, in which my ten-lira note was safely packed, he solemnly cursed Mr Sandbach, and Leyland, and myself, and Fate, because Eustace was dying in the upstairs room. Such is the working of the Southern mind; and I verily believe that he would not have moved even then, had not Leyland, that unspeakable idiot, upset the lamp with his elbow. It was a patent self-extinguishing lamp, bought by Signora Scafetti, at my special request, to replace the dangerous thing that she was using. The result was, that it went out; and the mere physical change from light to darkness had more power over the ignorant animal nature of Gennaro than the most obvious dictates of logic and reason.

I felt, rather than saw, that he had left the room, and shouted out to Mr Sandbach: 'Have you got the key to Eustace's room in your pocket?' But Mr Sandbach and Leyland were both on the floor, having mistaken each other for Gennaro, and some more precious time was wasted in finding a match. Mr Sandbach had only just time to say that he had left the key in the door, in case the Miss Robinsons wished to pay Eustace a visit, when we heard a noise on the stairs, and there was Gennaro, carrying Eustace down.

We rushed out and blocked up the passage, and they lost heart and retreated to the upper landing.

'Now they are caught,' cried Signora Scafetti. 'There is no other way out.'

We were cautiously ascending the staircase, when there

was a terrific scream from my wife's room, followed by a heavy thud on the asphalt path. They had leapt out of her window.

I reached the terrace just in time to see Eustace jumping over the parapet of the garden wall. This time I knew for certain he would be killed. But he alighted in an olive tree, looking like a great white moth, and from the tree he slid on to the earth. And as soon as his bare feet touched the clods of earth he uttered a strange loud cry, such as I should not have thought the human voice could have produced, and disappeared among the trees below.

'He has understood and he is saved,' cried Gennaro, who was still sitting on the asphalt path. 'Now, instead of dying he will live!'

'And you, instead of keeping the ten lire, will give them up,' I retorted, for at this theatrical remark I could contain myself no longer.

'The ten lire are mine,' he hissed back in a scarcely audible voice. He clasped his hand over his breast to protect his ill-gotten gains, and, as he did so, he swayed forward and fell upon his face on the path. He had not broken any limbs, and a leap like that would never have killed an Englishman, for the drop was not great. But those miserable Italians have no stamina. Something had gone wrong inside him, and he was dead.

The morning was still far off, but the morning breeze had begun, and more rose leaves fell on us as we carried him in. Signora Scafetti burst into screams at the sight of the dead body, and, far down the valley towards the sea, there still resounded the shouts and the laughter of the escaping boy.

# THE OTHER SIDE OF THE HEDGE

My pedometer told me that I was twenty-five; and, though it is a shocking thing to stop walking, I was so tired that I sat down on a milestone to rest. People outstripped me, jeering as they did so, but I was too apathetic to feel resentful, and even when Miss Eliza Dimbleby, the great educationist, swept past, exhorting me to persevere, I only smiled and raised my hat.

At first I thought I was going to be like my brother, whom I had had to leave by the roadside a year or two round the corner. He had wasted his breath on singing and his strength on helping others. But I had travelled more wisely, and now it was only the monotony of the highway that oppressed me – dust under foot and brown crackling hedges on either side, ever since I could remember.

And I had already dropped several things – indeed, the road behind was strewn with the things we all had dropped; and the white dust was settling down on them, so that already they looked no better than stones. My muscles were so weary that I could not even bear the weight of those things I still carried. I slid off the milestone into the road, and lay there prostrate, with my face to the great parched hedge, praying that I might give up.

A little puff of air revived me. It seemed to come from the hedge; and, when I opened my eyes, there was a glint of light through the tangle of boughs and dead leaves. The hedge could not be as thick as usual. In my weak, morbid state, I longed to force my way in, and see what was on the other side. No one was in sight, or I should not have dared to try. For we of the road do not admit in conversation that there is another side at all.

I yielded to the temptation, saying to myself that I would come back in a minute. The thorns scratched my face, and I had to use my arms as a shield, depending on my feet alone to push me forward. Half-way through I would have gone back, for in the passage all the things I was carrying were scraped off me, and my clothes were torn. But I was so wedged that return was impossible, and I had to wriggle blindly forward, expecting every moment that my strength would fail me and that I should perish in the undergrowth.

Suddenly cold water closed round my head, and I seemed sinking down for ever. I had fallen out of the hedge into a deep pool. I rose to the surface at last, crying for help, and I heard someone on the opposite bank laugh and say: 'Another!' And then I was twitched out and laid panting on the dry ground.

Even when the water was out of my eyes I was still dazed, for I had never been in so large a space, nor seen such grass and sunshine. The blue sky was no longer a strip, and beneath it the earth had risen grandly into hills – clean, bare buttresses, with beech trees in their folds, and meadows and clear pools at their feet. But the hills were not high, and there was in the landscape a sense of human occupation – so that one might have called it a park, or garden, if the words did not imply a certain triviality and constraint.

As soon as I got my breath, I turned to my rescuer and said: 'Where does this place lead to?'

'Nowhere, thank the Lord!' said he, and laughed. He was a man of fifty or sixty – just the kind of age we mistrust on the road – but there was no anxiety in his manner, and his voice was that of a boy of eighteen.

'But it must lead somewhere!' I cried, too much surprised at his answer to thank him for saving my life.

'He wants to know where it leads!' he shouted to some men on the hillside, and they laughed back and waved their caps.

I noticed then that the pool into which I had fallen was really a moat which bent round to the left and to the right, and that the hedge followed it continually. The hedge was green on this side – its roots showed through the clear water, and fish swam about in them – and it was wreathed over with dog-roses and Traveller's Joy. But it was a barrier, and in a moment I lost all pleasure in the grass, the sky, the trees, the happy men and women, and realized that the place was but a prison for all its beauty and extent.

We moved away from the boundary, and then followed a path almost parallel to it across the meadows. I found it difficult walking, for I was always trying to out-distance my companion, and there was no advantage in doing this if the place led nowhere. I had never kept step with anyone since I left my brother.

I amused him by stopping suddenly and saying disconsolately, 'This is perfectly terrible. One cannot advance: one cannot progress. Now we of the road —'

'Yes. I know.'

'I was going to say, we advance continually.'

'I know.'

'We are always learning, expanding, developing. Why, even in my short life I have seen a great deal of advance – the Transvaal War, the Fiscal Question, Christian Science, Radium. Here for example —'

I took out my pedometer, but it still marked twenty-five, not a degree more.

'Oh, it's stopped! I meant to show you. It should have registered all the time I was walking with you. But it makes me only twenty-five.'

'Many things don't work in here,' he said. 'One day a man brought in a Lee-Metford, and that wouldn't work.'

'The laws of science are universal in their application. It must be the water in the moat that has injured the machinery. In normal conditions everything works. Science and the spirit of emulation – those are the forces that have made us what we are.'

I had to break off and acknowledge the pleasant greetings of people whom we passed. Some of them were singing, some talking, some engaged in gardening, hay-making, or other rudimentary industries. They all seemed happy; and I might have been happy too, if I could have forgotten that the place led nowhere.

I was startled by a young man who came sprinting across our path, took a little fence in fine style, and went tearing over a ploughed field till he plunged into a lake, across which he began to swim. Here was true energy, and I exclaimed: 'A cross-country race! Where are the others?'

'There are no others,' my companion replied; and, later on, when we passed some long grass from which came the voice of a girl singing exquisitely to herself, he said again: 'There are no others.' I was bewildered at the waste in production, and murmured to myself, 'What does it all mean?'

He said: 'It means nothing but itself' – and he repeated the words slowly, as if I were a child.

'I understand,' I said quietly, 'but I do not agree. Every achievement is worthless unless it is a link in the chain of development. And I must not trespass on your kindness any longer. I must get back somehow to the road, and have my pedometer mended.'

'First you must see the gates,' he replied, 'for we have gates, though we never use them.'

I yielded politely, and before long we reached the moat again, at a point where it was spanned by a bridge. Over the bridge was a big gate, as white as ivory, which was fitted into a gap in the boundary hedge. The gate opened outwards, and I exclaimed in amazement, for from it ran a road – just such a road as I had left – dusty under foot, with brown crackling hedges on either side as far as the eye could reach.

'That's my road!' I cried.

He shut the gate and said: 'But not your part of the road. It is through this gate that humanity went out countless ages ago, when it was first seized with the desire to walk.'

I denied this, observing that the part of the road I myself had left was not more than two miles off. But with the obstinacy of his years he repeated: 'It is the same road. This is the beginning, and though it seems to run straight away from us, it doubles so often that it is never far from our boundary and sometimes touches it.' He stooped down by the moat, and traced on its moist margin an absurd figure like a maze. As we walked back through the meadows, I tried to convince him of his mistake.

'The road sometimes doubles, to be sure, but that is part of our discipline. Who can doubt that its general tendency is onward? To what goal we know not – it may be to some mountain where we shall touch the sky, it may be over precipices into the sea. But that it goes forward – who can doubt that? It is the thought of that that makes us strive to excel, each in his own way, and gives us an impetus which is lacking with you. Now that man who passed us – it's true that he ran well, and jumped well, and swam well; but we have men who can run better, and men who can jump better, and who can swim better. Specialization has produced results which would surprise you. Similarly, that girl —'

Here I interrupted myself to exclaim: 'Good gracious me! I could have sworn it was Miss Eliza Dimbleby over there, with her feet in the fountain!'

He believed that it was.

'Impossible! I left her on the road, and she is due to lecture this evening at Tunbridge Wells. Why, her train leaves Cannon Street in – of course my watch has stopped like everything else. She is the last person to be here.'

'People always are astonished at meeting each other. All kinds come through the hedge, and come at all times – when they are drawing ahead in the race, when they are lagging behind, when they are left for dead. I often stand near the boundary listening to the sounds of the road – you know what they are – and wonder if anyone will turn aside. It is my great happiness to help someone out of the moat, as I helped you. For our country fills up slowly, though it was meant for all mankind.'

'Mankind have other aims,' I said gently, for I thought him well-meaning; 'and I must join them.' I bade him good evening, for the sun was declining, and I wished to be on the road by nightfall. To my alarm, he caught hold of me, crying: 'You are not to go yet!' I tried to shake him off, for we had no interests in common, and his civility was becoming irksome to me. But for all my struggles the tiresome old man would not let go; and, as wrestling is not my speciality, I was obliged to follow him.

It was true that I could never have found alone the place where I came in, and I hoped that, when I had seen the other sights about which he was worrying, he would take me back to it. But I was determined not to sleep in the country, for I mistrusted it, and the people too, for all their friendliness. Hungry though I was, I would not join them in their evening meals of milk and fruit, and, when they gave me flowers, I flung them away as soon as I could do so unobserved. Already they were lying down for the night like cattle – some out on the bare hillside, others in groups under the beeches. In the light of an orange sunset I hurried on with my unwelcome guide, dead tired, faint for want of food, but murmuring indomitably: 'Give me life, with its struggles and victories, with its failures and hatreds, with its deep moral meaning and its unknown goal!'

At last we came to a place where the encircling moat was spanned by another bridge and where another gate interrupted the line of the boundary hedge. It was different from the first gate; for it was half transparent like horn, and opened inwards. But through it, in the waning light, I saw again just such a road as I had left – monotonous, dusty, with brown crackling hedges on either side, as far as the eye could reach.

I was strangely disquieted at the sight, which seemed to deprive me of all self-control. A man was passing us, returning for the night to the hills, with a scythe over his shoulder and a can of some liquid in his hand. I forgot the destiny of our race. I forgot the road that lay before my eyes, and I sprang at him, wrenched the can out of his hand, and began to drink.

It was nothing stronger than beer, but in my exhausted state it overcame me in a moment. As in a dream, I saw the old man shut the gate, and heard him say: 'This is where your road ends, and through this gate humanity – all that is left of it – will come in to us.'

Though my senses were sinking into oblivion, they seemed to expand ere they reached it. They perceived the magic song of nightingales, and the odour of invisible hay, and stars piercing the fading sky. The man whose beer I had stolen lowered me down gently to sleep off its effects, and, as he did so, I saw that he was my brother.

# THE CELESTIAL OMNIBUS

## I

THE boy who resided at Agathox Lodge, 28, Buckingham Park Road, Surbiton, had often been puzzled by the old sign-post that stood almost opposite. He asked his mother about it, and she replied that it was a joke, and not a very nice one, which had been made many years back by some naughty young men, and that the police ought to remove it. For there were two strange things about this sign-post: firstly, it pointed up a blank alley, and, secondly, it had painted on it, in faded characters, the words, 'To Heaven'.

'What kind of young men were they?' he asked.

'I think your father told me that one of them wrote verses, and was expelled from the University and came to grief in other ways. Still, it was a long time ago. You must ask your father about it. He will say the same as I do, that it was put up as a joke.'

'So it doesn't mean anything at all?'

She sent him upstairs to put on his best things, for the Bonses were coming to tea, and he was to hand the cake-stand.

It struck him, as he wrenched on his tightening trousers, that he might do worse than ask Mr Bons about the sign-post. His father, though very kind, always laughed at him – shrieked with laughter whenever he or any other child asked a question or spoke. But Mr Bons was serious as well as kind. He had a beautiful house and lent one books, he was a church-warden, and a candidate for the County Council; he had donated to the Free Library enormously; he presided over the Literary Society, and had Members of Parliament to stop with him – in short, he was probably the wisest person alive.

Yet even Mr Bons could only say that the sign-post was a joke – the joke of a person named Shelley.

'Of course!' cried the mother; 'I told you so, dear. That was the name.'

'Had you never heard of Shelley?' asked Mr Bons.

'No,' said the boy, and hung his head.

'But is there no Shelley in the house?'

'Why, yes!' exclaimed the lady, in much agitation. 'Dear Mr Bons, we aren't such Philistines as that. Two at the least. One a wedding present, and the other, smaller print, in one of the spare rooms.'

'I believe we have seven Shelleys,' said Mr Bons, with a slow smile. Then he brushed the cake crumbs off his stomach, and, together with his daughter, rose to go.

The boy, obeying a wink from his mother, saw them all the way to the garden gate, and when they had gone he did not at once return to the house, but gazed for a little up and down Buckingham Park Road.

His parents lived at the right end of it. After No. 39 the quality of the houses dropped very suddenly, and 64 had not even a separate servants' entrance. But at the present moment the whole road looked rather pretty, for the sun had just set in splendour, and the inequalities of rent were drowned in a saffron afterglow. Small birds twittered, and the breadwinners' train shrieked musically down through the cutting – that wonderful cutting which has drawn to itself the whole beauty out of Surbiton, and clad itself, like any Alpine valley, with the glory of the fir and the silver birch and the primrose. It was this cutting that had first stirred desires within the boy – desires for something just a little different, he knew not what, desires that would return whenever things were sunlit, as they were this evening, running up and down inside him, up and down, up and down, till he would feel quite unusual all over, and as likely as not would want to cry. This evening he was even sillier, for he slipped across the road towards the sign-post and began to run up the blank alley.

The alley runs between high walls – the walls of the

gardens of 'Ivanhoe' and 'Belle Vista' respectively. It smells a little all the way, and is scarcely twenty yards long, including the turn at the end. So not unnaturally the boy soon came to a standstill. 'I'd like to kick that Shelley,' he exclaimed, and glanced idly at a piece of paper which was pasted on the wall. Rather an odd piece of paper, and he read it carefully before he turned back. This is what he read:

S. AND C. R. C. C.

*Alteration in Service*

Owing to lack of patronage the Company are regretfully compelled to suspend the hourly service, and to retain only the

*Sunrise and Sunset Omnibuses,*

which will run as usual. It is to be hoped that the public will patronize an arrangement which is intended for their convenience. As an extra inducement, the Company will, for the first time, now issue

Return Tickets!

(available one day only), which may be obtained of the driver. Passengers are again reminded that *no tickets are issued at the other end*, and that no complaints in this connexion will receive consideration from the Company. Nor will the Company be responsible for any negligence or stupidity on the part of Passengers, nor for Hail-storms, Lightning, Loss of Tickets, nor for any Act of God.

For the Direction.

Now, he had never seen this notice before, nor could he imagine where the omnibus went to. S. of course was for Surbiton, and R.C.C. meant Road Car Company. But what was the meaning of the other C.? Coombe and Malden, perhaps, or possibly 'City'. Yet it could not hope to compete with the South-Western. The whole thing, the boy reflected, was run on hopelessly unbusiness-like lines. Why no tickets from the other end? And what an hour to start! Then he realized that unless the notice was a hoax, an omnibus must have been starting just as he was wishing the Bonses good-bye. He peered at the ground through the gathering dusk, and there he saw what might or might not be the marks of wheels. Yet nothing had come out of the alley. And he had never seen an omnibus at any time in the Buckingham Park Road. No: it must be a hoax, like the sign-posts, like the fairy-tales, like the dreams upon which he would wake suddenly in the night. And with a sigh he stepped from the alley – right into the arms of his father.

Oh, how his father laughed! 'Poor, poor Popsey!' he cried. 'Diddums! Diddums! Diddums think he'd walky-palky up to Evvink!' And his mother, also convulsed with laughter, appeared on the steps of Agathox Lodge. 'Don't, Bob!' she gasped. 'Don't be so naughty! Oh, you'll kill me! Oh, leave the boy alone!'

But all that evening the joke was kept up. The father implored to be taken too. Was it a very tiring walk? Need one wipe one's shoes on the door-mat? And the boy went to bed feeling faint and sore, and thankful for only one thing – that he had not said a word about the omnibus. It was a hoax, yet through his dreams it grew more and more real, and the streets of Surbiton, through which he saw it driving, seemed instead to become hoaxes and shadows. And very early in the morning he woke with a cry, for he had had a glimpse of its destination.

He struck a match, and its light fell not only on his watch but also on his calendar, so that he knew it to be half an hour to sunrise. It was pitch dark, for the fog had come down from London in the night, and all Surbiton was wrapped in its embraces. Yet he sprang out and dressed himself, for he was determined to settle once for all which was real: the omnibus or the streets. 'I shall be a fool one way or the other,' he thought, 'until I know.' Soon he was shivering in the road under the gas lamp that guarded the entrance to the alley.

To enter the alley itself required some courage. Not only was it horribly dark, but he now realized that it was an impossible terminus for an omnibus. If it had not been for a policeman, whom he heard approaching through the fog, he would never have made the attempt. The next moment he had made the attempt and failed. Nothing. Nothing but a blank alley and a very silly boy gaping at its dirty floor. It *was* a hoax. 'I'll tell papa and mamma,' he decided. 'I deserve it. I deserve that they should know. I am too silly to be alive.' And he went back to the gate of Agathox Lodge.

There he remembered that his watch was fast. The sun was not risen; it would not rise for two minutes. 'Give the bus every chance,' he thought cynically, and returned into the alley.

But the omnibus was there.

## II

It had two horses, whose sides were still smoking from their journey, and its two great lamps shone through the fog against the alley's walls, changing their cobwebs and moss into tissues of fairyland. The driver was huddled up in a cape. He faced the blank wall, and how he had managed to drive in so neatly and so silently was one of the many things that the boy never discovered. Nor could he imagine however he would drive out.

'Please,' his voice quavered through the foul brown air. 'Please, is that an omnibus?'

'Omnibus est,' said the driver, without turning round. There was a moment's silence. The policeman passed, coughing, by the entrance of the alley. The boy crouched in the shadow, for he did not want to be found out. He was pretty sure, too, that it was a Pirate; nothing else, he reasoned, would go from such odd places and at such odd hours.

'About when do you start?' He tried to sound nonchalant.

'At sunrise.'

'How far do you go?'

'The whole way.'

'And can I have a return ticket which will bring me all the way back?'

'You can.'

'Do you know, I half think I'll come.' The driver made no answer. The sun must have risen, for he unhitched the brake. And scarcely had the boy jumped in before the omnibus was off.

How? Did it turn? There was no room. Did it go forward? There was a blank wall. Yet it was moving – moving at a stately pace through the fog, which had turned from brown to yellow. The thought of warm bed and warmer breakfast made the boy feel faint. He wished he had not come. His parents would not have approved. He would have gone back to them if the weather had not made it impossible. The solitude was terrible; he was the only passenger. And the omnibus, though well-built, was cold and somewhat musty. He drew his coat round him, and in so doing chanced to feel his pocket. It was empty. He had forgotten his purse.

'Stop!' he shouted. 'Stop!' And then, being of a polite disposition, he glanced up at the painted notice-board so that he might call the driver by name. 'Mr Browne! stop; oh, do please stop!'

Mr Browne did not stop, but he opened a little window and looked in at the boy. His face was a surprise, so kind it was and modest.

'Mr Browne, I've left my purse behind. I've not got a penny. I can't pay for the ticket. Will you take my watch, please? I am in the most awful hole.'

'Tickets on this line,' said the driver, 'whether single or return, can be purchased by coinage from no terrene mint. And a chronometer, though it had solaced the vigils of Charlemagne or measured the slumbers of Laura, can acquire by no mutation the doublecake that charms the fangless Cerberus of Heaven!' So saying, he handed in the necessary ticket, and, while the boy said 'Thank you,' continued: 'Titular pretensions, I know it well, are vanity. Yet they merit no censure when uttered on a laughing lip, and in an homonymous world are in some sort useful, since they do serve to distinguish one Jack from his fellow. Remember me, therefore, as Sir Thomas Browne.'

'Are you a Sir? Oh, sorry!' He had heard of these gentlemen drivers. 'It *is* good of you about the ticket. But if you go on at this rate, however does your bus pay?'

'It does not pay. It was not intended to pay. Many are the faults of my equipage; it is compounded too curiously of foreign woods; its cushions tickle erudition rather than promote repose; and my horses are nourished not on the evergreen pastures of the moment, but on the dried bents and clovers of Latinity. But that it pays! – that error at all events was never intended and never attained.'

'Sorry again,' said the boy rather hopelessly. Sir Thomas looked sad, fearing that, even for a moment, he had been the cause of sadness. He invited the boy to come up and sit beside him on the box, and together they journeyed on through the fog, which was now changing from yellow to white. There were no houses by the road; so it must be either Putney Heath or Wimbledon Common.

'Have you been a driver always?'

'I was a physician once.'

'But why did you stop? Weren't you good?'

'As a healer of bodies I had scant success, and several score of my patients preceded me. But as a healer of the spirit I have succeeded beyond my hopes and my deserts. For though my draughts were not better nor subtler than those of other men, yet, by reason of the cunning goblets wherein I offered them, the queasy soul was ofttimes tempted to sip and be refreshed.'

'The queasy soul,' he murmured; 'if the sun sets with trees in front of it, and you suddenly come strange all over, is that a queasy soul?'

'Have you felt that?'

'Why yes.'

After a pause he told the boy a little, a very little, about the journey's end. But they did not chatter much, for the boy, when he liked a person, would as soon sit silent in his company as speak, and this, he discovered, was also the mind of Sir Thomas Browne and of many others with whom he was to be acquainted. He heard, however, about the young man Shelley, who was now quite a famous person, with a carriage of his own, and about some of the other drivers who are in the service of the Company. Meanwhile the light grew stronger, though the fog did not disperse. It was now more like mist than fog, and at times would travel quickly across them, as if it was part of a cloud. They had been ascending, too, in a most puzzling way; for over two hours the horses had been pulling against the collar, and even if it were Richmond Hill they ought to have been at the top long ago. Perhaps it was Epsom, or even the North Downs; yet the air seemed keener than that which blows on either. And as to the name of their destination, Sir Thomas Browne was silent.

Crash!

'Thunder, by Jove!' said the boy, 'and not so far off either. Listen to the echoes! It's more like mountains.'

He thought, not very vividly, of his father and mother. He saw them sitting down to sausages and listening to the storm. He saw his own empty place. Then there would be questions, alarms, theories, jokes, consolations. They would expect him back at lunch. To lunch he would not come, nor to tea, but he would be in for dinner, and so his day's truancy would be over. If he had had his purse he would have bought them presents – not that he should have known what to get them.

Crash!

The peal and the lightning came together. The cloud quivered as if it were alive, and torn streamers of mist rushed past. 'Are you afraid?' asked Sir Thomas Browne.

'What is there to be afraid of? Is it much farther?'

The horses of the omnibus stopped just as a ball of fire burst up and exploded with a ringing noise that was deafening but clear, like the noise of a blacksmith's forge. All the cloud was shattered.

'Oh, listen, Sir Thomas Browne! No, I mean look; we shall get a view at last. No, I mean listen; that sounds like a rainbow!'

The noise had died into the faintest murmur, beneath which another murmur grew, spreading stealthily, steadily, in a curve that widened but did not vary. And in widening curves a rainbow was spreading from the horses' feet into the dissolving mists.

'But how beautiful! What colours! Where will it stop? It is more like the rainbows you can tread on. More like dreams.'

The colour and the sound grew together. The rainbow spanned an enormous gulf. Clouds rushed under it and were pierced by it, and still it grew, reaching forward, conquering the darkness, until it touched something that seemed more solid than a cloud.

The boy stood up. 'What is that out there?' he called. 'What does it rest on, out at that other end?'

In the morning sunshine a precipice shone forth beyond the gulf. A precipice – or was it a castle? The horses moved. They set their feet upon the rainbow.

'Oh, look!' the boy shouted. 'Oh, listen! Those caves – or are they gateways? Oh, look between those cliffs at those ledges. I see people! I see trees!'

'Look also below,' whispered Sir Thomas. 'Neglect not the diviner Acheron.'

The boy looked below, past the flames of the rainbow that

licked against their wheels. The gulf also had cleared, and in its depths there flowed an everlasting river. One sunbeam entered and struck a green pool, and as they passed over he saw three maidens rise to the surface of the pool, singing, and playing with something that glistened like a ring.

'You down in the water —' he called.

They answered, 'You up on the bridge —' There was a burst of music. 'You up on the bridge, good luck to you. Truth in the depth, truth on the height.'

'You down in the water, what are you doing?'

Sir Thomas Browne replied: 'They sport in the mancipiary possession of their gold'; and the omnibus arrived.

## III

THE boy was in disgrace. He sat locked up in the nursery of Agathox Lodge, learning poetry for a punishment. His father had said, 'My boy! I can pardon anything but untruthfulness,' and had caned him, saying at each stroke, 'There is *no* omnibus, *no* driver, *no* bridge, *no* mountain; you are a *truant*, a *gutter-snipe*, a *liar*.' His father could be very stern at times. His mother had begged him to say he was sorry. But he could not say that. It was the greatest day of his life, in spite of the caning and the poetry at the end of it.

He had returned punctually at sunset – driven not by Sir Thomas Browne, but by a maiden lady who was full of quiet fun. They had talked of omnibuses and also of barouche landaus. How far away her gentle voice seemed now! Yet it was scarcely three hours since he had left her up the alley.

His mother called through the door. 'Dear, you are to come down and to bring your poetry with you.'

He came down, and found that Mr Bons was in the smoking-room with his father. It had been a dinner party.

'Here is the great traveller!' said his father grimly. 'Here is the young gentleman who drives in an omnibus over rainbows, while young ladies sing to him.' Pleased with his wit, he laughed.

'After all,' said Mr Bons, smiling, 'there is something a little like it in Wagner. It is odd how, in quite illiterate minds, you will find glimmers of Artistic Truth. The case interests me. Let me plead for the culprit. We have all romanced in our time, haven't we?'

'Hear how kind Mr Bons is,' said his mother, while his father said, 'Very well. Let him say his Poem, and that will do. He is going away to my sister on Tuesday, and *she* will cure him of this alley-slopering.' (Laughter.) 'Say your Poem.'

The boy began. ' "Standing aloof in giant ignorance." '

His father laughed again – roared. 'One for you, my son! "Standing aloof in giant ignorance!" I never knew these poets talked sense. Just describes you. Here, Bons, you go in for poetry. Put him through it, will you, while I fetch up the whisky?'

'Yes, give me the Keats,' said Mr Bons. 'Let him say his Keats to me.'

So for a few moments the wise man and the ignorant boy were left alone in the smoking-room.

' "Standing aloof in giant ignorance, of thee I dream and of the Cyclades, as one who sits ashore and longs perchance to visit —" '

'Quite right. To visit what?'

' "To visit dolphin coral in deep seas," ' said the boy, and burst into tears.

'Come, come! why do you cry?'

'Because – because all these words that only rhymed before, now that I've come back they're me.'

Mr Bons laid the Keats down. The case was more interesting than he had expected. '*You?*' he exclaimed. 'This sonnet, *you*?'

'Yes – and look farther on: "Aye, on the shores of darkness there is light, and precipices show untrodden green." It *is* so, sir. All these things are true.'

'I never doubted it,' said Mr Bons, with closed eyes.

'You – then you believe me? You believe in the omnibus and the driver and the storm and that return ticket I got for nothing and —'

'Tut, tut! No more of your yarns, my boy. I meant that I never doubted the essential truth of Poetry. Some day, when you have read more, you will understand what I mean.'

'But, Mr Bons, it *is* so. There *is* light upon the shores of darkness. I have seen it coming. Light and a wind.'

'Nonsense,' said Mr Bons.

'If I had stopped! They tempted me. They told me to give up my ticket – for you cannot come back if you lose your ticket. They called from the river for it, and indeed I was tempted, for I have never been so happy as among those precipices. But I thought of my mother and father, and that I must fetch them. Yet they will not come, though the road starts opposite our house. It has all happened as the people up there warned me, and Mr Bons has disbelieved me like everyone else. I have been caned. I shall never see that mountain again.'

'What's that about me?' said Mr Bons, sitting up in his chair very suddenly.

'I told them about you, and how clever you were, and how many books you had, and they said, "Mr Bons will certainly disbelieve you." '

'Stuff and nonsense, my young friend. You grow impertinent. I – well – I will settle the matter. Not a word to your father. I will cure you. To-morrow evening I will myself call here to take you for a walk, and at sunset we will go up this alley opposite and hunt for your omnibus, you silly little boy.'

His face grew serious, for the boy was not disconcerted, but leapt about the room singing, 'Joy! joy! I told them you would believe me. We will drive together over the rainbow. I told them that you would come.'

After all, could there be anything in the story? Wagner? Keats? Shelley? Sir Thomas Browne? Certainly the case was interesting.

And on the morrow evening, though it was pouring with rain, Mr Bons did not omit to call at Agathox Lodge.

The boy was ready, bubbling with excitement, and skipping about in a way that rather vexed the President of the Literary Society. They took a turn down Buckingham Park Road, and then – having seen that no one was watching them – slipped up the alley. Naturally enough (for the sun was setting) they ran straight against the omnibus.

'Good heavens!' exclaimed Mr Bons. 'Good gracious heavens!'

It was not the omnibus in which the boy had driven first, nor yet that in which he had returned. There were three horses – black, grey, and white, the grey being the finest. The driver, who turned round at the mention of goodness and of heaven, was a sallow man with terrifying jaws and sunken eyes. Mr Bons, on seeing him, gave a cry as if of recognition, and began to tremble violently.

The boy jumped in.

'Is it possible?' cried Mr Bons. 'Is the impossible possible?'

'Sir; come in, sir. It is such a fine omnibus. Oh, here is his name – Dan someone.'

Mr Bons sprang in too. A blast of wind immediately slammed the omnibus door, and the shock jerked down all the omnibus blinds, which were very weak on their springs.

'Dan ... Show me. Good gracious heavens! we're moving.'

'Hooray!' said the boy.

Mr Bons became flustered. He had not intended to be kidnapped. He could not find the door-handle nor push up the blinds. The omnibus was quite dark, and by the time he had struck a match, night had come on outside also. They were moving rapidly.

'A strange, a memorable adventure,' he said, surveying the

interior of the omnibus, which was large, roomy, and constructed with extreme regularity, every part exactly answering to every other part. Over the door (the handle of which was outside) was written, 'Lasciate ogni baldanza voi che entrate' – at least, that was what was written, but Mr Bons said that it was Lashy arty something, and that baldanza was a mistake for speranza. His voice sounded as if he was in church. Meanwhile, the boy called to the cadaverous driver for two return tickets. They were handed in without a word. Mr Bons covered his face with his hand and again trembled. 'Do you know who that is!' he whispered, when the little window had shut upon them. 'It is the impossible.'

'Well, I don't like him as much as Sir Thomas Browne, though I shouldn't be surprised if he had even more in him.'

'More in him?' He stamped irritably. 'By accident you have made the greatest discovery of the century, and all you can say is that there is more in this man. Do you remember those vellum books in my library, stamped with red lilies? This – sit still, I bring you stupendous news! – *this is the man who wrote them.*'

The boy sat quite still. 'I wonder if we shall see Mrs Gamp?' he asked, after a civil pause.

'Mrs — ?'

'Mrs Gamp and Mrs Harris. I like Mrs Harris. I came upon them quite suddenly. Mrs Gamp's bandboxes have moved over the rainbow so badly. All the bottoms have fallen out, and two of the pippins off her bedstead tumbled into the stream.'

'Out there sits the man who wrote my vellum books!' thundered Mr Bons, 'and you talk to me of Dickens and of Mrs Gamp?'

'I know Mrs Gamp so well,' he apologized. 'I could not help being glad to see her. I recognized her voice. She was telling Mrs Harris about Mrs Prig.'

'Did you spend the whole day in her elevating company?'

'Oh, no. I raced. I met a man who took me out beyond to a race-course. You run, and there are dolphins out at sea.'

'Indeed. Do you remember the man's name?'

'Achilles. No; he was later. Tom Jones.'

Mr Bons sighed heavily. 'Well, my lad, you have made a miserable mess of it. Think of a cultured person with your opportunities! A cultured person would have known all these characters and known what to have said to each. He would not have wasted his time with a Mrs Gamp or a Tom Jones. The creations of Homer, of Shakespeare, and of Him who drives us now, would alone have contented him. He would not have raced. He would have asked intelligent questions.'

'But, Mr Bons,' said the boy humbly, 'you will be a cultured person. I told them so.'

'True, true, and I beg you not to disgrace me when we arrive. No gossiping. No running. Keep close to my side, and never speak to these Immortals unless they speak to you. Yes, and give me the return tickets. You will be losing them.'

The boy surrendered the tickets, but felt a little sore. After all, he had found the way to this place. It was hard first to be disbelieved and then to be lectured. Meanwhile, the rain had stopped, and moonlight crept into the omnibus through the cracks in the blinds.

'But how is there to be a rainbow?' cried the boy.

'You distract me,' snapped Mr Bons. 'I wish to meditate on beauty. I wish to goodness I was with a reverent and sympathetic person.'

The lad bit his lip. He made a hundred good resolutions. He would imitate Mr Bons all the visit. He would not laugh, or run, or sing, or do any of the vulgar things that must have disgusted his new friends last time. He would be very careful to pronounce their names properly, and to remember who knew whom. Achilles did not know Tom Jones – at least, so Mr Bons said. The Duchess of Malfi was older than Mrs

Gamp – at least, so Mr Bons said. He would be self-conscious, reticent, and prim. He would never say he liked anyone. Yet when the blind flew up at a chance touch of his head, all these good resolutions went to the winds, for the omnibus had reached the summit of a moonlit hill, and there was the chasm, and there, across it, stood the old precipices, dreaming, with their feet in the everlasting river. He exclaimed, 'The mountain! Listen to the new tune in the water! Look at the camp-fires in the ravines,' and Mr Bons, after a hasty glance, retorted, 'Water? Camp-fires? Ridiculous rubbish. Hold your tongue. There is nothing at all.'

Yet under his eyes a rainbow formed, compounded not of sunlight and storm, but of moonlight and the spray of the river. The three horses put their feet upon it. He thought it the finest rainbow he had seen, but did not dare to say so, since Mr Bons said that nothing was there. He leant out – the window had opened – and sang the tune that rose from the sleeping waters.

'The prelude to Rhinegold?' said Mr Bons suddenly. 'Who taught you these *leit motifs*?' He, too, looked out of the window. Then he behaved very oddly. He gave a choking cry, and fell back on to the omnibus floor. He writhed and kicked. His face was green.

'Does the bridge make you dizzy?' the boy asked.

'Dizzy!' gasped Mr Bons. 'I want to go back. Tell the driver.'

But the driver shook his head.

'We are nearly there,' said the boy. 'They are asleep. Shall I call? They will be so pleased to see you, for I have prepared them.'

Mr Bons moaned. They moved over the lunar rainbow, which ever and ever broke away behind their wheels. How still the night was! Who would be sentry at the Gate?

'I am coming,' he shouted, again forgetting the hundred resolutions. 'I am returning – I, the boy.'

'The boy is returning,' cried a voice to other voices, who repeated, 'The boy is returning.'

'I am bringing Mr Bons with me.'

Silence.

'I should have said Mr Bons is bringing me with him.'

Profound silence.

'Who stands sentry?'

'Achilles.'

And on the rocky causeway, close to the springing of the rainbow bridge, he saw a young man who carried a wonderful shield.

'Mr Bons, it is Achilles, armed.'

'I want to go back,' said Mr Bons.

The last fragment of the rainbow melted, the wheels sang upon the living rock, the door of the omnibus burst open. Out leapt the boy – he could not resist – and sprang to meet the warrior, who, stooping suddenly, caught him on his shield.

'Achilles!' he cried, 'let me get down, for I am ignorant and vulgar, and I must wait for that Mr Bons of whom I told you yesterday.'

But Achilles raised him aloft. He crouched on the wonderful shield, on heroes and burning cities, on vineyards graven in gold, on every dear passion, every joy, on the entire image of the Mountain that he had discovered, encircled, like it, with an everlasting stream. 'No, no,' he protested, 'I am not worthy. It is Mr Bons who must be up here.'

But Mr Bons was whimpering, and Achilles trumpeted and cried, 'Stand upright upon my shield!'

'Sir, I did not mean to stand! Something made me stand. Sir, why do you delay? Here is only the great Achilles, whom you knew.'

Mr Bons screamed, 'I see no one. I see nothing. I want to go back.' Then he cried to the driver, 'Save me! Let me stop in your chariot. I have honoured you. I have quoted you. I have bound you in vellum. Take me back to my world.'

The driver replied, 'I am the means and not the end. I am the food and not the life. Stand by yourself, as that boy has stood. I cannot save you. For poetry is a spirit; and they that would worship it must worship in spirit and in truth.'

Mr Bons – he could not resist – crawled out of the beautiful omnibus. His face appeared, gaping horribly. His hands followed, one gripping the step, the other beating the air. Now his shoulders emerged, his chest, his stomach. With a shriek of 'I see London,' he fell – fell against the hard, moonlit rock, fell into it as if it were water, fell through it, vanished, and was seen by the boy no more.

'Where have you fallen to, Mr Bons? Here is a procession arriving to honour you with music and torches. Here come the men and women whose names you know. The mountain is awake, the river is awake, over the race-course the sea is awaking those dolphins, and it is all for you. They want you —'

There was the touch of fresh leaves on his forehead. Some one had crowned him.

*ΤΕΛΟΣ*

. . . . .

From the *Kingston Gazette, Surbiton Times,*
and *Raynes Park Observer.*

The body of Mr Septimus Bons has been found in a shockingly mutilated condition in the vicinity of the Bermondsey gas-works. The deceased's pockets contained a sovereign-purse, a silver cigar-case, a bijou pronouncing dictionary, and a couple of omnibus tickets. The unfortunate gentleman had apparently been hurled from a considerable height. Foul play is suspected, and a thorough investigation is pending by the authorities.

# OTHER KINGDOM

I

'"QUEM, whom; *fugis*, are you avoiding; *ah demens*, you silly ass; *habitarunt di quoque*, gods too have lived in; *silvas*, the woods." Go ahead!'

I always brighten the classics – it is part of my system – and therefore I translated *demens* by 'silly ass'. But Miss Beaumont need not have made a note of the translation, and Ford, who knows better, need not have echoed after me, 'Whom are you avoiding, you silly ass, gods too have lived in the woods.'

'Ye–es,' I replied, with scholarly hesitation. 'Ye–es. *Silvas* – woods, wooded spaces, the country generally. Yes. *Demens*, of course, is *de–mens*. "Ah, witless fellow! Gods, I say, even gods have dwelt in the woods ere now."'

'But I thought gods always lived in the sky,' said Mrs Worters, interrupting our lesson for I think the third-and-twentieth time.

'Not always,' answered Miss Beaumont. As she spoke she inserted 'witless fellow' as an alternative to 'silly ass'.

'I always thought they lived in the sky.'

'Oh, no, Mrs Worters,' the girl repeated. 'Not always.' And finding her place in the note-book she read as follows: 'Gods. Where. Chief deities – Mount Olympus. Pan – most places, as name implies. Oreads – mountains. Sirens, Tritons, Nereids – water (salt). Naiads – water (fresh). Satyrs, Fauns, etc. – woods. Dryads – trees.'

'Well, dear, you have learnt a lot. And will you now tell me what good it has done you?'

'It has helped me —' faltered Miss Beaumont. She was very earnest over her classics. She wished she could have said what good they had done her.

Ford came to her rescue. 'Of course it's helped you. The classics are full of tips. They teach you how to dodge things.'

I begged my young friend not to dodge his Virgil lesson.

'But they do!' he cried. 'Suppose that long-haired brute Apollo wants to give you a music lesson. Well, out you pop into the laurels. Or Universal Nature comes along. You aren't feeling particularly keen on Universal Nature, so you turn into a reed.'

'Is Jack mad?' asked Mrs Worters.

But Miss Beaumont had caught the allusions – which were quite ingenious, I must admit. 'And Croesus?' she inquired. 'What was it one turned into to get away from Croesus?'

I hastened to tidy up her mythology. 'Midas, Miss Beaumont, not Croesus. And he turns you – you don't turn yourself: he turns you into gold.'

'There's no dodging Midas,' said Ford.

'Surely —' said Miss Beaumont. She had been learning Latin not quite a fortnight, but she would have corrected the Regius Professor.

He began to tease her. 'Oh, there's no dodging Midas! He just comes, he touches you, and you pay him several thousand per cent at once. You're gold – a young golden lady – if he touches you.'

'I won't be touched!' she cried, relapsing into her habitual frivolity.

'Oh, but he'll touch you.'

'He shan't!'

'He will.'

'He shan't!'

'He will.'

Miss Beaumont took up her Virgil and smacked Ford over the head with it.

'Evelyn! Evelyn!' said Mrs Worters. 'Now you are forgetting yourself. And you also forget my question. What good has Latin done you?'

'Mr Ford – what good has Latin done you?'

'Mr Inskip – what good has Latin done us?'

So I was let in for the classical controversy. The arguments for the study of Latin are perfectly sound, but they are difficult to remember, and the afternoon sun was hot and I needed my tea. But I had to justify my existence as a coach, so I took off my eye-glasses and breathed on them and said, 'My dear Ford, what a question!'

'It's all right for Jack,' said Mrs Worters. 'Jack has to pass his entrance examination. But what's the good of it for Evelyn? None at all.'

'No, Mrs Worters,' I persisted, pointing my eye-glasses at her. 'I cannot agree. Miss Beaumont is – in a sense – new to our civilization. She is entering it, and Latin is one of the subjects in her entrance examination also. No one can grasp modern life without some knowledge of its origins.'

'But why should she grasp modern life?' said the tiresome woman.

'Well, there you are!' I retorted, and shut up my eye-glasses with a snap.

'Mr Inskip, I am not there. Kindly tell me what's the good of it all. Oh, I've been through it myself: Jupiter, Venus, Juno, I know the lot of them. And many of the stories not at all proper.'

'Classical education,' I said dryly, 'is not entirely confined to classical mythology. Though even the mythology has its value. Dreams if you like, but there is value in dreams.'

'I too have dreams,' said Mrs Worters, 'but I am not so foolish as to mention them afterwards.'

Mercifully we were interrupted. A rich virile voice close behind us said, 'Cherish your dreams!' We had been joined by our host, Harcourt Worters – Mrs Worters' son, Miss Beaumont's *fiancé*, Ford's guardian, my employer: I must speak of him as Mr Worters.

'Let us cherish our dreams!' he repeated. 'All day I've

been fighting, haggling, bargaining. And to come out on to this lawn and see you all learning Latin, so happy, so passionless, so Arcadian —'

He did not finish the sentence, but sank into the chair next to Miss Beaumont, and possessed himself of her hand. As he did so she sang: 'Ah yoù sílly àss, góds live in woóds!'

'What have we here?' said Mr Worters with a slight frown.

With the other hand she pointed to me.

'Virgil —' I stammered. 'Colloquial translation —'

'Oh, I see; a colloquial translation of poetry.' Then his smile returned. 'Perhaps if gods live in woods, that is why woods are so dear. I have just bought Other Kingdom Copse!'

Loud exclamations of joy. Indeed, the beeches in that copse are as fine as any in Hertfordshire. Moreover, it, and the meadow by which it is approached, have always made an ugly notch in the rounded contours of the Worters estate. So we were all very glad that Mr Worters had purchased Other Kingdom. Only Ford kept silent, stroking his head where the Virgil had hit it, and smiling a little to himself as he did so.

'Judging from the price I paid, I should say there was a god in every tree. But price, this time, was no object.' He glanced at Miss Beaumont. 'You admire beeches, Evelyn, do you not?'

'I forget always which they are. Like this?'

She flung her arms up above her head, close together, so that she looked like a slender column. Then her body swayed and her delicate green dress quivered over it with the suggestion of countless leaves.

'My dear child!' exclaimed her lover.

'No: that is a silver birch,' said Ford.

'Oh, of course. Like this, then.' And she twitched up her skirts so that for a moment they spread out in great horizontal layers, like the layers of a beech.

We glanced at the house, but none of the servants were

looking. So we laughed, and said she ought to go on the variety stage.

'Ah, this is the kind I like!' she cried, and practised the beech-tree again.

'I thought so,' said Mr Worters. 'I thought so. Other Kingdom Copse is yours.'

'Mine —?' She had never had such a present in her life. She could not realize it.

'The purchase will be drawn up in your name. You will sign the deed. Receive the wood, with my love. It is a second engagement ring.'

'But is it – is it mine? Can I – do what I like there?'

'You can,' said Mr Worters, smiling.

She rushed at him and kissed him. She kissed Mrs Worters. She would have kissed myself and Ford if we had not extruded elbows. The joy of possession had turned her head.

'It's mine! I can walk there, work there, live there. A wood of my own! Mine for ever.'

'Yours, at all events, for ninety-nine years.'

'Ninety-nine years?' I regret to say there was a tinge of disappointment in her voice.

'My dear child! Do you expect to live longer?'

'I suppose I can't,' she replied, and flushed a little. 'I don't know.'

'Ninety-nine seems long enough to most people. I have got this house, and the very lawn you are standing on, on a lease of ninety-nine years. Yet I call them my own, and I think I am justified. Am I not?'

'Oh, yes.'

'Ninety-nine years is practically for ever. Isn't it?'

'Oh, yes. It must be.'

Ford possesses a most inflammatory note-book. Outside it is labelled 'Private', inside it is headed 'Practically a book'. I saw him make an entry in it now, 'Eternity: practically ninety-nine years'.

Mr Worters, as if speaking to himself, now observed: 'My goodness! My goodness! How land has risen! Perfectly astounding.'

I saw that he was in need of a Boswell, so I said: 'Has it, indeed?'

'My dear Inskip. Guess what I could have got that wood for ten years ago! But I refused. Guess why.'

We could not guess why.

'Because the transaction would not have been straight.' A most becoming blush spread over his face as he uttered the noble word. 'Not straight. Straight legally. But not morally straight. We were to force the hands of the man who owned it. I refused. The others – decent fellows in their way – told me I was squeamish. I said, "Yes. Perhaps I am. My name is plain Harcourt Worters – not a well-known name if you go outside the City and my own country, but a name which, where it is known, carries, I flatter myself, some weight. And I will not sign my name to this. That is all. Call me squeamish if you like. But I will not sign. It is just a fad of mine. Let us call it a fad." ' He blushed again. Ford believes that his guardian blushes all over – that if you could strip him and make him talk nobly he would look like a boiled lobster. There is a picture of him in this condition in the note-book.

'So the man who owned it then didn't own it now?' said Miss Beaumont, who had followed the narrative with some interest.

'Oh, no!' said Mr Worters.

'Why no!' said Mrs Worters absently, as she hunted in the grass for her knitting-needle. 'Of course not. It belongs to the widow.'

'Tea!' cried her son, springing vivaciously to his feet. 'I see tea and I want it. Come, Mother. Come along, Evelyn. I can tell you it's no joke, a hard day in the battle of life. For life is practically a battle. To all intents and purposes a battle. Except for a few lucky fellows who can read books, and so avoid the realities. But I —'

His voice died away as he escorted the two ladies over the smooth lawn and up the stone steps to the terrace, on which the footman was placing tables and little chairs and a silver kettle-stand. More ladies came out of the house. We could just hear their shouts of excitement as they also were told of the purchase of Other Kingdom.

I like Ford. The boy has the makings of a scholar and – though for some reason he objects to the word – of a gentleman. It amused me now to see his lip curl with the vague cynicism of youth. He cannot understand the footman and the solid silver kettle-stand. They make him cross. For he has dreams – not exactly spiritual dreams: Mr Worters is the man for those – but dreams of the tangible and the actual: robust dreams, which take him, not to heaven, but to another earth. There are no footmen in this other earth, and the kettle-stands, I suppose, will not be made of silver, and I know that everything is to be itself, and not practically something else. But what this means, and, if it means anything, what the good of it is, I am not prepared to say. For though I have just said 'there is value in dreams', I only said it to silence old Mrs Worters.

'Go ahead, man! We can't have tea till we've got through something.'

He turned his chair away from the terrace, so that he could sit looking at the meadows, and at the stream that runs through the meadows, and at the beech-trees of Other Kingdom that rise beyond the stream. Then, most gravely and admirably, he began to construe the Eclogues of Virgil.

## II

OTHER KINGDOM COPSE is just like any other beech copse, and I am therefore spared the fatigue of describing it. And the stream in front of it, like many other streams, is not crossed by a bridge in the right place, and you must either walk round a mile or else you must paddle. Miss Beaumont suggested that we should paddle.

Mr Worters accepted the suggestion tumultuously. It only became evident gradually that he was not going to adopt it.

'What fun! what fun! We will paddle to your kingdom. If only – if only it wasn't for the tea-things.'

'But you can carry the tea-things on your back.'

'Why, yes! so I can. Or the servants could.'

'Harcourt – no servants. This is my picnic, and my wood. I'm going to settle everything. I didn't tell you: I've got all the food. I've been in the village with Mr Ford.'

'In the village —'

'Yes. We got biscuits and oranges and half a pound of tea. That's all you'll have. He carried them up. And he'll carry them over the stream. I want you just to lend me some tea-things – not the best ones. I'll take care of them. That's all.'

'Dear creature—'

'Evelyn,' said Mrs Worters, 'how much did you and Jack pay for that tea?'

'For the half-pound, tenpence.'

Mrs Worters received the announcement in gloomy silence.

'Mother!' cried Mr Worters. 'Why, I forgot! How could we go paddling with mother?'

'Oh, but, Mrs Worters, we could carry you over.'

'Thank you, dearest child. I am sure you could.'

'Alas! alas! Evelyn. Mother is laughing at us. She would sooner die than be carried. And alas! there are my sisters, and Mrs Osgood: she has a cold, tiresome woman. No: we shall have to go round by the bridge.'

'But some of us—' began Ford. His guardian cut him short with a quick look.

So we went round – a procession of eight. Miss Beaumont led us. She was full of fun – at least so I thought at the time, but when I reviewed her speeches afterwards I could not find in them anything amusing. It was all this kind of thing:

'Single file! Pretend you're in church and don't talk. Mr Ford, turn out your toes. Harcourt – at the bridge throw to the Naiad a pinch of tea. She has a headache. She has had a headache for nineteen hundred years.' All that she said was quite stupid. I cannot think why I liked it at the time.

As we approached the copse she said, 'Mr Inskip, sing, and we'll sing after you: Ah yoù sílly àss, góds live in woóds.' I cleared my throat and gave out the abominable phrase, and we all chanted it as if it were a litany. There was something attractive about Miss Beaumont. I was not surprised that Harcourt had picked her out of 'Ireland' and had brought her home, without money, without connexions, almost without antecedents, to be his bride. It was daring of him, but he knew himself to be a daring fellow. She brought him nothing; but that he could afford, he had so vast a surplus of spiritual and commercial goods. 'In time,' I heard him tell his mother, 'in time Evelyn will repay me a thousandfold.' Meanwhile there was something attractive about her. If it were my place to like people, I could have liked her very much.

'Stop singing!' she cried. We had entered the wood. 'Welcome, all of you.' We bowed. Ford, who had not been laughing, bowed down to the ground. 'And now be seated. Mrs Worters – will you sit there – against that tree with a green trunk? It will show up your beautiful dress.'

'Very well, dear, I will,' said Mrs Worters.

'Anna – there. Mr Inskip next to her. Then Ruth and Mrs Osgood. Oh, Harcourt – do sit a little forward, so that you'll hide the house. I don't want to see the house at all.'

'I won't!' laughed her lover. 'I want my back against a tree, too.'

'Miss Beaumont,' asked Ford, 'where shall I sit?' He was standing at attention, like a soldier.

'Oh, look at all these Worters,' she cried, 'and one little Ford in the middle of them!' For she was at that state of civilization which appreciates a pun.

'Shall I stand, Miss Beaumont? Shall I hide the house from you if I stand?'

'Sit down, Jack, you baby!' cried his guardian, breaking in with needless asperity. 'Sit down!'

'He may just as well stand if he will,' said she. 'Just pull back your soft hat, Mr Ford. Like a halo. Now you hide even the smoke from the chimneys. And it makes you look beautiful.'

'Evelyn! Evelyn! You are too hard on the boy. You'll tire him. He's one of those bookworms. He's not strong. Let him sit down.'

'Aren't you strong?' she asked.

'I am strong!' he cried. It is quite true. Ford has no right to be strong, but he is. He never did his dumb-bells or played in his school fifteen. But the muscles came. He thinks they came while he was reading Pindar.

'Then you may just as well stand, if you will.'

'Evelyn! Evelyn! childish, selfish maiden! If poor Jack gets tired I will take his place. Why don't you want to see the house? Eh?'

Mrs Worters and the Miss Worters moved uneasily. They saw that their Harcourt was not quite pleased. Theirs not to question why. It was for Evelyn to remove his displeasure, and they glanced at her.

'Well, why don't you want to see your future home? I must say – though I practically planned the house myself – that it looks very well from here. I like the gables. Miss! Answer me!'

I felt for Miss Beaumont. A home-made gable is an awful thing, and Harcourt's mansion looked like a cottage with the dropsy. But what would she say?

She said nothing.

'Well?'

It was as if he had never spoken. She was as merry, as smiling, as pretty as ever, and she said nothing. She had not realized that a question requires an answer.

For us the situation was intolerable. I had to save it by making a tactful reference to the view, which, I said, reminded me a little of the country near Veii. It did not – indeed it could not, for I have never been near Veii. But it is part of my system to make classical allusions. And at all events I saved the situation.

Miss Beaumont was serious and rational at once. She asked me the date of Veii. I made a suitable answer.

'I do like the classics,' she informed us. 'They are so natural. Just writing down things.'

'Ye–es,' said I. 'But the classics have their poetry as well as their prose. They're more than a record of facts.'

'Just writing down things,' said Miss Beaumont, and smiled as if the silly definition pleased her.

Harcourt had recovered himself. 'A very just criticism,' said he. 'It is what I always feel about the ancient world. It takes us but a very little way. It only writes things down.'

'What do you mean?' asked Evelyn.

'I mean this – though it is presumptuous to speak in the presence of Mr Inskip. This is what I mean. The classics are not everything. We owe them an enormous debt; I am the last to undervalue it; I, too, went through them at school. They are full of elegance and beauty. But they are not everything. They were written before men began to really feel.' He coloured crimson. 'Hence, the chilliness of classical art – its lack of – of a something. Whereas later things – Dante – a Madonna of Raphael – some bars of Mendelssohn —' His voice tailed reverently away. We sat with our eyes on the ground, not liking to look at Miss Beaumont. It is a fairly open secret that she also lacks a something. She has not yet developed her soul.

The silence was broken by the still small voice of Mrs Worters saying that she was faint with hunger.

The young hostess sprang up. She would let none of us help her: it was her party. She undid the basket and emptied out the biscuits and oranges from their bags, and boiled the kettle and poured out the tea, which was horrible. But we laughed and talked with the frivolity that suits the open air, and even Mrs Worters expectorated her flies with a smile. Over us all there stood the silent, chivalrous figure of Ford, drinking tea carefully lest it should disturb his outline. His guardian, who is a wag, chaffed him and tickled his ankles and calves.

'Well, this is nice!' said Miss Beaumont. 'I am happy.'

'Your wood, Evelyn!' said the ladies.

'Her wood for ever!' cried Mr Worters. 'It is an unsatisfactory arrangement, a ninety-nine years' lease. There is no feeling of permanency. I reopened negotiations. I have bought her the wood for ever – all right, dear, all right: don't make a fuss.'

'But I must!' she cried. 'For everything's perfect! Everyone so kind – and I didn't know most of you a year ago. Oh, it is so wonderful – and now a wood – a wood of my own – a wood for ever. All of you coming to tea with me here! Dear Harcourt – dear people – and just where the house would come and spoil things, there is Mr Ford!'

'Ha! ha!' laughed Mr Worters, and slipped his hand up round the boy's ankle. What happened I do not know, but Ford collapsed on to the ground with a sharp cry. To an outsider it might have sounded like a cry of anger or pain. We, who knew better, laughed uproariously.

'Down he goes! Down he goes!' and they struggled playfully, kicking up the mould and the dry leaves.

'Don't hurt my wood!' cried Miss Beaumont.

Ford gave another sharp cry. Mr Worters withdrew his hand. 'Victory!' he exclaimed. 'Evelyn! behold the family seat!' But Miss Beaumont, in her butterfly fashion, had left us, and was strolling away into her wood.

We packed up the tea-things and then split into groups. Ford went with the ladies. Mr Worters did me the honour to stop by me.

'Well!' he said, in accordance with his usual formula, 'and how goes the classics?'

'Fairly well.'

'Does Miss Beaumont show any ability?'

'I should say that she does. At all events she has enthusiasm.'

'You do not think it is the enthusiasm of a child? I will be frank with you, Mr Inskip. In many ways Miss Beaumont's practically a child. She has everything to learn: she acknowledges as much herself. Her new life is so different – so strange. Our habits – our thoughts – she has to be initiated into them all.'

I saw what he was driving at, but I am not a fool, and I replied: 'And how can she be initiated better than through the classics?'

'Exactly, exactly,' said Mr Worters. In the distance we heard her voice. She was counting the beech-trees. 'The only question is – this Latin and Greek – what will she do with it? Can she make anything of it? Can she – well, it's not as if she will ever have to teach it to others.'

'That is true.' And my features might have been observed to become undecided.

'Whether, since she knows so little – I grant you she has enthusiasm. But ought one not to divert her enthusiasm – say to English literature? She scarcely knows her Tennyson at all. Last night in the conservatory I read her that wonderful scene between Arthur and Guinevere. Greek and Latin are all very well, but I sometimes feel we ought to begin at the beginning.'

'You feel,' said I, 'that for Miss Beaumont the classics are something of a luxury.'

'A luxury. That is the exact word, Mr Inskip. A luxury. A whim. It is all very well for Jack Ford. And here we come to another point. Surely she keeps Jack back? Her knowledge must be elementary.'

'Well, her knowledge *is* elementary: and I must say that it's difficult to teach them together. Jack has read a good deal, one way and another, whereas Miss Beaumont, though diligent and enthusiastic —'

'So I have been feeling. The arrangement is scarcely fair on Jack?'

'Well, I must admit —'

'Quite so. I ought never to have suggested it. It must come to an end. Of course, Mr Inskip, it shall make no difference to you, this withdrawal of a pupil.'

'The lessons shall cease at once, Mr Worters.'

Here she came up to us. 'Harcourt, there are seventy-eight trees. I have had such a count.'

He smiled down at her. Let me remember to say that he is tall and handsome, with a strong chin and liquid brown eyes, and a high forehead and hair not at all grey. Few things are more striking than a photograph of Mr Harcourt Worters.

'Seventy-eight trees?'

'Seventy-eight.'

'Are you pleased?'

'Oh, Harcourt —!'

I began to pack up the tea-things. They both saw and heard me. It was their own fault if they did not go further.

'I'm looking forward to the bridge,' said he. 'A rustic bridge at the bottom, and then, perhaps, an asphalt path from the house over the meadow, so that in all weathers we can walk here dry-shod. The boys come into the wood – look at all these initials – and I thought of putting a simple fence, to prevent anyone but ourselves —'

'Harcourt!'

'A simple fence,' he continued, 'just like what I have put round my garden and the fields. Then at the other side of the copse, away from the house, I would put a gate, and have keys – two keys, I think – one for me and one for you – not more; and I would bring the asphalt path —'

'But, Harcourt —'

'But, Evelyn!'

'I – I – I —'

'You – you – you —?'

'I – I don't want an asphalt path.'

'No? Perhaps you are right. Cinders perhaps. Yes. Or even gravel.'

'But, Harcourt – I don't want a path at all. I – I – can't afford a path.'

He gave a roar of triumphant laughter. 'Dearest! As if you were going to be bothered? The path's part of my present.'

'The wood is your present,' said Miss Beaumont. 'Do you know – I don't care for the path. I'd rather always come as we came to-day. And I don't want a bridge. No – nor a fence either. I don't mind the boys and their initials. They and the girls have always come up to Other Kingdom and cut their names together in the bark. It's called the Fourth Time of Asking. I don't want it to stop.'

'Ugh!' He pointed to a large heart transfixed by an arrow. 'Ugh! Ugh!' I suspect that he was gaining time.

'They cut their names and go away, and when the first child is born they come again and deepen the cuts. So for each child. That's how you know: the initials that go right through to the wood are the fathers and mothers of large families, and the scratches in the bark that soon close up are boys and girls who were never married at all.'

'You wonderful person! I've lived here all my life and never heard a word of this. Fancy folk-lore in Hertfordshire! I must tell the Archdeacon: he will be delighted —'

'And, Harcourt, I don't want this to stop.'

'My dear girl, the villagers will find other trees! There's nothing particular in Other Kingdom.'

'But —'

'Other Kingdom shall be for us. You and I alone. Our initials only.' His voice sank to a whisper.

'I don't want it fenced in.' Her face was turned to me; I saw that it was puzzled and frightened. 'I hate fences. And bridges. And all paths. It is my wood. Please: you gave me the wood.'

'Why, yes!' he replied, soothing her. But I could see that he was angry. 'Of course. But aha! Evelyn, the meadow's mine; I have a right to fence there – between my domain and yours!'

'Oh, fence me out, if you like! Fence me out as much as you like! But never in. Oh, Harcourt, never in. I must be on the outside, I must be where anyone can reach me. Year by year – while the initials deepen – the only thing worth feeling – and at last they close up – but one has felt them.'

'Our initials!' he murmured, seizing upon the one word which he had understood and which was useful to him. 'Let us carve our initials now. You and I – a heart if you like it, and an arrow and everything. H. W. – E. B.'

'H. W.,' she repeated, 'and E. B.'

He took out his pen-knife and drew her away in search of an unsullied tree. 'E. B., Eternal Blessing. Mine! Mine! My haven from the world! My temple of purity. Oh, the spiritual exaltation – you cannot understand it, but you will! Oh, the seclusion of Paradise. Year after year alone together, all in all to each other – year after year, soul to soul, E. B., Everlasting Bliss!'

He stretched out his hand to cut the initials. As he did so she seemed to awake from a dream. 'Harcourt!' she cried, 'Harcourt! What's that? What's that red stuff on your finger and thumb?'

III

OH, my goodness! Oh, all ye goddesses and gods! Here's a mess. Mr Worters has been reading Ford's inflammatory note-book.

'It is my own fault,' said Ford. 'I should have labelled it "Practically Private". How could he know he was not meant to look inside?'

I spoke out severely, as an *employé* should. 'My dear boy, none of that. The label came unstuck. That was why Mr Worters opened the book. He never suspected it was private. See – the label's off.'

'Scratched off,' Ford retorted grimly, and glanced at his ankle.

I affected not to understand. 'The point is this. Mr Worters is thinking the matter over for four-and-twenty hours. If you take my advice you will apologize before that time elapses.'

'And if I don't?'

'You know your own affairs of course. But don't forget that you are young and practically ignorant of life, and that you have scarcely any money of your own. As far as I can see, your career practically depends on the favour of Mr Worters. You have laughed at him. He does not like being laughed at. It seems to me that your course is obvious.'

'Apology?'

'Complete.'

'And if I don't?'

'Departure.'

He sat down on the stone steps and rested his head on his knees. On the lawn below us was Miss Beaumont, draggling about with some croquet balls. Her lover was out in the meadow, superintending the course of the asphalt path. For the path is to be made, and so is the bridge, and the fence is to be built round Other Kingdom after all. In time Miss Beaumont saw how unreasonable were her objections. Of her own accord, one evening in the drawing-room, she gave her Harcourt permission to do what he liked. 'That wood looks nearer,' said Ford.

'The inside fences have gone: that brings it nearer. But my dear boy – you must settle what you're going to do.'

'How much has he read?'

'Naturally he only opened the book. From what you showed me of it, one glance would be enough.'

'Did he open at the poems?'

'Poems?'

'Did he speak of the poems?'

'No. Were they about him?'

'They were not about him.'

'Then it wouldn't matter if he saw them.'

'It is sometimes a compliment to be mentioned,' said Ford, looking up at me. The remark had a stinging fragrance about it – such a fragrance as clings to the mouth after admirable wine. It did not taste like the remark of a boy. I was sorry that my pupil was likely to wreck his career; and I told him again that he had better apologize.

'I won't speak of Mr Worters' claim for an apology. That's an aspect on which I prefer not to touch. The point is, if you don't apologize, you go – where?'

'To an aunt at Peckham.'

I pointed to the pleasant, comfortable landscape, full of cows and carriage-horses out at grass, and civil retainers. In the midst of it stood Mr Worters, radiating energy and wealth, like a terrestrial sun. 'My dear Ford – don't be heroic! Apologize.'

Unfortunately I raised my voice a little, and Miss Beaumont heard me, down on the lawn.

'Apologize?' she cried. 'What about?' And as she was not interested in the game, she came up the steps towards us, trailing her croquet mallet behind her. Her walk was rather listless. She was toning down at last.

'Come indoors!' I whispered. 'We must get out of this.'

'Not a bit of it!' said Ford.

'What is it?' she asked, standing beside him on the step.

He swallowed something as he looked up at her. Suddenly I understood. I knew the nature and the subject of his poems.

I was not so sure now that he had better apologize. The sooner he was kicked out of the place the better.

In spite of my remonstrances, he told her about the book, and her first remark was: 'Oh, do let me see it!' She had no 'proper feeling' of any kind. Then she said: 'But why do you both look so sad?'

'We are awaiting Mr Worters' decision,' said I.

'Mr Inskip! What nonsense! Do you suppose Harcourt'll be angry?'

'Of course he is angry, and rightly so.'

'But why?'

'Ford has laughed at him.'

'But what's that!' And for the first time there was anger in her voice. 'Do you mean to say he'll punish someone who laughs at him? Why, for what else – for whatever reason are we all here? Not to laugh at each other! I laugh at people all day. At Mr Ford. At you. And so does Harcourt. Oh, you've misjudged him! He won't – he couldn't be angry with people who laughed.'

'Mine is not nice laughter,' said Ford. 'He could not well forgive me.'

'You're a silly boy.' She sneered at him. 'You don't know Harcourt. So generous in every way. Why, he'd be as furious as I should be if you apologized. Mr Inskip, isn't that so?'

'He has every right to an apology, I think.'

'Right? What's a right? You use too many new words. "Rights" – "apologies" – "society" – "position" – I don't follow it. What are we all here for, anyhow?'

Her discourse was full of trembling lights and shadows – frivolous one moment, the next moment asking why Humanity is here. I did not take the Moral Science Tripos, so I could not tell her.

'One thing I know – and that is that Harcourt isn't as stupid as you two. He soars above conventions. He doesn't care about "rights" and "apologies". He knows that all laughter is nice, and that the other nice things are money and the soul and so on.'

The soul and so on! I wonder that Harcourt out in the meadows did not have an apoplectic fit.

'Why, what a poor business your life would be,' she continued, 'if you all kept taking offence and apologizing! Forty million people in England and all of them touchy! How one would laugh if it was true! Just imagine!' And she did laugh. 'Look at Harcourt though. He knows better. He isn't petty like that. Mr Ford! He isn't petty like that. Why, what's wrong with your eyes?'

He rested his head on his knees again, and we could see his eyes no longer. In dispassionate tones she informed me that she thought he was crying. Then she tapped him on the hair with her mallet and said: 'Cry-baby! Cry-cry-baby! Crying about nothing!' and ran laughing down the steps. 'All right!' she shouted from the lawn. 'Tell the cry-baby to stop. I'm going to speak to Harcourt!'

We watched her go in silence. Ford had scarcely been crying. His eyes had only become large and angry. He used such swear-words as he knew, and then got up abruptly and went into the house. I think he could not bear to see her disillusioned. I had no such tenderness, and it was with considerable interest that I watched Miss Beaumont approach her lord.

She walked confidently across the meadow, bowing to the workmen as they raised their hats. Her languor had passed, and with it her suggestion of 'tone'. She was the same crude, unsophisticated person that Harcourt had picked out of Ireland – beautiful and ludicrous in the extreme, and – if you go in for pathos – extremely pathetic.

I saw them meet, and soon she was hanging on his arm. The motion of his hand explained to her the construction of bridges. Twice she interrupted him: he had to explain everything again. Then she got in her word, and what followed was a good deal better than a play. Their two little figures parted and met and parted again, she gesticulating, he most pompous and calm. She pleaded, she argued and – if satire can carry half a mile – she tried to be satirical. To enforce one of her childish points she made two steps back. Splash! She was floundering in the little stream.

That was the *dénouement* of the comedy. Harcourt rescued her, while the workmen crowded round in an agitated chorus. She was wet quite as far as her knees, and muddy over her ankles. In this state she was conducted towards me, and in time I began to hear words. 'Influenza – a slight immersion – clothes are of no consequence beside health – pray, dearest, don't worry – yes, it must have been a shock – bed! bed! I insist on bed! Promise? Good girl. Up the steps to bed then.'

They parted on the lawn, and she came obediently up the steps. Her face was full of terror and bewilderment.

'So you've had a wetting, Miss Beaumont!'

'Wetting? Oh, yes. But, Mr Inskip – I don't understand: I've failed.'

I expressed surprise.

'Mr Ford is to go – at once. I've failed.'

'I'm sorry.'

'I've failed with Harcourt. He's offended. He won't laugh. He won't let me do what I want. Latin and Greek began it: I wanted to know about gods and heroes and he wouldn't let me: then I wanted no fence round Other Kingdom and no bridge and no path – and look! Now I ask that Mr Ford, who has done nothing, shan't be punished for it – and he is to go away for ever.'

'Impertinence is not "nothing," Miss Beaumont.' For I must keep in with Harcourt.

'Impertinence is nothing!' she cried. 'It doesn't exist. It's a sham, like "claims" and "position" and "rights". It's part of the great dream.'

'What "great dream"?' I asked, trying not to smile.

'Tell Mr Ford – here comes Harcourt; I must go to bed.

Give my love to Mr Ford, and tell him "to guess". I shall never see him again, and I won't stand it. Tell him to guess. I am sorry I called him a cry-baby. He was not crying like a baby. He was crying like a grown-up person, and now I have grown up too.'

I judged it right to repeat this conversation to my employer.

## IV

THE bridge is built, the fence finished, and Other Kingdom lies tethered by a ribbon of asphalt to our front door. The seventy-eight trees therein certainly seem nearer, and during the windy nights that followed Ford's departure we could hear their branches sighing, and would find in the morning that beech-leaves had been blown right up against the house. Miss Beaumont made no attempt to go out, much to the relief of the ladies, for Harcourt had given the word that she was not to go out unattended, and the boisterous weather deranged their petticoats. She remained indoors, neither reading nor laughing, and dressing no longer in green, but in brown.

Not noticing her presence, Mr Worters looked in one day and said with a sigh of relief: 'That's all right. The circle's completed.'

'Is it indeed!' she replied.

'You there, you quiet little mouse? I only meant that our lords, the British workmen, have at last condescended to complete their labours, and have rounded us off from the world. I – in the end I was a naughty, domineering tyrant, and disobeyed you. I didn't have the gate out at the farther side of the copse. Will you forgive me?'

'Anything, Harcourt, that pleases you, is certain to please me.'

The ladies smiled at each other, and Mr Worters said: 'That's right, and as soon as the wind goes down we'll all progress together to your wood, and take possession of it formally, for it didn't really count that last time.'

'No, it didn't really count that last time,' Miss Beaumont echoed.

'Evelyn says this wind never will go down,' remarked Mrs Worters. 'I don't know how she knows.'

'It will never go down as long as I am in the house.'

'Really?' he said gaily. 'Then come out now, and send it down with me.'

They took a few turns up and down the terrace. The wind lulled for a moment, but blew fiercer than ever during lunch. As we ate, it roared and whistled down the chimney at us, and the trees of Other Kingdom frothed like the sea. Leaves and twigs flew from them, and a bough, a good-sized bough, was blown on to the smooth asphalt path, and actually switch-backed over the bridge, up the meadow, and across our very lawn. (I venture to say 'our', as I am now staying on as Harcourt's secretary.) Only the stone steps prevented it from reaching the terrace and perhaps breaking the dining-room window. Miss Beaumont sprang up and, napkin in hand, ran out and touched it.

'Oh, Evelyn —' the ladies cried.

'Let her go,' said Mr Worters tolerantly. 'It certainly is a remarkable incident, remarkable. We must remember to tell the Archdeacon about it.'

'Harcourt,' she cried, with the first hint of returning colour in her cheeks, 'mightn't we go up to the copse after lunch, you and I?'

Mr Worters considered.

'Of course, not if you don't think best.'

'Inskip, what's your opinion?'

I saw what his own was, and cried, 'Oh, let's go!' though I detest the wind as much as anyone.

'Very well. Mother, Anna, Ruth, Mrs Osgood – we'll all go.'

And go we did, a lugubrious procession; but the gods were good to us for once, for as soon as we were started, the tempest dropped, and there ensued an extraordinary calm. After all, Miss Beaumont was something of a weather prophet. Her spirits improved every minute. She tripped in front of us along the asphalt path, and ever and anon turned round to say to her lover some gracious or alluring thing. I admired her for it. I admire people who know on which side their bread is buttered.

'Evelyn, come here!'

'Come here yourself.'

'Give me a kiss.'

'Come and take it, then.'

He ran after her, and she ran away, while all our party laughed melodiously.

'Oh, I am so happy!' she cried. 'I think I've everything I want in all the world. Oh dear, those last few days indoors! But oh, I am so happy now!' She had changed her brown dress for the old flowing green one, and she began to do her skirt dance in the open meadow, lit by sudden gleams of the sunshine. It was really a beautiful sight, and Mr Worters did not correct her, glad perhaps that she should recover her spirits, even if she lost her tone. Her feet scarcely moved, but her body so swayed and her dress spread so gloriously around her that we were transported with joy. She danced to the song of a bird that sang passionately in Other Kingdom, and the river held back its waves to watch her (one might have supposed), and the winds lay spell-bound in their cavern, and the great clouds spell-bound in the sky. She danced away from our society and our life, back, back through the centuries till houses and fences fell and the earth lay wild to the sun. Her garment was as foliage upon her, the strength of her limbs as boughs, her throat the smooth upper branch that salutes the morning or glistens to the rain. Leaves move, leaves hide it as hers was hidden by the motion of her hair.

Leaves move again and it is ours, as her throat was ours again when, parting the tangle, she faced us crying, 'Oh!' crying, 'Oh, Harcourt! I never was so happy. I have all that there is in the world.'

But he, entrammelled in love's ecstasy, forgetting certain Madonnas of Raphael, forgetting, I fancy, his soul, sprang to inarm her with, 'Evelyn! Eternal Bliss! Mine to eternity! Mine! and she sprang away. Music was added and she sang, 'Oh Ford! oh Ford, among all these Worters, I am coming through you to my Kingdom. Oh Ford, my lover while I was a woman, I will never forget you, never, as long as I have branches to shade you from the sun,' and, singing, crossed the stream.

Why he followed her so passionately, I do not know. It was play, she was in his own domain which a fence surrounds, and she could not possibly escape him. But he dashed round by the bridge as if all their love was at stake, and pursued her with fierceness up the hill. She ran well, but the end was a foregone conclusion, and we only speculated whether he would catch her outside or inside the copse. He gained on her inch by inch; now they were in the shadow of the trees; he had practically grasped her, he had missed; she had disappeared into the trees themselves, he following.

'Harcourt is in high spirits,' said Mrs Osgood, Anna, and Ruth.

'Evelyn!' we heard him shouting within.

We proceeded up the asphalt path.

'Evelyn! Evelyn!'

'He's not caught her yet, evidently.'

'Where are you, Evelyn?'

'Miss Beaumont must have hidden herself rather cleverly.'

'Look here,' cried Harcourt, emerging, 'have you seen Evelyn?'

'Oh, no, she's certainly inside.'

'So I thought.'

'Evelyn must be dodging round one of the trunks. You go this way, I that. We'll soon find her.'

We searched, gaily at first, and always with a feeling that Miss Beaumont was close by, that the delicate limbs were just behind this bole, the hair and the drapery quivering among those leaves. She was beside us, above us; here was her footstep on the purple-brown earth – her bosom, her neck – she was everywhere and nowhere. Gaiety turned to irritation, irritation to anger and fear. Miss Beaumont was apparently lost. 'Evelyn! Evelyn!' we continued to cry. 'Oh, really, it is beyond a joke.'

Then the wind arose, the more violent for its lull, and we were driven into the house by a terrific storm. We said, 'At all events she will come back now.' But she did not come, and the rain hissed and rose up from the dry meadows like incense smoke, and smote the quivering leaves to applause. Then it lightened. Ladies screamed, and we saw Other Kingdom as one who claps the hands, and heard it as one who roars with laughter in the thunder. Not even the Archdeacon can remember such a storm. All Harcourt's seedlings were ruined, and the tiles flew off his gables right and left. He came to me presently with a white, drawn face, saying: 'Inskip, can I trust you?'

'You can indeed.'

'I have long suspected it; she has eloped with Ford.'

'But how —' I gasped.

'The carriage is ready – we'll talk as we drive.' Then, against the rain he shouted: 'No gate in the fence, I know, but what about a ladder? While I blunder, she's over the fence, and he —'

'But you were so close. There was not the time.'

'There is time for anything,' he said venomously, 'where a treacherous woman is concerned. I found her no better than a savage, I trained her, I educated her. But I'll break them both. I can do that; I'll break them soul and body.'

No one can break Ford now. The task is impossible. But I trembled for Miss Beaumont.

We missed the train. Young couples had gone by it, several young couples, and we heard of more young couples in London, as if all the world were mocking Harcourt's solitude. In desperation we sought the squalid suburb that is now Ford's home. We swept past the dirty maid and the terrified aunt, swept upstairs, to catch him if we could red-handed. He was seated at the table, reading the *Oedipus Coloneus* of Sophocles.

'That won't take me in!' shouted Harcourt. 'You've got Miss Beaumont with you, and I know it.'

'No such luck,' said Ford.

He stammered with rage. 'Inskip – you hear that? "No such luck!" Quote the evidence against him. I can't speak.'

So I quoted her song. ' "Oh Ford! Oh Ford, among all these Worters, I am coming through you to my Kingdom! Oh Ford, my lover while I was a woman, I will never forget you, never, as long as I have branches to shade you from the sun." Soon after that, we lost her.'

'And – and on another occasion she sent a message of similar effect. Inskip, bear witness. He was to "guess" something.'

'I have guessed it,' said Ford.

'So you practically —'

'Oh, no, Mr Worters, you mistake me. I have not practically guessed. I have guessed. I could tell you if I chose, but it would be no good, for she has not practically escaped you. She has escaped you absolutely, for ever and ever, as long as there are branches to shade men from the sun.'

# THE CURATE'S FRIEND

It is uncertain how the Faun came to be in Wiltshire. Perhaps he came over with the Roman legionaries to live with his friends in camp, talking to them of Lucretilis, or Garganus or of the slopes of Etna; they in the joy of their recall forgot to take him on board, and he wept in exile; but at last he found that our hills also understood his sorrows, and rejoiced when he was happy. Or, perhaps he came to be there because he had been there always. There is nothing particularly classical about a faun: it is only that the Greeks and Italians have ever had the sharpest eyes. You will find him in the 'Tempest' and the 'Benedicite'; and any country which has beech clumps and sloping grass and very clear streams may reasonably produce him.

How I came to see him is a more difficult question. For to see him there is required a certain quality, for which truthfulness is too cold a name and animal spirits too coarse a one, and he alone knows how this quality came to be in me. No man has the right to call himself a fool, but I may say that I then presented the perfect semblance of one. I was facetious without humour and serious without conviction. Every Sunday I would speak to my rural parishioners about the other world in the tone of one who has been behind the scenes, or I would explain to them the errors of the Pelagians, or I would warn them against hurrying from one dissipation to another. Every Tuesday I gave what I called 'straight talks to my lads' – talks which led straight past anything awkward. And every Thursday I addressed the Mothers' Union on the duties of wives or widows, and gave them practical hints on the management of a family of ten.

I took myself in, and for a time I certainly took in Emily. I have never known a girl attend so carefully to my sermons, or laugh so heartily at my jokes. It is no wonder that I became engaged. She has made an excellent wife, freely correcting her husband's absurdities, but allowing no one else to breathe a word against them; able to talk about the subconscious self in the drawing-room, and yet have an ear for the children crying in the nursery or the plates breaking in the scullery. An excellent wife – better than I ever imagined. But she has not married me.

Had we stopped indoors that afternoon nothing would have happened. It was all owing to Emily's mother, who insisted on our tea-ing out. Opposite the village, across the stream, was a small chalk down, crowned by a beech copse and a few Roman earthworks. (I lectured very vividly on those earthworks: they have since proved to be Saxon.) Hither did I drag up a tea-basket and a heavy rug for Emily's mother, while Emily and a little friend went on in front. The little friend – who has played all through a much less important part than he supposes – was a pleasant youth, full of intelligence and poetry, especially of what he called the poetry of earth. He longed to wrest earth's secret from her, and I have seen him press his face passionately into the grass, even when he has believed himself to be alone. Emily was at that time full of vague aspirations, and, though I should have preferred them all to centre in me, yet it seemed unreasonable to deny her such other opportunities for self-culture as the neighbourhood provided.

It was then my habit, on reaching the top of any eminence, to exclaim facetiously 'And who will stand on either hand and keep the bridge with me?' at the same moment violently agitating my arms or casting my wide-awake at an imaginary foe. Emily and the friend received my sally as usual, nor could I detect any insincerity in their mirth. Yet I was convinced that someone was present who did not think I had been funny, and any public speaker will understand my growing uneasiness.

I was somewhat cheered by Emily's mother, who puffed up exclaiming, 'Kind Harry, to carry the things! What should we do without you, even now! Oh, what a view! Can you see the dear Cathedral? No. Too hazy. Now *I'm* going to sit *right* on the rug.' She smiled mysteriously. 'The downs in September, you know.'

We gave some perfunctory admiration to the landscape, which is indeed only beautiful to those who admire land, and to them perhaps the most beautiful in England. For here is the body of the great chalk spider who straddles over our island – whose legs are the south downs and the north downs and the Chilterns, and the tips of whose toes poke out at Cromer and Dover. He is a clean creature, who grows as few trees as he can, and those few in tidy clumps, and he loves to be tickled by quickly flowing streams. He is pimpled all over with earthworks, for from the beginning of time men have fought for the privilege of standing on him, and the oldest of our temples is built upon his back.

But in those days I liked my country snug and pretty, full of gentlemen's residences and shady bowers and people who touch their hats. The great sombre expanses on which one may walk for miles and hardly shift a landmark or meet a genteel person were still intolerable to me. I turned away as soon as propriety allowed and said, 'And may I now prepare the cup that cheers?'

Emily's mother replied: 'Kind man, to help me. I always do say that tea out is worth the extra effort. I wish we led simpler lives.' We agreed with her. I spread out the food. 'Won't the kettle stand? Oh, but *make* it stand.' I did so. There was a little cry, faint but distinct, as of something in pain.

'How silent it all is up here!' said Emily.

I dropped a lighted match on the grass, and again I heard the little cry.

'What is that?' I asked.

'I only said it was so silent,' said Emily.

'Silent, indeed,' echoed the little friend.

Silent! the place was full of noises. If the match had fallen in a drawing-room it could not have been worse, and the loudest noise came from beside Emily herself. I had exactly the sensation of going to a great party, of waiting to be announced in the echoing hall, where I could hear the voices of the guests but could not yet see their faces. It is a nervous moment for a self-conscious man, especially if all the voices should be strange to him and he has never met his host.

'My dear Harry!' said the elder lady, 'never mind about that match. That'll smoulder away and harm no one. Tea-ee-ee! I always say – and you will find Emily the same – that as the magic hour of five approaches, no matter how good a lunch, one begins to feel a sort of —'

Now the Faun is of the kind who capers upon the Neo-Attic reliefs, and if you do not notice his ears or see his tail, you take him for a man and are horrified.

'Bathing!' I cried wildly. 'Such a thing for our village lads, but I quite agree – more supervision – I blame myself. Go away, bad boy, go away!'

'What will he think of next!' said Emily, while the creature beside her stood up and beckoned to me. I advanced struggling and gesticulating with tiny steps and horrified cries, exorcising the apparition with my hat. Not otherwise had I advanced the day before, when Emily's nieces showed me their guinea pigs. And by no less hearty laughter was I greeted now. Until the strange fingers closed upon me, I still thought that here was one of my parishioners and did not cease to exclaim, 'Let me go, naughty boy, let go!' And Emily's mother, believing herself to have detected the joke, replied, 'Well, I must confess they are naughty boys and reach one even on the rug: the downs in September, as I said before.'

Here I caught sight of the tail, uttered a wild shriek and fled into the beech copse behind.

'Harry would have been a born actor,' said Emily's mother as I left them.

I realized that a great crisis in my life was approaching, and that if I failed in it I might permanently lose my self-esteem. Already in the wood I was troubled by a multitude of voices – the voices of the hill beneath me, of the trees over my head, of the very insects in the bark of the tree. I could even hear the stream licking little pieces out of the meadows, and the meadows dreamily protesting. Above the din – which is no louder than the flight of a bee – rose the Faun's voice saying, 'Dear priest, be placid, be placid: why are you frightened?'

'I am not frightened,' said I – and indeed I was not. 'But I am grieved: you have disgraced me in the presence of ladies.'

'No one else has seen me,' he said, smiling idly. 'The women have tight boots and the man has long hair. Those kinds never see. For years I have only spoken to children, and they lose sight of me as soon as they grow up. But you will not be able to lose sight of me, and until you die you will be my friend. Now I begin to make you happy: lie upon your back or run races, or climb trees, or shall I get you blackberries, or harebells, or wives —'

In a terrible voice I said to him, 'Get thee behind me!' He got behind me. 'Once for all,' I continued, 'let me tell you that it is vain to tempt one whose happiness consists in giving happiness to others.'

'I cannot understand you,' he said ruefully. 'What is to tempt?'

'Poor woodland creature!' said I, turning round. 'How could you understand? It was idle of me to chide you. It is not in your little nature to comprehend a life of self-denial. Ah! if only I could reach you!'

'You have reached him,' said the hill.

'If only I could touch you!'

'You have touched him,' said the hill.

'But I will never leave you,' burst out the Faun. 'I will sweep out your shrine for you, I will accompany you to the meetings of matrons. I will enrich you at the bazaars.'

I shook my head. 'For these things I care not at all. And indeed I was minded to reject your offer of service altogether. There I was wrong. You shall help me – you shall help me to make others happy.'

'Dear priest, what a curious life! People whom I have never seen – people who cannot see me – why should I make them happy?'

'My poor lad – perhaps in time you will learn why. Now begone: commence. On this very hill sits a young lady for whom I have a high regard. Commence with her. Aha! your face falls. I thought as much. You *cannot* do anything. Here is the conclusion of the whole matter!'

'I can make her happy,' he replied, 'if you order me; and when I have done so, perhaps you will trust me more.'

Emily's mother had started home, but Emily and the little friend still sat beside the tea-things – she in her white piqué dress and biscuit straw, he in his rough but well-cut summer suit. The great pagan figure of the Faun towered insolently above them.

The friend was saying, 'And have you never felt the appalling loneliness of a crowd?'

'All that,' replied Emily, 'have I felt, and very much more —'

Then the Faun laid his hands upon them. They, who had only intended a little cultured flirtation, resisted him as long as they could, but were gradually urged into each other's arms, and embraced with passion.

'Miscreant!' I shouted, bursting from the wood. 'You have betrayed me.'

'I know it: I care not,' cried the little friend. 'Stand aside. You are in the presence of that which you do not understand. In the great solitude we have found ourselves at last.'

'Remove your accursed hands!' I shrieked to the Faun.

He obeyed and the little friend continued more calmly: 'It is idle to chide. What should you know, poor clerical creature, of the mystery of love of the eternal man and the eternal woman, of the self-effectuation of a soul?'

'That is true,' said Emily angrily. 'Harry, you would never have made me happy. I shall treat you as a friend, but how could I give myself to a man who makes such silly jokes? When you played the buffoon at tea, your hour was sealed. I must be treated seriously: I must see infinities broadening around me as I rise. You may not approve of it, but so I am. In the great solitude I have found myself at last.'

'Wretched girl!' I cried. 'Great solitude! O pair of helpless puppets —'

The little friend began to lead Emily away, but I heard her whisper to him: 'Dear, we can't possibly leave the basket for Harry after this: and mother's rug; do you mind having that in the other hand?'

So they departed and I flung myself upon the ground with every appearance of despair.

'Does he cry?' said the Faun.

'He does not cry,' answered the hill. 'His eyes are as dry as pebbles.'

My tormentor made me look at him. 'I see happiness at the bottom of your heart,' said he.

'I trust I have my secret springs,' I answered stiffly. And then I prepared a scathing denunciation, but of all the words I might have said, I only said one and it began with 'D'.

He gave a joyful cry, 'Oh, now you really belong to us. To the end of your life you will swear when you are cross and laugh when you are happy. Now laugh!'

There was a great silence. All nature stood waiting, while a curate tried to conceal his thoughts not only from nature but from himself. I thought of my injured pride, of my baffled unselfishness, of Emily, whom I was losing through no fault of her own, of the little friend, who just then slipped beneath the heavy tea basket, and that decided me, and I laughed.

That evening, for the first time, I heard the chalk downs singing to each other across the valleys, as they often do when the air is quiet and they have had a comfortable day. From my study window I could see the sunlit figure of the Faun, sitting before the beech copse as a man sits before his house. And as night came on I knew for certain that not only was he asleep but that the hills and woods were asleep also. The stream, of course, never slept, any more than it ever freezes. Indeed, the hour of darkness is really the hour of water, which has been somewhat stifled all day by the great pulsings of the land. That is why you can feel it and hear it from a greater distance in the night, and why a bath after sundown is most wonderful.

The joy of that first evening is still clear in my memory, in spite of all the happy years that have followed. I remember it when I ascend my pulpit – I have a living now – and look down upon the best people sitting beneath me pew after pew, generous and contented, upon the worse people, crowded in the aisles, upon the whiskered tenors of the choir, and the high-browed curates and the churchwardens fingering their bags, and the supercilious vergers who turn late-comers from the door. I remember it also when I sit in my comfortable bachelor rectory, amidst the carpet slippers that good young ladies have worked for me, and the oak brackets that have been carved for me by good young men; amidst my phalanx of presentation teapots and my illuminated testimonials and all the other offerings of people who believe that I have given them a helping hand, and who really have helped me out of the mire themselves. And though I try to communicate that joy to others – as I try to communicate anything else that seems good – and though I sometimes succeed, yet I can tell no one exactly how it came to me. For if I breathed one word of that, my present life, so agreeable and profitable, would come to an end, my congregation would depart, and so should I, and instead of being an asset to my parish, I might find myself an expense to the nation. Therefore in the place of the lyrical and rhetorical treatment, so suitable to the subject, so congenial to my profession, I have been forced to use the unworthy medium of a narrative, and to delude you by declaring that this is a short story, suitable for reading in the train.

# THE ROAD FROM COLONUS

## I

FOR no very intelligible reason, Mr Lucas had hurried ahead of his party. He was perhaps reaching the age at which independence becomes valuable, because it is so soon to be lost. Tired of attention and consideration, he liked breaking away from the younger members, to ride by himself and to dismount unassisted. Perhaps he also relished that more subtle pleasure of being kept waiting for lunch, and of telling the others on their arrival that it was of no consequence.

So, with childish impatience, he battered the animal's sides with his heels, and made the muleteer bang it with a thick stick and prick it with a sharp one, and jolted down the hill-sides through clumps of flowering shrubs and stretches of anemones and asphodel, till he heard the sound of running water, and came in sight of the group of plane trees where they were to have their meal.

Even in England those trees would have been remarkable, so huge were they, so interlaced, so magnificently clothed in quivering green. And here in Greece they were unique, the one cool spot in that hard brilliant landscape, already scorched by the heat of an April sun. In their midst was hidden a tiny Khan or country inn, a frail mud building with a broad wooden balcony in which sat an old woman spinning, while a small brown pig, eating orange peel, stood beside her. On the wet earth below squatted two children, playing some primaeval game with their fingers; and their mother, none too clean either, was messing with some rice inside. As Mrs Forman would have said, it was all very Greek, and the fastidious Mr Lucas felt thankful that they were bringing their own food with them and should eat it in the open air.

Still, he was glad to be there – the muleteer had helped

him off – and glad that Mrs Forman was not there to forestall his opinions – glad even that he should not see Ethel for quite half an hour. Ethel was his youngest daughter, still unmarried. She was unselfish and affectionate, and it was generally understood that she was to devote her life to her father and be the comfort of his old age. Mrs Forman always referred to her as Antigone, and Mr Lucas tried to settle down to the role of Oedipus, which seemed the only one that public opinion allowed him.

He had this in common with Oedipus, that he was growing old. Even to himself it had become obvious. He had lost interest in other people's affairs, and seldom attended when they spoke to him. He was fond of talking himself but often forgot what he was going to say, and even when he succeeded, it seldom seemed worth the effort. His phrases and gestures had become stiff and set, his anecdotes, once so successful, fell flat, his silence was as meaningless as his speech. Yet he had led a healthy, active life, had worked steadily, made money, educated his children. There was nothing and no one to blame: he was simply growing old.

At the present moment, here he was in Greece, and one of the dreams of his life was realized. Forty years ago he had caught the fever of Hellenism, and all his life he had felt that could he but visit that land, he would not have lived in vain. But Athens had been dusty, Delphi wet, Thermopylae flat, and he had listened with amazement and cynicism to the rapturous exclamations of his companions. Greece was like England: it was a man who was growing old, and it made no difference whether that man looked at the Thames or the Eurotas. It was his last hope of contradicting that logic of experience, and it was failing.

Yet Greece had done something for him, though he did not know it. It had made him discontented, and there are stirrings of life in discontent. He knew that he was not the victim of continual ill-luck. Something great was wrong, and he was pitted against no mediocre or accidental enemy. For the last month a strange desire had possessed him to die fighting.

'Greece is the land for young people,' he said to himself as he stood under the plane trees, 'but I will enter into it, I will possess it. Leaves shall be green again, water shall be sweet, the sky shall be blue. They were so forty years ago, and I will win them back. I do mind being old, and I will pretend no longer.'

He took two steps forward, and immediately cold waters were gurgling over his ankle.

'Where does the water come from?' he asked himself. 'I do not even know that.' He remembered that all the hillsides were dry; yet here the road was suddenly covered with flowing streams.

He stopped still in amazement saying: 'Water out of a tree – out of a hollow tree? I never saw nor thought of that before.'

For the enormous plane that leant towards the Khan was hollow – it had been burnt out for charcoal – and from its living trunk there gushed an impetuous spring, coating the bark with fern and moss, and flowing over the mule track to create fertile meadows beyond. The simple country folk had paid to beauty and mystery such tribute as they could, for in the rind of the tree a shrine was cut, holding a lamp and a little picture of the Virgin, inheritor of the Naiad's and Dryad's joint abode.

'I never saw anything so marvellous before,' said Mr Lucas. 'I could even step inside the trunk and see where the water comes from.'

For a moment he hesitated to violate the shrine. Then he remembered with a smile his own thought – 'the place shall be mine; I will enter it and possess it' – and leapt almost aggressively on to a stone within.

The water pressed up steadily and noiselessly from the

hollow roots and hidden crevices of the plane, forming a wonderful amber pool ere it spilt over the lip of bark on to the earth outside. Mr Lucas tasted it and it was sweet, and when he looked up the black funnel of the trunk he saw sky which was blue, and some leaves which were green; and he remembered, without smiling, another of his thoughts.

Others had been before him – indeed he had a curious sense of companionship. Little votive offerings to the presiding Power were fastened on to the bark – tiny arms and legs and eyes in tin, grotesque models of the brain or the heart – all tokens of some recovery of strength or wisdom or love. There was no such thing as the solitude of nature, for the sorrows and joys of humanity had pressed even into the bosom of a tree. He spread out his arms and steadied himself against the soft charred wood, and then slowly leant back, till his body was resting on the trunk behind. His eyes closed, and he had the strange feeling of one who is moving, yet at peace – the feeling of the swimmer, who, after long struggling with chopping seas, finds that after all the tide will sweep him to his goal.

So he lay motionless, conscious only of the stream below his feet, and that all things were a stream, in which he was moving.

He was aroused at last by a shock – the shock of an arrival perhaps, for when he opened his eyes, something unimagined, indefinable, had passed over all things, and made them intelligible and good.

There was meaning in the stoop of the old woman over her work, and in the quick motions of the little pig, and in her diminishing globe of wool. A young man came singing over the streams on a mule, and there was beauty in his pose and sincerity in his greeting. The sun made no accidental patterns upon the spreading roots of the trees, and there was intention in the nodding clumps of asphodel, and in the music of the water. To Mr Lucas, who, in a brief space of time, had discovered not only Greece, but England and all the world and life, there seemed nothing ludicrous in the desire to hang within the tree another votive offering – a little model of an entire man.

'Why, here's papa, playing at being Merlin.'

All unnoticed they had arrived – Ethel, Mrs Forman, Mr Graham, and the English-speaking dragoman. Mr Lucas peered out at them suspiciously. They had suddenly become unfamiliar, and all that they did seemed strained and coarse.

'Allow me to give you a hand,' said Mr Graham, a young man who was always polite to his elders.

Mr Lucas felt annoyed 'Thank you, I can manage. perfectly well by myself,' he replied. His foot slipped as he stepped out of the tree, and went into the spring.

'Oh, papa, my papa!' said Ethel, 'what are you doing? Thank goodness I have got a change for you on the mule.'

She tended him carefully, giving him clean socks and dry boots, and then sat him down on the rug beside the lunch basket, while she went with the others to explore the grove.

They came back in ecstasies, in which Mr Lucas tried to join. But he found them intolerable. Their enthusiasm was superficial, commonplace, and spasmodic. They had no perception of the coherent beauty that was flowering around them. He tried at least to explain his feelings, and what he said was:

'I am altogether pleased with the appearance of this place. It impresses me very favourably. The trees are fine, remarkably fine for Greece, and there is something very poetic in the spring of clear running water. The people too seem kindly and civil. It is decidedly an attractive place.'

Mrs Forman upbraided him for his tepid praise.

'Oh, it is a place in a thousand!' she cried. 'I could live and die here! I really would stop if I had not to be back at Athens! It reminds me of the Colonus of Sophocles.'

'Well, *I* must stop,' said Ethel. 'I positively must.'

'Yes, do! You and your father! Antigone and Oedipus. Of course you must stop at Colonus!'

Mr Lucas was almost breathless with excitement. When he stood within the tree, he had believed that his happiness would be independent of locality. But these few minutes' conversation had undeceived him. He no longer trusted himself to journey through the world, for old thoughts, old wearinesses might be waiting to rejoin him as soon as he left the shade of the planes and the music of the virgin water. To sleep in the Khan with the gracious, kind-eyed country people, to watch the bats flit about within the globe of shade, and see the moon turn the golden patterns into silver – one such night would place him beyond relapse, and confirm him for ever in the kingdom he had regained. But all his lips could say was: 'I should be willing to put in a night here.'

'You mean a week, papa! It would be sacrilege to put in less.'

'A week then, a week,' said his lips, irritated at being corrected, while his heart was leaping with joy. All through lunch he spoke to them no more, but watched the place he should know so well, and the people who would so soon be his companions and friends. The inmates of the Khan only consisted of an old woman, a middle-aged woman, a young man and two children, and to none of them had he spoken, yet he loved them as he loved everything that moved or breathed or existed beneath the benedictory shade of the planes.

'*En route!*' said the shrill voice of Mrs Forman. 'Ethel! Mr Graham! The best of things must end.'

'To-night,' thought Mr Lucas, 'they will light the little lamp by the shrine. And when we all sit together on the balcony, perhaps they will tell me which offerings they put up.'

'I beg your pardon, Mr Lucas,' said Graham, 'but they want to fold up the rug you are sitting on.'

Mr Lucas got up, saying to himself: 'Ethel shall go to bed

first, and then I will try to tell them about my offering too – for it is a thing I must do. I think they will understand if I am left with them alone.'

Ethel touched him on the cheek. 'Papa! I've called you three times. All the mules are here.'

'Mules? What mules?'

'Our mules. We're all waiting. Oh, Mr Graham, do help my father on.'

'I don't know what you're talking about, Ethel.'

'My dearest papa, we must start. You know we have to get to Olympia to-night.'

Mr Lucas in pompous, confident tones replied: 'I always did wish, Ethel, that you had a better head for plans. You know perfectly well that we are putting in a week here. It is your own suggestion.'

Ethel was startled into impoliteness. 'What a perfectly ridiculous idea. You must have known I was joking. Of course I meant I wished we could.'

'Ah! if we could only do what we wished!' sighed Mrs Forman, already seated on her mule.

'Surely,' Ethel continued in calmer tones, 'you didn't think I meant it.'

'Most certainly I did. I have made all my plans on the supposition that we are stopping here, and it will be extremely inconvenient, indeed, impossible for me to start.'

He delivered this remark with an air of great conviction, and Mrs Forman and Mr Graham had to turn away to hide their smiles.

'I am sorry I spoke so carelessly; it was wrong of me. But, you know, we can't break up our party, and even one night here would make us miss the boat at Patras.'

Mrs Forman, in an aside, called Mr Graham's attention to the excellent way in which Ethel managed her father.

'I don't mind about the Patras boat. You said that we should stop here, and we are stopping.'

It seemed as if the inhabitants of the Khan had divined in some mysterious way that the altercation touched them. The old woman stopped her spinning, while the young man and the two children stood behind Mr Lucas, as if supporting him.

Neither arguments nor entreaties moved him. He said little, but he was absolutely determined, because for the first time he saw his daily life aright. What need had he to return to England? Who would miss him? His friends were dead or cold. Ethel loved him in a way, but, as was right, she had other interests. His other children he seldom saw. He had only one other relative, his sister Julia, whom he both feared and hated. It was no effort to struggle. He would be a fool as well as a coward if he stirred from the place which brought him happiness and peace.

At last Ethel, to humour him, and not disinclined to air her modern Greek, went into the Khan with the astonished dragoman to look at the rooms. The woman inside received them with loud welcomes, and the young man, when no one was looking, began to lead Mr Lucas' mule to the stable.

'Drop it, you brigand!' shouted Graham, who always declared that foreigners could understand English if they chose. He was right, for the man obeyed, and they all stood waiting for Ethel's return.

She emerged at last, with close-gathered skirts, followed by the dragoman bearing the little pig, which he had bought at a bargain.

'My dear papa, I will do all I can for you, but stop in that Khan – no.'

'Are there – fleas?' asked Mrs Forman.

Ethel intimated that 'fleas' was not the word.

'Well, I am afraid that settles it,' said Mrs Forman, 'I know how particular Mr Lucas is.'

'It does not settle it,' said Mr Lucas. 'Ethel, you go on. I do not want you. I don't know why I ever consulted you. I shall stop here alone.'

'That is absolute nonsense,' said Ethel, losing her temper. 'How can you be left alone at your age? How would you get your meals or your bath? All your letters are waiting for you at Patras. You'll miss the boat. That means missing the London operas, and upsetting all your engagements for the month. And as if you could travel by yourself!'

'They might knife you,' was Mr Graham's contribution.

The Greeks said nothing; but whenever Mr Lucas looked their way, they beckoned him towards the Khan. The children would even have drawn him by the coat, and the old woman on the balcony stopped her almost completed spinning, and fixed him with mysterious appealing eyes. As he fought, the issue assumed gigantic proportions, and he believed that he was not merely stopping because he had regained youth or seen beauty or found happiness, but because in that place and with those people a supreme event was awaiting him which would transfigure the face of the world. The moment was so tremendous that he abandoned words and arguments as useless, and rested on the strength of his mighty unrevealed allies: silent men, murmuring water, and whispering trees. For the whole place called with one voice, articulate to him, and his garrulous opponents became every minute more meaningless and absurd. Soon they would be tired and go chattering away into the sun, leaving him to the cool grove and the moonlight and the destiny he foresaw.

Mrs Forman and the dragoman had indeed already started, amid the piercing screams of the little pig, and the struggle might have gone on indefinitely if Ethel had not called in Mr Graham.

'Can you help me?' she whispered. 'He is absolutely unmanageable.'

'I'm no good at arguing – but if I could help you in any

other way —' and he looked down complacently at his well-made figure.

Ethel hesitated. Then she said: 'Help me in any way you can. After all, it is for his good that we do it.'

'Then have his mule led up behind him.'

So when Mr Lucas thought he had gained the day, he suddenly felt himself lifted off the ground, and sat sideways on the saddle, and at the same time the mule started off at a trot. He said nothing, for he had nothing to say, and even his face showed little emotion as he felt the shade pass and heard the sound of the water cease. Mr Graham was running at his side, hat in hand, apologizing.

'I know I had no business to do it, and I do beg your pardon awfully. But I do hope that some day you too will feel that I was – damn!'

A stone had caught him in the middle of the back. It was thrown by the little boy, who was pursuing them along the mule track. He was followed by his sister, also throwing stones.

Ethel screamed to the dragoman, who was some way ahead with Mrs Forman, but before he could rejoin them, another adversary appeared. It was the young Greek, who had cut them off in front, and now dashed down at Mr Lucas' bridle. Fortunately Graham was an expert boxer, and it did not take him a moment to beat down the youth's feeble defence, and to send him sprawling with a bleeding mouth into the asphodel. By this time the dragoman had arrived, the children, alarmed at the fate of their brother, had desisted, and the rescue party, if such it is to be considered, retired in disorder to the trees.

'Little devils!' said Graham, laughing with triumph. 'That's the modern Greek all over. Your father meant money if he stopped, and they consider we were taking it out of their pocket.'

'Oh, they are terrible – simple savages! I don't know how I shall ever thank you. You've saved my father.'

'I only hope you didn't think me brutal.'

'No,' replied Ethel with a little sigh. 'I admire strength.'

Meanwhile the cavalcade reformed, and Mr Lucas, who, as Mrs Forman said, bore his disappointment wonderfully well, was put comfortably on to his mule. They hurried up the opposite hillside, fearful of another attack, and it was not until they had left the eventful place far behind that Ethel found an opportunity to speak to her father and ask his pardon for the way she had treated him.

'You seemed so different, dear father, and you quite frightened me. Now I feel that you are your old self again.'

He did not answer, and she concluded that he was not unnaturally offended at her behaviour.

By one of those curious tricks of mountain scenery, the place they had left an hour before suddenly reappeared far below them. The Khan was hidden under the green dome, but in the open there still stood three figures, and through the pure air rose up a faint cry of defiance or farewell.

Mr Lucas stopped irresolutely, and let the reins fall from his hand.

'Come, father dear,' said Ethel gently.

He obeyed, and in another moment a spur of the hill hid the dangerous scene for ever.

## II

It was breakfast time, but the gas was alight, owing to the fog. Mr Lucas was in the middle of an account of a bad night he had spent. Ethel, who was to be married in a few weeks, had her arms on the table, listening.

'First the door bell rang, then you came back from the theatre. Then the dog started, and after the dog the cat. And at three in the morning a young hooligan passed by singing. Oh yes: then there was the water gurgling in the pipe above my head.'

'I think that was only the bath water running away,' said Ethel, looking rather worn.

'Well, there's nothing I dislike more than running water. It's perfectly impossible to sleep in the house. I shall give it up. I shall give notice next quarter. I shall tell the landlord plainly, "The reason I am giving up the house is this: it is perfectly impossible to sleep in it." If he says – says – well, what has he got to say?'

'Some more toast, father?'

'Thank you, my dear.' He took it, and there was an interval of peace.

But he soon recommenced. 'I'm not going to submit to the practising next door as tamely as they think. I wrote and told them so – didn't I?'

'Yes,' said Ethel, who had taken care that the letter should not reach. 'I have seen the governess, and she has promised to arrange it differently. And Aunt Julia hates noise. It will sure to be all right.'

Her aunt, being the only unattached member of the family, was coming to keep house for her father when she left him. The reference was not a happy one, and Mr Lucas commenced a series of half articulate sighs, which was only stopped by the arrival of the post.

'Oh, what a parcel!' cried Ethel. 'For me! What can it be! Greek stamps. This is most exciting!'

It proved to be some asphodel bulbs, sent by Mrs Forman from Athens for planting in the conservatory.

'Doesn't it bring it all back! You remember the asphodels, father. And all wrapped up in Greek newspapers. I wonder if I can read them still. I used to be able to, you know.'

She rattled on, hoping to conceal the laughter of the children next door – a favourite source of querulousness at breakfast time.

'Listen to me! "A rural disaster." Oh, I've hit on something sad. But never mind. "Last Tuesday at Plataniste, in the province of Messenia, a shocking tragedy occurred. A large tree" – aren't I getting on well? – "blew down in the night and" – wait a minute – oh dear! "crushed to death the five occupants of the little Khan there, who had apparently been sitting in the balcony. The bodies of Maria Rhomaides, the aged proprietress, and of her daughter, aged forty-six, were easily recognizable, whereas that of her grandson" – oh, the rest is really too horrid; I wish I had never tried it, and what's more I feel to have heard the name Plataniste before. We didn't stop there, did we, in the spring?'

'We had lunch,' said Mr Lucas, with a faint expression of trouble on his vacant face. 'Perhaps it was where the dragoman bought the pig.'

'Of course,' said Ethel in a nervous voice. 'Where the dragoman bought the little pig. How terrible!'

'Very terrible!' said her father, whose attention was wandering to the noisy children next door. Ethel suddenly started to her feet with genuine interest.

'Good gracious!' she exclaimed. 'This is an old paper. It happened not lately but in April – the night of Tuesday the eighteenth – and we – we must have been there in the afternoon.'

'So we were,' said Mr Lucas. She put her hand to her heart, scarcely able to speak.

'Father, dear father, I must say it: you wanted to stop there. All those people, those poor half savage people, tried to keep you, and they're dead. The whole place, it says, is in ruins, and even the stream has changed its course. Father dear, if it had not been for me, and if Arthur had not helped me, you must have been killed.'

Mr Lucas waved his hand irritably. 'It is not a bit of good speaking to the governess, I shall write to the landlord and say, "The reason I am giving up the house is this: the dog barks, the children next door are intolerable, and I cannot stand the noise of running water."'

Ethel did not check his babbling. She was aghast at the narrowness of the escape, and for a long time kept silence. At last she said: 'Such a marvellous deliverance does make one believe in Providence.'

Mr Lucas, who was still composing his letter to the landlord, did not reply.

# THE MACHINE STOPS

## PART I

### THE AIR-SHIP

IMAGINE, if you can, a small room, hexagonal in shape like the cell of a bee. It is lighted neither by window nor by lamp, yet it is filled with a soft radiance. There are no apertures for ventilation, yet the air is fresh. There are no musical instruments, and yet, at the moment that my meditation opens, this room is throbbing with melodious sounds. An arm-chair is in the centre, by its side a reading-desk – that is all the furniture. And in the arm-chair there sits a swaddled lump of flesh – a woman, about five feet high, with a face as white as a fungus. It is to her that the little room belongs.

An electric bell rang.

The woman touched a switch and the music was silent.

'I suppose I must see who it is,' she thought, and set her chair in motion. The chair, like the music, was worked by machinery, and it rolled her to the other side of the room, where the bell still rang importunately.

'Who is it?' she called. Her voice was irritable, for she had been interrupted often since the music began. She knew several thousand people; in certain directions human intercourse had advanced enormously.

But when she listened into the receiver, her white face wrinkled into smiles, and she said:

'Very well. Let us talk, I will isolate myself. I do not expect anything important will happen for the next five minutes – for I can give you fully five minutes, Kuno. Then I must deliver my lecture on "Music during the Australian Period".'

She touched the isolation knob, so that no one else could speak to her. Then she touched the lighting apparatus, and the little room was plunged into darkness.

'Be quick!' she called, her irritation returning. 'Be quick, Kuno; here I am in the dark wasting my time.'

But it was fully fifteen seconds before the round plate that she held in her hands began to glow. A faint blue light shot across it, darkening to purple, and presently she could see the image of her son, who lived on the other side of the earth, and he could see her.

'Kuno, how slow you are.'

He smiled gravely.

'I really believe you enjoy dawdling.'

'I have called you before, mother, but you were always busy or isolated. I have something particular to say.'

'What is it, dearest boy? Be quick. Why could you not send it by pneumatic post?'

'Because I prefer saying such a thing. I want —'

'Well?'

'I want you to come and see me.'

Vashti watched his face in the blue plate.

'But I can see you!' she exclaimed. 'What more do you want?'

'I want to see you not through the Machine,' said Kuno. 'I want to speak to you not through the wearisome Machine.'

'Oh, hush!' said his mother, vaguely shocked. 'You mustn't say anything against the Machine.'

'Why not?'

'One mustn't.'

'You talk as if a god had made the Machine,' cried the other. 'I believe that you pray to it when you are unhappy. Men made it, do not forget that. Great men, but men. The Machine is much, but it is not everything. I see something like you in this plate, but I do not see you. I hear something like you through this telephone, but I do not hear you. That is why I want you to come. Come and stop with me. Pay me a visit, so that we can meet face to face, and talk about the hopes that are in my mind.'

She replied that she could scarcely spare the time for a visit.

'The air-ship barely takes two days to fly between me and you.'

'I dislike air-ships.'

'Why?'

'I dislike seeing the horrible brown earth, and the sea, and the stars when it is dark. I get no ideas in an air-ship.'

'I do not get them anywhere else.'

'What kind of ideas can the air give you?'

He paused for an instant.

'Do you not know four big stars that form an oblong, and three stars close together in the middle of the oblong, and hanging from these stars, three other stars?'

'No, I do not. I dislike the stars. But did they give you an idea? How interesting; tell me.'

'I had an idea that they were like a man.'

'I do not understand.'

'The four big stars are the man's shoulders and his knees. The three stars in the middle are like the belts that men wore once, and the three stars hanging are like a sword.'

'A sword?'

'Men carried swords about with them, to kill animals and other men.'

'It does not strike me as a very good idea, but it is certainly original. When did it come to you first?'

'In the air-ship —' He broke off, and she fancied that he looked sad. She could not be sure, for the Machine did not transmit *nuances* of expression. It only gave a general idea of people – an idea that was good enough for all practical purposes, Vashti thought. The imponderable bloom, declared by a discredited philosophy to be the actual essence of intercourse, was rightly ignored by the Machine, just as the imponderable bloom of the grape was ignored by the manufacturers of artificial fruit. Something 'good enough' had long since been accepted by our race.

'The truth is,' he continued, 'that I want to see these stars again. They are curious stars. I want to see them not from the air-ship, but from the surface of the earth, as our ancestors did, thousands of years ago. I want to visit the surface of the earth.'

She was shocked again.

'Mother, you must come, if only to explain to me what is the harm of visiting the surface of the earth.'

'No harm,' she replied, controlling herself. 'But no advantage. The surface of the earth is only dust and mud, no life remains on it, and you would need a respirator, or the cold of the outer air would kill you. One dies immediately in the outer air.'

'I know; of course I shall take all precautions.'

'And besides —'

'Well?'

She considered, and chose her words with care. Her son had a queer temper, and she wished to dissuade him from the expedition.

'It is contrary to the spirit of the age,' she asserted.

'Do you mean by that, contrary to the Machine?'

'In a sense, but —'

His image in the blue plate faded.

'Kuno!'

He had isolated himself.

For a moment Vashti felt lonely.

Then she generated the light, and the sight of her room, flooded with radiance and studded with electric buttons, revived her. There were buttons and switches everywhere – buttons to call for food, for music, for clothing. There was the hot-bath button, by pressure of which a basin of (imitation) marble rose out of the floor, filled to the brim with a warm deodorized liquid. There was the cold-bath button. There was the button that produced literature. And there were of course the buttons by which she communicated with her friends. The room, though it contained nothing, was in touch with all that she cared for in the world.

Vashti's next move was to turn off the isolation-switch, and all the accumulations of the last three minutes burst upon her. The room was filled with the noise of bells, and speaking-tubes. What was the new food like? Could she recommend it? Had she had any ideas lately? Might one tell her one's own ideas? Would she make an engagement to visit the public nurseries at an early date? – say this day month.

To most of these questions she replied with irritation – a growing quality in that accelerated age. She said that the new food was horrible. That she could not visit the public nurseries through press of engagements. That she had no ideas of her own but had just been told one – that four stars and three in the middle were like a man: she doubted there was much in it. Then she switched off her correspondents, for it was time to deliver her lecture on Australian music.

The clumsy system of public gatherings had been long since abandoned; neither Vashti nor her audience stirred from their rooms. Seated in her arm-chair she spoke, while they in their arm-chairs heard her, fairly well, and saw her, fairly well. She opened with a humorous account of music in the pre-Mongolian epoch, and went on to describe the great outburst of song that followed the Chinese conquest. Remote and primaeval as were the methods of I-San-So and the Brisbane school, she yet felt (she said) that study of them might repay the musician of to-day: they had freshness; they had, above all, ideas.

Her lecture, which lasted ten minutes, was well received and at its conclusion she and many of her audience listened to a lecture on the sea; there were ideas to be got from the sea;

the speaker had donned a respirator and visited it lately. Then she fed, talked to many friends, had a bath, talked again, and summoned her bed.

The bed was not to her liking. It was too large, and she had a feeling for a small bed. Complaint was useless, for beds were of the same dimension all over the world, and to have had an alternative size would have involved vast alterations in the Machine. Vashti isolated herself – it was necessary, for neither day nor night existed under the ground – and reviewed all that had happened since she had summoned the bed last. Ideas? Scarcely any. Events – was Kuno's invitation an event?

By her side, on the little reading-desk, was a survival from the ages of litter – one book. This was the Book of the Machine. In it were instructions against every possible contingency. If she was hot or cold or dyspeptic or at a loss for a word, she went to the book, and it told her which button to press. The Central Committee published it. In accordance with a growing habit, it was richly bound.

Sitting up in the bed, she took it reverently in her hands. She glanced round the glowing room as if someone might be watching her. Then, half ashamed, half joyful, she murmured 'O Machine! O Machine!' and raised the volume to her lips. Thrice she kissed it, thrice inclined her head, thrice she felt the delirium of acquiescence. Her ritual performed, she turned to page 1367, which gave the times of the departure of the air-ships from the island in the southern hemisphere, under whose soil she lived, to the island in the northern hemisphere, whereunder lived her son.

She thought, 'I have not the time.'

She made the room dark and slept; she awoke and made the room light; she ate and exchanged ideas with her friends, and listened to music and attended lectures; she made the room dark and slept. Above her, beneath her, and around her, the Machine hummed eternally; she did not notice the noise, for she had been born with it in her ears. The earth, carrying her, hummed as it sped through silence, turning her now to the invisible sun, now to the invisible stars. She awoke and made the room light.

'Kuno!'

'I will not talk to you,' he answered, 'until you come.'

'Have you been on the surface of the earth since we spoke last?'

His image faded.

Again she consulted the book. She became very nervous and lay back in her chair palpitating. Think of her as without teeth or hair. Presently she directed the chair to the wall, and pressed an unfamiliar button. The wall swung apart slowly. Through the opening she saw a tunnel that curved slightly, so that its goal was not visible. Should she go to see her son, here was the beginning of the journey.

Of course she knew all about the communication-system. There was nothing mysterious in it. She would summon a car and it would fly with her down the tunnel until it reached the lift that communicated with the air-ship station: the system had been in use for many, many years, long before the universal establishment of the Machine. And of course she had studied the civilization that had immediately preceded her own – the civilization that had mistaken the functions of the system, and had used it for bringing people to things, instead of for bringing things to people. Those funny old days, when men went for change of air instead of changing the air in their rooms! And yet – she was frightened of the tunnel: she had not seen it since her last child was born. It curved – but not quite as she remembered; it was brilliant – but not quite as brilliant as a lecturer had suggested. Vashti was seized with the terrors of direct experience. She shrank back into the room, and the wall closed up again.

'Kuno,' she said, 'I cannot come to see you. I am not well.'

Immediately an enormous apparatus fell on to her out of

the ceiling, a thermometer was automatically inserted between her lips, a stethoscope was automatically laid upon her heart. She lay powerless. Cool pads soothed her forehead. Kuno had telegraphed to her doctor.

So the human passions still blundered up and down in the Machine. Vashti drank the medicine that the doctor projected into her mouth, and the machinery retired into the ceiling. The voice of Kuno was heard asking how she felt.

'Better.' Then with irritation: 'But why do you not come to me instead?'

'Because I cannot leave this place.'

'Why?'

'Because, any moment, something tremendous may happen.'

'Have you been on the surface of the earth yet?'

'Not yet.'

'Then what is it?'

'I will not tell you through the machine.'

She resumed her life.

But she thought of Kuno as a baby, his birth, his removal to the public nurseries, her one visit to him there, his visits to her – visits which stopped when the Machine had assigned him a room on the other side of the earth. 'Parents, duties of,' said the book of the Machine, 'cease at the moment of birth. P. 422327483.' True, but there was something special about Kuno – indeed there had been something special about all her children – and, after all, she must brave the journey if he desired it. And 'something tremendous might happen'. What did that mean? The nonsense of a youthful man, no doubt, but she must go. Again she pressed the unfamiliar button, again the wall swung back, and she saw the tunnel that curved out of sight. Clasping the Book, she rose, tottered on to the platform, and summoned the car. Her room closed behind her: the journey to the northern hemisphere had begun.

Of course it was perfectly easy. The car approached and

in it she found arm-chairs exactly like her own. When she signalled, it stopped, and she tottered into the lift. One other passenger was in the lift, the first fellow creature she had seen face to face for months. Few travelled in these days, for, thanks to the advance of science, the earth was exactly alike all over. Rapid intercourse, from which the previous civilization had hoped so much, had ended by defeating itself. What was the good of going to Pekin when it was just like Shrewsbury? Why return to Shrewsbury when it would be just like Pekin? Men seldom moved their bodies; all unrest was concentrated in the soul.

The air-ship service was a relic from the former age. It was kept up, because it was easier to keep it up than to stop it or to diminish it, but it now far exceeded the wants of the population. Vessel after vessel would rise from the vomitories of Rye or of Christchurch (I use the antique names), would sail into the crowded sky, and would draw up at the wharves of the south – empty. So nicely adjusted was the system, so independent of meteorology, that the sky, whether calm or cloudy, resembled a vast kaleidoscope whereon the same patterns periodically recurred. The ship on which Vashti sailed started now at sunset, now at dawn. But always, as it passed above Rheims, it would neighbour the ship that served between Helsingfors and the Brazils, and, every third time it surmounted the Alps, the fleet of Palermo would cross its track behind. Night and day, wind and storm, tide and earthquake, impeded man no longer. He had harnessed Leviathan. All the old literature, with its praise of Nature and its fear of Nature, rang false as the prattle of a child.

Yet as Vashti saw the vast flank of the ship, stained with exposure to the outer air, her horror of direct experience returned. It was not quite like the air-ship in the cinematophote. For one thing it smelt – not strongly or unpleasantly, but it did smell, and with her eyes shut she should have known that a new thing was close to her. Then she had to walk to it from the lift, had to submit to glances from the other passengers. The man in front dropped his Book – no great matter, but it disquieted them all. In the rooms, if the Book was dropped, the floor raised it mechanically, but the gangway to the air-ship was not so prepared, and the sacred volume lay motionless. They stopped – the thing was unforeseen – and the man, instead of picking up his property, felt the muscles of his arm to see how they had failed him. Then someone actually said with direct utterance: 'We shall be late' – and they trooped on board, Vashti treading on the pages as she did so.

Inside, her anxiety increased. The arrangements were old-fashioned and rough. There was even a female attendant, to whom she would have to announce her wants during the voyage. Of course a revolving platform ran the length of the boat, but she was expected to walk from it to her cabin. Some cabins were better than others, and she did not get the best. She thought the attendant had been unfair, and spasms of rage shook her. The glass valves had closed, she could not go back. She saw, at the end of the vestibule, the lift in which she had ascended going quietly up and down, empty. Beneath those corridors of shining tiles were rooms, tier below tier, reaching far into the earth, and in each room there sat a human being, eating, or sleeping, or producing ideas. And buried deep in the hive was her own room. Vashti was afraid.

'O Machine! O Machine!' she murmured, and caressed her Book, and was comforted.

Then the sides of the vestibule seemed to melt together, as do the passages that we see in dreams, the lift vanished, the Book that had been dropped slid to the left and vanished, polished tiles rushed by like a stream of water, there was a slight jar, and the air-ship, issuing from its tunnel, soared above the waters of a tropical ocean.

It was night. For a moment she saw the coast of Sumatra edged by the phosphorescence of waves, and crowned by lighthouses, still sending forth their disregarded beams. These also vanished, and only the stars distracted her. They were not motionless, but swayed to and fro above her head, thronging out of one skylight into another, as if the universe and not the air-ship was careening. And, as often happens on clear nights, they seemed now to be in perspective, now on a plane; now piled tier beyond tier into the infinite heavens, now concealing infinity, a roof limiting for ever the visions of men. In either case they seemed intolerable. 'Are we to travel in the dark?' called the passengers angrily, and the attendant, who had been careless, generated the light and pulled down the blinds of pliable metal. When the air-ships had been built, the desire to look direct at things still lingered in the world. Hence the extraordinary number of skylights and windows, and the proportionate discomfort to those who were civilized and refined. Even in Vashti's cabin one star peeped through a flaw in the blind, and after a few hours' uneasy slumber, she was disturbed by an unfamiliar glow, which was the dawn.

Quick as the ship had sped westwards, the earth had rolled eastwards quicker still, and had dragged back Vashti and her companions towards the sun. Science could prolong the night, but only for a little, and those high hopes of neutralizing the earth's diurnal revolution had passed, together with hopes that were possibly higher. To 'keep pace with the sun', or even to outstrip it, had been the aim of the civilization preceding this. Racing aeroplanes had been built for the purpose, capable of enormous speed, and steered by the greatest intellects of the epoch. Round the globe they went, round and round, westward, westward, round and round, amidst humanity's applause. In vain. The globe went eastward quicker still, horrible accidents occurred, and the Committee of the Machine, at the time rising into prominence, declared the pursuit illegal, unmechanical, and punishable by Homelessness.

Of Homelessness more will be said later.

Doubtless the Committee was right. Yet the attempt to 'defeat the sun' aroused the last common interest that our race experienced about the heavenly bodies, or indeed about anything. It was the last time that men were compacted by thinking of a power outside the world. The sun had conquered, yet it was the end of his spiritual dominion. Dawn, midday, twilight, the zodiacal path, touched neither men's lives nor their hearts, and science retreated into the ground, to concentrate herself upon problems that she was certain of solving.

So when Vashti found her cabin invaded by a rosy finger of light, she was annoyed and tried to adjust the blind. But the blind flew up altogether, and she saw through the skylight small pink clouds, swaying against a background of blue, and as the sun crept higher, its radiance entered direct, brimming down the wall, like a golden sea. It rose and fell with the air-ship's motion, just as waves rise and fall, but it advanced steadily, as a tide advances. Unless she was careful, it would strike her face. A spasm of horror shook her and she rang for the attendant. The attendant too was horrified, but she could do nothing; it was not her place to mend the blind. She could only suggest that the lady should change her cabin, which she accordingly prepared to do.

People were almost exactly alike all over the world, but the attendant of the air-ship, perhaps owing to her exceptional duties, had grown a little out of the common. She had often to address passengers with direct speech, and this had given her a certain roughness and originality of manner. When Vashti swerved away from the sunbeams with a cry, she behaved barbarically – she put out her hand to steady her.

'How dare you!' exclaimed the passenger. 'You forget yourself!'

The woman was confused, and apologized for not having let her fall. People never touched one another. The custom had become obsolete, owing to the Machine.

'Where are we now?' asked Vashti haughtily.

'We are over Asia,' said the attendant, anxious to be polite.

'Asia?'

'You must excuse my common way of speaking. I have got into the habit of calling places over which I pass by their unmechanical names.'

'Oh, I remember Asia. The Mongols came from it.'

'Beneath us, in the open air, stood a city that was once called Simla.'

'Have you ever heard of the Mongols and of the Brisbane school?'

'No.'

'Brisbane also stood in the open air.'

'Those mountains to the right – let me show you them.' She pushed back a metal blind. The main chain of the Himalayas was revealed. 'They were once called the Roof of the World, those mountains.'

'What a foolish name!'

'You must remember that, before the dawn of civilization, they seemed to be an impenetrable wall that touched the stars. It was supposed that no one but the gods could exist above their summits. How we have advanced, thanks to the Machine!'

'How we have advanced, thanks to the Machine!' said Vashti.

'How we have advanced, thanks to the Machine!' echoed the passenger who had dropped his Book the night before and who was standing in the passage.

'And that white stuff in the cracks? – what is it?'

'I have forgotten its name.'

'Cover the window, please. These mountains give me no ideas.'

The northern aspect of the Himalayas was in deep shadow: on the Indian slope the sun had just prevailed. The forests had been destroyed during the literature epoch for the purpose of making newspaper-pulp, but the snows were awakening to their morning glory, and clouds still hung on the breasts of Kinchinjunga. In the plain were seen the ruins of cities, with diminished rivers creeping by their walls, and by the sides of these were sometimes the signs of vomitories, marking the cities of to-day. Over the whole prospect air-ships rushed, crossing and inter-crossing with incredible *aplomb*, and rising nonchalantly when they desired to escape the perturbations of the lower atmosphere and to traverse the Roof of the World.

'We have indeed advanced, thanks to the Machine,' repeated the attendant, and hid the Himalayas behind a metal blind.

The day dragged wearily forward. The passengers sat each in his cabin, avoiding one another with an almost physical repulsion and longing to be once more under the surface of the earth. There were eight or ten of them, mostly young males, sent out from the public nurseries to inhabit the rooms of those who had died in various parts of the earth. The man who had dropped his Book was on the homeward journey. He had been sent to Sumatra for the purpose of propagating the race. Vashti alone was travelling by her private will.

At midday she took a second glance at the earth. The air-ship was crossing another range of mountains, but she could see little, owing to clouds. Masses of black rock hovered below her and merged indistinctly into grey. Their shapes were fantastic; one of them resembled a prostrate man.

'No ideas here,' murmured Vashti, and hid the Caucasus behind a metal blind.

In the evening she looked again. They were crossing a golden sea, in which lay many small islands and one peninsula.

She repeated, 'No ideas here,' and hid Greece behind a metal blind.

# PART II

## THE MENDING APPARATUS

BY a vestibule, by a lift, by a tubular railway, by a platform, by a sliding door – by reversing all the steps of her departure did Vashti arrive at her son's room, which exactly resembled her own. She might well declare that the visit was superfluous. The buttons, the knobs, the reading-desk with the Book, the temperature, the atmosphere, the illumination – all were exactly the same. And if Kuno himself, flesh of her flesh, stood close beside her at last, what profit was there in that? She was too well-bred to shake him by the hand.

Averting her eyes, she spoke as follows:

'Here I am. I have had the most terrible journey and greatly retarded the development of my soul. It is not worth it, Kuno, it is not worth it. My time is too precious. The sunlight almost touched me, and I have met with the rudest people. I can only stop a few minutes. Say what you want to say, and then I must return.'

'I have been threatened with Homelessness,' said Kuno.

She looked at him now.

'I have been threatened with Homelessness, and I could not tell you such a thing through the Machine.'

Homelessness means death. The victim is exposed to the air, which kills him.

'I have been outside since I spoke to you last. The tremendous thing has happened, and they have discovered me.'

'But why shouldn't you go outside?' she exclaimed. 'It is perfectly legal, perfectly mechanical, to visit the surface of the earth. I have lately been to a lecture on the sea; there is no objection to that; one simply summons a respirator and gets an Egression-permit. It is not the kind of thing that spiritually-minded people do, and I begged you not to do it, but there is no legal objection to it.'

'I did not get an Egression-permit.'

'Then how did you get out?'

'I found out a way of my own.'

The phrase conveyed no meaning to her, and he had to repeat it.

'A way of your own?' she whispered. 'But that would be wrong.'

'Why?'

The question shocked her beyond measure.

'You are beginning to worship the Machine,' he said coldly. 'You think it irreligious of me to have found out a way of my own. It was just what the Committee thought, when they threatened me with Homelessness.'

At this she grew angry. 'I worship nothing!' she cried. 'I am most advanced. I don't think you irreligious, for there is no such thing as religion left. All the fear and the superstition that existed once have been destroyed by the Machine. I only meant that to find out a way of your own was — Besides, there is no new way out.'

'So it is always supposed.'

'Except through the vomitories, for which one must have an Egression-permit, it is impossible to get out. The Book says so.'

'Well, the Book's wrong, for I have been out on my feet.'

For Kuno was possessed of a certain physical strength.

By these days it was a demerit to be muscular. Each infant was examined at birth, and all who promised undue strength were destroyed. Humanitarians may protest, but it would have been no true kindness to let an athlete live; he would never have been happy in that state of life to which the Machine had called him; he would have yearned for trees to climb, rivers to bathe in, meadows and hills against which he might measure his body. Man must be adapted to his surroundings, must he not? In the dawn of the world our weakly must be exposed on Mount Taygetus, in its twilight our strong will suffer euthanasia, that the Machine may progress, that the Machine may progress, that the Machine may progress eternally.

'You know that we have lost the sense of space. We say "space is annihilated", but we have annihilated not space but the sense thereof. We have lost a part of ourselves. I determined to recover it, and I began by walking up and down the platform of the railway outside my room. Up and down, until I was tired, and so did recapture the meaning of "Near" and "Far". "Near" is a place to which I can get quickly *on my feet*, not a place to which the train or the air-ship will take me quickly. "Far" is a place to which I cannot get quickly on my feet; the vomitory is "far", though I could be there in thirty-eight seconds by summoning the train. Man is the measure. That was my first lesson. Man's feet are the measure for distance, his hands are the measure for ownership, his body is the measure for all that is lovable and desirable and strong. Then I went further: it was then that I called to you for the first time, and you would not come.

'This city, as you know, is built deep beneath the surface of the earth, with only the vomitories protruding. Having paced the platform outside my own room, I took the lift to the next platform and paced that also, and so with each in turn, until I came to the topmost, above which begins the earth. All the platforms were exactly alike, and all that I gained by visiting them was to develop my sense of space and my muscles. I think I should have been content with this – it is not a little thing – but as I walked and brooded, it occurred to me that our cities had been built in the days when men still breathed the outer air, and that there had been ventilation shafts for the workmen. I could think of nothing but these ventilation shafts. Had they been destroyed by all the food-tubes and medicine-tubes and music-tubes that the Machine has evolved lately? Or did traces of them remain? One thing was certain. If I came upon them anywhere, it would be in the railway-tunnels of the topmost story. Everywhere else, all space was accounted for.

'I am telling my story quickly, but don't think that I was not a coward or that your answers never depressed me. It is not the proper thing, it is not mechanical, it is not decent to walk along a railway-tunnel. I did not fear that I might tread upon a live rail and be killed. I feared something far more intangible – doing what was not contemplated by the Machine. Then I said to myself, "Man is the measure", and I went, and after many visits I found an opening.

'The tunnels, of course, were lighted. Everything is light, artificial light; darkness is the exception. So when I saw a black gap in the tiles, I knew that it was an exception, and rejoiced. I put in my arm – I could put in no more at first – and waved it round and round in ecstasy. I loosened another tile, and put in my head, and shouted into the darkness: "I am coming, I shall do it yet", and my voice reverberated down endless passages. I seemed to hear the spirits of those dead workmen who had returned each evening to the starlight and to their wives, and all the generations who had lived in the open air called back to me, "You will do it yet, you are coming".'

He paused, and, absurd as he was, his last words moved her. For Kuno had lately asked to be a father, and his request had been refused by the Committee. His was not a type that the Machine desired to hand on.

'Then a train passed. It brushed by me, but I thrust my head and arms into the hole. I had done enough for one day, so I crawled back to the platform, went down in the lift, and summoned my bed. Ah, what dreams! And again I called you, and again you refused.'

She shook her head and said:

'Don't. Don't talk of these terrible things. You make me

miserable. You are throwing civilization away.'

'But I had got back the sense of space and a man cannot rest then. I determined to get in at the hole and climb the shaft. And so I exercised my arms. Day after day I went through ridiculous movements, until my flesh ached, and I could hang by my hands and hold the pillow of my bed outstretched for many minutes. Then I summoned a respirator, and started.

'It was easy at first. The mortar had somehow rotted, and I soon pushed some more tiles in, and clambered after them into the darkness, and the spirits of the dead comforted me. I don't know what I mean by that. I just say what I felt. I felt, for the first time, that a protest had been lodged against corruption, and that even as the dead were comforting me, so I was comforting the unborn. I felt that humanity existed, and that it existed without clothes. How can I possibly explain this? It was naked, humanity seemed naked, and all these tubes and buttons and machineries neither came into the world with us, nor will they follow us out, nor do they matter supremely while we are here. Had I been strong, I would have torn off every garment I had, and gone out into the outer air unswaddled. But this is not for me, nor perhaps for my generation. I climbed with my respirator and my hygienic clothes and my dietetic tabloids! Better thus than not at all.

'There was a ladder, made of some primaeval metal. The light from the railway fell upon its lowest rungs, and I saw that it led straight upwards out of the rubble at the bottom of the shaft. Perhaps our ancestors ran up and down it a dozen times daily, in their building. As I climbed, the rough edges cut through my gloves so that my hands bled. The light helped me for a little, and then came darkness and, worse still, silence which pierced my ears like a sword. The Machine hums! Did you know that? Its hum penetrates our blood, and may even guide our thoughts. Who knows! I was getting beyond its power. Then I thought: "This silence means that I am doing wrong." But I heard voices in the silence, and again they strengthened me.' He laughed. 'I had need of them. The next moment I cracked my head against something.'

She sighed.

'I had reached one of those pneumatic stoppers that defend us from the outer air. You may have noticed them on the air-ship. Pitch dark, my feet on the rungs of an invisible ladder, my hands cut; I cannot explain how I lived through this part, but the voices still comforted me, and I felt for fastenings. The stopper, I suppose, was about eight feet across. I passed my hand over it as far as I could reach. It was perfectly smooth. I felt it almost to the centre. Not quite to the centre, for my arm was too short. Then the voice said: "Jump. It is worth it. There may be a handle in the centre, and you may catch hold of it and so come to us your own way. And if there is no handle, so that you may fall and are dashed to pieces – it is still worth it: you will still come to us your own way." So I jumped. There was a handle, and —'

He paused. Tears gathered in his mother's eyes. She knew that he was fated. If he did not die to-day he would die to-morrow. There was not room for such a person in the world. And with her pity disgust mingled. She was ashamed at having borne such a son, she who had always been so respectable and so full of ideas. Was he really the little boy to whom she had taught the use of his stops and buttons, and to whom she had given his first lessons in the Book? The very hair that disfigured his lip showed that he was reverting to some savage type. On atavism the Machine can have no mercy.

'There was a handle, and I did catch it. I hung tranced over the darkness and heard the hum of these workings as the last whisper in a dying dream. All the things I had cared about and all the people I had spoken to through tubes appeared infinitely little. Meanwhile the handle revolved.

My weight had set something in motion and I span slowly, and then —

'I cannot describe it. I was lying with my face to the sunshine. Blood poured from my nose and ears and I heard a tremendous roaring. The stopper, with me clinging to it, had simply been blown out of the earth, and the air that we make down here was escaping through the vent into the air above. It burst up like a fountain. I crawled back to it – for the upper air hurts – and, as it were, I took great sips from the edge. My respirator had flown goodness knows where, my clothes were torn. I just lay with my lips close to the hole, and I sipped until the bleeding stopped. You can imagine nothing so curious. This hollow in the grass – I will speak of it in a minute – the sun shining into it, not brilliantly but through marbled clouds – the peace, the nonchalance, the sense of space, and, brushing my cheek, the roaring fountain of our artificial air! Soon I spied my respirator, bobbing up and down in the current high above my head, and higher still were many air-ships. But no one ever looks out of air-ships, and in any case they could not have picked me up. There I was, stranded. The sun shone a little way down the shaft, and revealed the topmost rung of the ladder, but it was hopeless trying to reach it. I should either have been tossed up again by the escape, or else have fallen in, and died. I could only lie on the grass, sipping and sipping, and from time to time glancing around me.

'I knew that I was in Wessex, for I had taken care to go to a lecture on the subject before starting. Wessex lies above the room in which we are talking now. It was once an important state. Its kings held all the southern coast from the Andredswald to Cornwall, while the Wansdyke protected them on the north, running over the high ground. The lecturer was only concerned with the rise of Wessex, so I do not know how long it remained an international power, nor would the knowledge have assisted me. To tell the truth, I could do nothing but laugh during this part. There was I, with a pneumatic stopper by my side and a respirator bobbing over my head, imprisoned, all three of us, in a grass-grown hollow that was edged with fern.'

Then he grew grave again.

'Lucky for me that it was a hollow. For the air began to fall back into it and to fill it as water fills a bowl. I could crawl about. Presently I stood. I breathed a mixture, in which the air that hurts predominated whenever I tried to climb the sides. This was not so bad. I had not lost my tabloids and remained ridiculously cheerful, and as for the Machine, I forgot about it altogether. My one aim now was to get to the top, where the ferns were, and to view whatever objects lay beyond.

'I rushed the slope. The new air was still too bitter for me and I came rolling back, after a momentary vision of something grey. The sun grew very feeble, and I remembered that he was in Scorpio – I had been to a lecture on that too. If the sun is in Scorpio and you are in Wessex, it means that you must be as quick as you can or it will get too dark. (This is the first bit of useful information I have ever got from a lecture, and I expect it will be the last.) It made me try frantically to breathe the new air, and to advance as far as I dared out of my pond. The hollow filled so slowly. At times I thought that the fountain played with less vigour. My respirator seemed to dance nearer the earth; the roar was decreasing.'

He broke off.

'I don't think this is interesting you. The rest will interest you even less. There are no ideas in it, and I wish that I had not troubled you to come. We are too different, mother.'

She told him to continue.

'It was evening before I climbed the bank. The sun had very nearly slipped out of the sky by this time, and I could not get a good view. You, who have just crossed the Roof of the World, will not want to hear an account of the little hills that I saw – low colourless hills. But to me they were living and the turf that covered them was a skin, under which their muscles rippled, and I felt that those hills had called with incalculable force to men in the past, and that men had loved them. Now they sleep – perhaps for ever. They commune with humanity in dreams. Happy the man, happy the woman, who awakes the hills of Wessex. For though they sleep, they will never die.'

His voice rose passionately.

'Cannot you see, cannot all you lecturers see, that it is we that are dying, and that down here the only thing that really lives is the Machine? We created the Machine, to do our will, but we cannot make it do our will now. It has robbed us of the sense of space and of the sense of touch, it has blurred every human relation and narrowed down love to a carnal act, it has paralysed our bodies and our wills, and now it compels us to worship it. The Machine develops – but not on our lines. The Machine proceeds – but not to our goal. We only exist as the blood corpuscles that course through its arteries, and if it could work without us, it would let us die. Oh, I have no remedy – or, at least, only one – to tell men again and again that I have seen the hills of Wessex as Aelfrid saw them when he overthrew the Danes.

'So the sun set. I forgot to mention that a belt of mist lay between my hill and other hills, and that it was the colour of pearl.'

He broke off for the second time.

'Go on,' said his mother wearily.

He shook his head.

'Go on. Nothing that you say can distress me now. I am hardened.'

'I had meant to tell you the rest, but I cannot: I know that I cannot: good-bye.'

Vashti stood irresolute. All her nerves were tingling with his blasphemies. But she was also inquisitive.

'This is unfair,' she complained. 'You have called me across the world to hear your story, and hear it I will. Tell me – as briefly as possible, for this is a disastrous waste of time – tell me how you returned to civilization.'

'Oh – that!' he said, starting. 'You would like to hear about civilization. Certainly. Had I got to where my respirator fell down?'

'No – but I understand everything now. You put on your respirator, and managed to walk along the surface of the earth to a vomitory, and there your conduct was reported to the Central Committee.'

'By no means.'

He passed his hand over his forehead, as if dispelling some strong impression. Then, resuming his narrative, he warmed to it again.

'My respirator fell about sunset. I had mentioned that the fountain seemed feebler, had I not?'

'Yes.'

'About sunset, it let the respirator fall. As I said, I had entirely forgotten about the Machine, and I paid no great attention at the time, being occupied with other things. I had my pool of air, into which I could dip when the outer keenness became intolerable, and which would possibly remain for days, provided that no wind sprang up to disperse it. Not until it was too late did I realize what the stoppage of the escape implied. You see – the gap in the tunnel had been mended; the Mending Apparatus; the Mending Apparatus, was after me.

'One other warning I had, but I neglected it. The sky at night was clearer than it had been in the day, and the moon, which was about half the sky behind the sun, shone into the dell at moments quite brightly. I was in my usual place – on the boundary between the two atmospheres – when I thought I saw something dark move across the bottom of the dell, and vanish into the shaft. In my folly, I ran down. I bent over and listened, and I thought I heard a faint scraping noise in the depths.

'At this – but it was too late – I took alarm. I determined to put on my respirator and to walk right out of the dell. But my respirator had gone. I knew exactly where it had fallen – between the stopper and the aperture – and I could even feel the mark that it had made in the turf. It had gone, and I realized that something evil was at work, and I had better escape to the other air, and, if I must die, die running towards the cloud that had been the colour of a pearl. I never started. Out of the shaft – it is too horrible. A worm, a long white worm, had crawled out of the shaft and was gliding over the moonlit grass.

'I screamed. I did everything that I should not have done, I stamped upon the creature instead of flying from it, and it at once curled round the ankle. Then we fought. The worm let me run all over the dell, but edged up my leg as I ran. "Help!" I cried. (That part is too awful. It belongs to the part that you will never know.) "Help!" I cried. (Why cannot we suffer in silence?) "Help!" I cried. Then my feet were wound together, I fell, I was dragged away from the dear ferns and the living hills, and past the great metal stopper (I can tell you this part), and I thought it might save me again if I caught hold of the handle. It also was enwrapped, it also. Oh, the whole dell was full of the things. They were searching it in all directions, they were denuding it, and the white snouts of others peeped out of the hole, ready if needed. Everything that could be moved they brought – brushwood, bundles of fern, everything, and down we all went intertwined into hell. The last things that I saw, ere the stopper closed after us, were certain stars, and I felt that a man of my sort lived in the sky. For I did fight, I fought till the very end, and it was only my head hitting against the ladder that quieted me. I woke up in this room. The worms had vanished, I was surrounded by artificial air, artificial light, artificial peace, and my friends were calling to me down speaking-tubes to know whether I had come across any new ideas lately.'

Here his story ended. Discussion of it was impossible, and Vashti turned to go.

'It will end in Homelessness,' she said quietly.

'I wish it would,' retorted Kuno.

'The Machine has been most merciful.'

'I prefer the mercy of God.'

'By that superstitious phrase, do you mean that you could live in the outer air?'

'Yes.'

'Have you ever seen, round the vomitories, the bones of those who were extruded after the Great Rebellion?'

'Yes.'

'They were left where they perished for our edification. A few crawled away, but they perished, too – who can doubt it? And so with the Homeless of our own day. The surface of the earth supports life no longer.'

'Indeed.'

'Ferns and a little grass may survive, but all higher forms have perished. Has any air-ship detected them?'

'No.'

'Has any lecturer dealt with them?'

'No.'

'Then why this obstinacy?'

'Because I have seen them,' he exploded.

'Seen *what*?'

'Because I have seen her in the twilight – because she came to my help when I called – because she, too, was entangled by the worms, and, luckier than I, was killed by one of them piercing her throat.'

He was mad. Vashti departed, nor, in the troubles that followed, did she ever see his face again.

# PART III

## THE HOMELESS

DURING the years that followed Kuno's escapade, two important developments took place in the Machine. On the surface they were revolutionary, but in either case men's minds had been prepared beforehand, and they did but express tendencies that were latent already.

The first of these was the abolition of respirators.

Advanced thinkers, like Vashti, had always held it foolish to visit the surface of the earth. Air-ships might be necessary, but what was the good of going out for mere curiosity and crawling along for a mile or two in a terrestrial motor? The habit was vulgar and perhaps faintly improper: it was unproductive of ideas, and had no connexion with the habits that really mattered. So respirators were abolished, and with them, of course, the terrestrial motors, and except for a few lecturers, who complained that they were debarred access to their subject-matter, the development was accepted quietly. Those who still wanted to know what the earth was like had after all only to listen to some gramophone or to look into some cinematophote. And even the lecturers acquiesced when they found that a lecture on the sea was none the less stimulating when compiled out of other lectures that had already been delivered on the same subject. 'Beware of first-hand ideas!' exclaimed one of the most advanced of them. 'First-hand ideas do not really exist. They are but the physical impressions produced by love and fear, and on this gross foundation who could erect a philosophy? Let your ideas be second-hand, and if possible tenth-hand, for then they will be far removed from that disturbing element – direct observation. Do not learn anything about this subject of mine – the

French Revolution. Learn instead what I think that Enicharmon thought Urizen thought Gutch thought Ho-Yung thought Chi-Bo-Sing thought Lafcadio Hearn thought Carlyle thought Mirabeau said about the French Revolution. Through the medium of these ten great minds the blood that was shed at Paris and the windows that were broken at Versailles will be clarified to an idea which you may employ most profitably in your daily lives. But be sure that the intermediates are many and varied, for in history one authority exists to counteract another. Urizen must counteract the scepticism of Ho-Yung and Enicharmon, I must myself counteract the impetuosity of Gutch. You who listen to me are in a better position to judge about the French Revolution than I am. Your descendants will be even in a better position than you, for they will learn what you think. I think, and yet another intermediate will be added to the chain. And in time' – his voice rose – 'there will come a generation that has got beyond facts, beyond impressions, a generation absolutely colourless, a generation

*seraphically free*
*From taint of personality,*

which will see the French Revolution not as it happened, nor as they would like it to have happened, but as it would have happened had it taken place in the days of the Machine.'

Tremendous applause greeted this lecture, which did but voice a feeling already latent in the minds of men – a feeling that terrestrial facts must be ignored, and that the abolition of respirators was a positive gain. It was even suggested that air-ships should be abolished too. This was not done, because air-ships had somehow worked themselves into the Machine's system. But year by year they were used less, and mentioned less by thoughtful men.

The second great development was the re-establishment of religion.

This, too, had been voiced in the celebrated lecture. No one could mistake the reverent tone in which the peroration had concluded, and it awakened a responsive echo in the heart of each. Those who had long worshipped silently now began to talk. They described the strange feeling of peace that came over them when they handled the Book of the Machine, the pleasure that it was to repeat certain numerals out of it, however little meaning those numerals conveyed to the outward ear, the ecstasy of touching a button however unimportant, or of ringing an electric bell however superfluously.

'The Machine,' they exclaimed, 'feeds us and clothes us and houses us; through it we speak to one another, through it we see one another, in it we have our being. The Machine is the friend of ideas and the enemy of superstition: the Machine is omnipotent, eternal; blessed is the Machine.' And before long this allocution was printed on the first page of the Book, and in subsequent editions the ritual swelled into a complicated system of praise and prayer. The word 'religion' was sedulously avoided, and in theory the Machine was still the creation and the implement of man. But in practice all, save a few retrogrades, worshipped it as divine. Nor was it worshipped in unity. One believer would be chiefly impressed by the blue optic plates, through which he saw other believers; another by the mending apparatus, which sinful Kuno had compared to worms; another by the lifts, another by the Book. And each would pray to this or to that, and ask it to intercede for him with the Machine as a whole. Persecution – that also was present. It did not break out, for reasons that will be set forward shortly. But it was latent, and all who did not accept the minimum known as 'undenominational Mechanism' lived in danger of Homelessness, which means death, as we know.

To attribute these two great developments to the Central Committee is to take a very narrow view of civilization. The Central Committee announced the developments, it is true, but they were no more the cause of them than were the kings of the imperialistic period the cause of war. Rather did they yield to some invincible pressure, which came no one knew whither, and which, when gratified, was succeeded by some new pressure equally invincible. To such a state of affairs it is convenient to give the name of progress. No one confessed the Machine was out of hand. Year by year it was served with increased efficiency and decreased intelligence. The better a man knew his own duties upon it, the less he understood the duties of his neighbour, and in all the world there was not one who understood the monster as a whole. Those master brains had perished. They had left full directions, it is true, and their successors had each of them mastered a portion of those directions. But Humanity, in its desire for comfort, had overreached itself. It had exploited the riches of nature too far. Quietly and complacently, it was sinking into decadence, and progress had come to mean the progress of the Machine.

As for Vashti, her life went peacefully forward until the final disaster. She made her room dark and slept; she awoke and made the room light. She lectured and attended lectures. She exchanged ideas with her innumerable friends and believed she was growing more spiritual. At times a friend was granted Euthanasia, and left his or her room for the homelessness that is beyond all human conception. Vashti did not much mind. After an unsuccessful lecture, she would sometimes ask for Euthanasia herself. But the death-rate was not permitted to exceed the birth-rate, and the Machine had hitherto refused it to her.

The troubles began quietly, long before she was conscious of them.

One day she was astonished at receiving a message from her son. They never communicated, having nothing in common, and she had only heard indirectly that he was still alive, and had been transferred from the northern hemisphere, where he had behaved so mischievously, to the southern – indeed, to a room not far from her own.

'Does he want me to visit him?' she thought. 'Never again, never. And I have not the time.'

No, it was madness of another kind.

He refused to visualize his face upon the blue plate, and speaking out of the darkness with solemnity said:

'The Machine stops.'

'What do you say?'

'The Machine is stopping, I know it, I know the signs.'

She burst into a peal of laughter. He heard her and was angry, and they spoke no more.

'Can you imagine anything more absurd?' she cried to a friend. 'A man who was my son believes that the Machine is stopping. It would be impious if it was not mad.'

'The Machine is stopping?' her friend replied. 'What does that mean? The phrase conveys nothing to me.'

'Nor to me.'

'He does not refer, I suppose, to the trouble there has been lately with the music?'

'Oh no, of course not. Let us talk about music.'

'Have you complained to the authorities?'

'Yes, and they say it wants mending, and referred me to the Committee of the Mending Apparatus. I complained of those curious gasping sighs that disfigure the symphonies of the Brisbane school. They sound like someone in pain. The Committee of the Mending Apparatus say that it shall be remedied shortly.'

Obscurely worried, she resumed her life. For one thing, the defect in the music irritated her. For another thing, she could not forget Kuno's speech. If he had known that the music was out of repair – he could not know it, for he detested music – if he had known that it was wrong, 'the Machine stops' was exactly the venomous sort of remark he would have made. Of course he had made it at a venture, but the coincidence annoyed her, and she spoke with some petulance to the Committee of the Mending Apparatus.

They replied, as before, that the defect would be set right shortly.

'Shortly! At once!' she retorted. 'Why should I be worried by imperfect music? Things are always put right at once. If you do not mend it at once, I shall complain to the Central Committee.'

'No personal complaints are received by the Central Committee,' the Committee of the Mending Apparatus replied.

'Through whom am I to make my complaint, then?'

'Through us.'

'I complain then.'

'Your complaint shall be forwarded in its turn.'

'Have others complained?'

This question was unmechanical, and the Committee of the Mending Apparatus refused to answer it.

'It is too bad!' she exclaimed to another of her friends. 'There never was such an unfortunate woman as myself. I can never be sure of my music now. It gets worse and worse each time I summon it.'

'I too have my troubles,' the friend replied. 'Sometimes my ideas are interrupted by a slight jarring noise.'

'What is it?'

'I do not know whether it is inside my head or inside the wall.'

'Complain in either case.'

'I have complained, and my complaint will be forwarded in its turn to the Central Committee.'

Time passed, and they resented the defects no longer. The defects had not been remedied, but the human tissues in that latter day had become so subservient that they readily adapted themselves to every caprice of the Machine. The sigh at the crisis of the Brisbane symphony no longer irritated Vashti; she accepted it as part of the melody. The jarring noise, whether in the head or in the wall, was no longer resented by her friend. And so with the mouldy artificial fruit, so with the bath water that began to stink, so with the defective rhymes that the poetry machine had taken to emit. All were bitterly complained of at first, and then acquiesced in and forgotten. Things went from bad to worse unchallenged.

It was otherwise with the failure of the sleeping apparatus. That was a more serious stoppage. There came a day when over the whole world – in Sumatra, in Wessex, in the innumerable cities of Courland and Brazil – the beds, when summoned by their tired owners, failed to appear. It may seem a ludicrous matter, but from it we may date the collapse of humanity. The Committee responsible for the failure was assailed by complaints, whom it referred, as usual, to the Committee of the Mending Apparatus, who in its turn assured them that their complaints would be forwarded to the Central Committee. But the discontent grew, for mankind was not yet sufficiently adaptable to do without sleeping.

'Someone is meddling with the Machine —' they began.

'Someone is trying to make himself king, to reintroduce the personal element.'

'Punish that man with Homelessness.'

'To the rescue! Avenge the Machine! Avenge the Machine!'

'War! Kill the man!'

But the Committee of the Mending Apparatus now came forward, and allayed the panic with well-chosen words. It confessed that the Mending Apparatus was itself in need of repair.

The effect of this frank confession was admirable.

'Of course,' said a famous lecturer – he of the French Revolution, who gilded each new decay with splendour – 'of course we shall not press our complaints now. The Mending Apparatus has treated us so well in the past that we all sympathize with it, and will wait patiently for its recovery. In its own good time it will resume its duties. Meanwhile let us do without our beds, our tabloids, our other little wants. Such, I feel sure, would be the wish of the Machine.'

Thousands of miles away his audience applauded. The Machine still linked them. Under the seas, beneath the roots of the mountains, ran the wires through which they saw and heard, the enormous eyes and ears that were their heritage, and the hum of many workings clothed their thoughts in one garment of subserviency. Only the old and the sick remained ungrateful, for it was rumoured that Euthanasia, too, was out of order, and that pain had reappeared among men.

It became difficult to read. A blight entered the atmosphere and dulled its luminosity. At times Vashti could scarcely see across her room. The air, too, was foul. Loud were the complaints, impotent the remedies, heroic the tone of the lecturer as he cried: 'Courage! courage! What matter so long as the Machine goes on? To it the darkness and the light are one.' And though things improved again after a time, the old brilliancy was never recaptured, and humanity never recovered from its entrance into twilight. There was an hysterical talk of 'measures,' of 'provisional dictatorship,' and the inhabitants of Sumatra were asked to familiarize themselves with the workings of the central power station, the said power station being situated in France. But for the most part panic reigned, and men spent their strength praying to their Books, tangible proofs of the Machine's omnipotence. There were gradations of terror – at times came rumours of hope – the Mending Apparatus was almost mended – the enemies of the Machine had been got under – new 'nerve-centres' were evolving which would do the work even more magnificently than before. But there came a day when, without the slightest warning, without any previous hint of feebleness, the entire communication-system broke down, all over the world, and the world, as they understood it, ended.

Vashti was lecturing at the time and her earlier remarks had been punctuated with applause. As she proceeded the audience became silent, and at the conclusion there was no sound. Somewhat displeased, she called to a friend who was a specialist in sympathy. No sound: doubtless the friend was sleeping. And so with the next friend whom she tried to summon, and so with the next, until she remembered Kuno's cryptic remark, 'The Machine stops.'

The phrase still conveyed nothing. If Eternity was stopping it would of course be set going shortly.

For example, there was still a little light and air – the atmosphere had improved a few hours previously. There was still the Book, and while there was the Book there was security.

Then she broke down, for with the cessation of activity came an unexpected terror – silence.

She had never known silence, and the coming of it nearly killed her – it did kill many thousands of people outright. Ever since her birth she had been surrounded by the steady hum. It was to the ear what artificial air was to the lungs, and agonizing pains shot across her head. And scarcely knowing what she did, she stumbled forward and pressed the unfamiliar button, the one that opened the door of her cell.

Now the door of the cell worked on a simple hinge of its own. It was not connected with the central power station, dying far away in France. It opened, rousing immoderate hopes in Vashti, for she thought that the Machine had been mended. It opened, and she saw the dim tunnel that curved far away towards freedom. One look, and then she shrank back. For the tunnel was full of people – she was almost the last in that city to have taken alarm.

People at any time repelled her, and these were nightmares from her worst dreams. People were crawling about, people were screaming, whimpering, gasping for breath, touching each other, vanishing in the dark, and ever and anon being pushed off the platform on to the live rail. Some were fighting round the electric bells, trying to summon trains which could not be summoned. Others were yelling for Euthanasia or for respirators, or blaspheming the Machine. Others stood at the doors of their cells fearing, like herself, either to stop in them or to leave them, and behind all the uproar was silence – the silence which is the voice of the earth and of the generations who have gone.

No – it was worse than solitude. She closed the door again and sat down to wait for the end. The disintegration went on, accompanied by horrible cracks and rumbling. The valves that restrained the Medical Apparatus must have been weakened, for it ruptured and hung hideously from the ceiling. The floor heaved and fell and flung her from her chair. A tube oozed towards her serpent fashion. And at last the final horror approached – light began to ebb, and she knew that civilization's long day was closing.

She whirled round, praying to be saved from this, at any rate, kissing the Book, pressing button after button. The uproar outside was increasing, and even penetrated the wall. Slowly the brilliancy of her cell was dimmed, the reflections faded from her metal switches. Now she could not see the reading-stand, now not the Book, though she held it in her hand. Light followed the flight of sound, air was following light, and the original void returned to the cavern from which it had been so long excluded. Vashti continued to whirl, like the devotees of an earlier religion, screaming, praying, striking at the buttons with bleeding hands.

It was thus that she opened her prison and escaped – escaped in the spirit: at least so it seems to me, ere my meditation closes. That she escapes in the body – I cannot perceive that. She struck, by chance, the switch that released the door, and the rush of foul air on her skin, the loud throbbing whispers in her ears, told her that she was facing the tunnel again, and that tremendous platform on which she had seen men fighting. They were not fighting now. Only the whispers remained, and the little whimpering groans. They were dying by hundreds out in the dark.

She burst into tears.

Tears answered her.

They wept for humanity, those two, not for themselves. They could not bear that this should be the end. Ere silence was completed their hearts were opened, and they knew what had been important on the earth. Man, the flower of all flesh, the noblest of all creatures visible, man who had once made god in his image, and had mirrored his strength on the constellations, beautiful naked man was dying, strangled in the garments that he had woven. Century after century had he toiled, and here was his reward. Truly the garment had seemed heavenly at first, shot with the colours of culture, sewn with the threads of self-denial. And heavenly it had been so long as it was a garment and no more, so long as man could shed it at will and live by the essence that is his soul, and the essence, equally divine, that is his body. The sin against the body – it was for that they wept in chief; the centuries of wrong against the muscles and the nerves, and those five portals by which we can alone apprehend – glozing it over with talk of evolution, until the body was white pap, the home of ideas as colourless, last sloshy stirrings of a spirit that had grasped the stars.

'Where are you?' she sobbed.

His voice in the darkness said, 'Here.'

'Is there any hope, Kuno?'

'None for us.'

'Where are you?'

She crawled towards him over the bodies of the dead. His blood spurted over her hands.

'Quicker,' he gasped, 'I am dying – but we touch, we talk, not through the Machine.'

He kissed her.

'We have come back to our own. We die, but we have recaptured life, as it was in Wessex, when Aelfrid overthrew the Danes. We know what they know outside, they who dwelt in the cloud that is the colour of a pearl.'

'But, Kuno, is it true? Are there still men on the surface of the earth? Is this – this tunnel, this poisoned darkness – really not the end?'

He replied:

'I have seen them, spoken to them, loved them. They are hiding in the mist and the ferns until our civilization stops. To-day they are the Homeless – to-morrow —'

'Oh, to-morrow – some fool will start the Machine again, to-morrow.'

'Never,' said Kuno, 'never. Humanity has learnt its lesson.'

As he spoke the whole city was broken like a honeycomb. An air-ship had sailed in through the vomitory into a ruined wharf. It crashed downwards, exploding as it went, rending gallery after gallery with its wings of steel. For a moment they saw the nations of the dead, and, before they joined them, scraps of the untainted sky.

# THE POINT OF IT

I

'I DON'T see the point of it,' said Micky, through much imbecile laughter.

Harold went on rowing. They had spent too long on the sand-dunes, and now the tide was running out of the estuary strongly. The sun was setting, the fields on the opposite bank shone bright, and the farm-house where they were stopping glowed from its upper windows as though filled to the brim with fire.

'We're going to be carried out to sea,' Micky continued. 'You'll never win unless you bust yourself a bit, and you a poor invalid, too. I back the sea.'

They were reaching the central channel, the backbone, as it were, of the retreating waters. Once past it, the force of the tide would slacken, and they would have easy going until they beached under the farm. It was a glorious evening. It had been a most glorious day. They had rowed out to the dunes at the slack, bathed, raced, eaten, slept, bathed and raced and eaten again. Micky was in roaring spirits. God had never thwarted him hitherto, and he could not suppose that they would really be made late for supper by an ebbing tide. When they came to the channel, and the boat, which had been slowly edging upstream, hung motionless among the moving waters, he lost all semblance of sanity, and shouted:

*It may be that the gulfs will wash us down,*
*It may be we shall touch the Happy Isles,*
*And see the great Achilles, whom we knew.*

Harold, who did not care for poetry, only shouted. His spirits also were roaring, and he neither looked nor felt a poor invalid. Science had talked to him seriously of late, shaking her head at his sunburnt body. What should Science know? She had sent him down to the sea to recruit, and Micky to see that he did not tire himself. Micky had been a nuisance at first, but common sense had prevailed, as it always does among the young. A fortnight ago, he would not let the patient handle an oar. Now he bid him bust himself, and Harold took him at his word and did so. He made himself all will and muscle. He began not to know where he was. The thrill of the stretcher against his feet, and of the tide up his arms, merged with his friend's voice towards one nameless sensation; he was approaching the mystic state that is the athlete's true though unacknowledged goal: he was beginning to be.

Micky chanted, 'One, two – one, two,' and tried to help by twitching the rudder. But Micky had imagination. He looked at the flaming windows and fancied that the farm was a star and the boat its attendant satellite. Then the tide was the rushing ether stream of the universe, the interstellar surge that beats for ever. How jolly! He did not formulate his joys, after the wary fashion of older people. He was far too happy to be thankful. 'Remember now thy Creator in the days of thy youth' are the words of one who has left his youth behind, and all that Micky sang was 'One, two'.

Harold laughed without hearing. Sweat poured off his forehead. He put on a spurt, as did the tide.

'Wish the doctor could see you,' cried Micky.

No answer. Setting his teeth, he went berserk. His ancestors called to him that it was better to die than to be beaten by the sea. He rowed with gasps and angry little cries, while the voice of the helmsman lashed him to fury.

'That's right – one, two – plug it in harder.... Oh, I say, this is a bit stiff, though. Let's give it up, old man, perhaps.'

The gulls were about them now. Some wheeled overhead, others bobbed past on the furrowed waters. The song of a lark came faintly from the land, and Micky saw the doctor's trap driving along the road that led to the farm. He felt ashamed.

'Look here, Harold, you oughtn't to – I oughtn't to have let you. I – I don't see the point of it.'

'Don't you?' said Harold with curious distinctness. 'Well, you will some day', and so saying dropped both oars. The boat spun round at this, the farm, the trap, the song of the lark vanished, and he fell heavily against the rowlock. Micky caught at him. He had strained his heart. Half in the boat and half out of it, he died, a rotten business.

II

A ROTTEN business. It happened when Michael was twenty-two, and he expected never to be happy again. The sound of his own voice shouting as he was carried out, the doctor's voice saying 'I consider you responsible', the coming of Harold's parents, the voice of the curate summarizing Harold's relations with the unseen – all these things affected him so deeply that he supposed they would affect him for ever. They did not, because he lived to be over seventy, and with the best will in the world, it is impossible to remember clearly for so long. The mind, however sensitive and affectionate, is coated with new experiences daily; it cannot clear itself of the steady accretion, and is forced either to forget the past or to distort it. So it was with Michael. In time only the more dramatic incidents survived. He remembered Harold's final gesture (one hand grasping his own, the other plunged deep into the sea), because there was a certain aesthetic quality about it, not because it was the last of his friend. He remembered the final words for the same reason. 'Don't you see the point of it? Well, you will some day.' The phrase struck his fancy, and passed into his own stock; after thirty or forty years he forgot its origin. He is not to blame; the business of life snowed him under.

There is also this to say: he and Harold had nothing in common except youth. No spiritual bond could survive. They had never discussed theology or social reform, or any of the problems that were thronging Michael's brain, and consequently, though they had been intimate enough, there was nothing to remember. Harold melted the more one thought of him. Robbed of his body, he was so shadowy. Nor could one imagine him as a departed spirit, for the world beyond death is surely august. Neither in heaven nor hell is there place for athletics and aimless good temper, and if these were taken from Harold, what was left? Even if the unseen life should prove an archetype of this, even if it should contain a sun and stars of its own, the sunburn of earth must fade off our faces as we look at it, the muscles of earth must wither before we can go rowing on its infinite sea. Michael sadly resigned his friend to God's mercy. He himself could do nothing, for men can only immortalize those who leave behind them some strong impression of poetry or wisdom.

For himself he expected another fate. With all humility, he knew that he was not as Harold. It was no merit of his own, but he had been born of a more intellectual stock, and had inherited powers that rendered him worthier of life, and of whatever may come after it. He cared for the universe, for the tiny tangle in it that we call civilization, for his fellowmen who had made the tangle and who transcended it. Love, the love of humanity, warmed him; and even when he was thinking of other matters, was looking at Orion perhaps in the cold winter evenings, a pang of joy, too sweet for description, would thrill him, and he would feel sure that our highest impulses have some eternal value, and will be completed hereafter. So full a nature could not brood over death.

To summarize his career.

Soon after the tragedy, when he in his turn was recruiting, he met the woman who was to become his helpmate through life. He had met her once before, and had not liked her; she had seemed uncharitable and hard. Now he saw that her hardness sprang from a morality that he himself lacked. If he believed in love, Janet believed in truth. She tested all men and all things. She had no patience with the sentimentalist who shelters from the world's rough and tumble. Engaged at that time to another man, she spoke more freely to Michael than she would otherwise have done, and told him that it is not enough to feel good and to feel that others are good; one's business is to make others better, and she urged him to adopt a profession. The beauty of honest work dawned upon the youth as she spoke. Mentally and physically, he came to full manhood, and, after due preparation, he entered the Home Civil Service – the British Museum.

Here began a career that was rather notable and wholly beneficial to humanity. With his ideals of conduct and culture, Michael was not content with the official routine. He desired to help others, and, since he was gifted with tact, they consented to the operation. Before long he became a conciliatory force in his department. He could mollify his superiors, encourage his inferiors, soothe foreign scholars, and show that there is something to be said for all sides. Janet, who watched his rise, taxed him again with instability. But now she was wrong. The young man was not a mere opportunist. He always had a sincere opinion of his own, or he could not have retained the respect of his colleagues. It was really the inherent sweetness of his nature at work, turned by a woman's influence towards fruitful ends.

At the end of a ten years' acquaintance the two married. In the interval Janet had suffered much pain, for the man to whom she had been engaged had proved unworthy of her. Her character was set when she came to Michael, and, as he knew, strongly contrasted with his own; and perhaps they had already interchanged all the good they could. But the marriage proved durable and sufficiently happy. He, in particular, made endless allowances, for toleration and sympathy were becoming the cardinal points of his nature. If his wife was unfair to the official mind, or if his brother-in-law, an atheist, denounced religion, he would say to himself, 'They cannot help it; they are made thus, and have the qualities of their defects. Let me rather think of my own, and strive for a wider outlook ceaselessly.' He grew sweeter every day.

It was partly this desire for a wider outlook that turned him to literature. As he was crossing the forties it occurred to him to write a few essays, somewhat retrospective in tone, and thoughtful rather than profound in content. They had some success. Their good taste, their lucid style, the tempered Christianity of their ethics, whetted the half-educated public and made it think and feel. They were not, and were not intended to be, great literature, but they opened the doors to it, and were indubitably a power for good. The first volume was followed by 'The Confessions of a Middle-aged Man'. In it Michael paid melodious tribute to youth, but showed that ripeness is all. Experience, he taught, is the only humanizer; sympathy, balance and many-sidedness cannot come to a man until he is elderly. It is always pleasant to be told that the best is yet to be, and the sale of the book was large. Perhaps he would have become a popular author, but his wife's influence restrained him from writing anything that he did not sincerely feel. She had borne him three children by now – Henry, Catherine, and Adam. On the whole they were a happy family. Henry never gave any trouble. Catherine took after her mother. Adam, who was wild and uncouth, caused his father some anxiety. He could not understand him, in spite of careful observation, and they never became real friends. Still, it was but a little cloud in a large horizon. At home, as in his work, Michael was more successful than most men.

Thus he slipped into the fifties. On the death of his father he inherited a house in the Surrey hills, and Janet, whose real interests were horticultural, settled down there. After all, she had not proved an intellectual woman. Her fierce manner had misled him and perhaps herself into believing it. She was efficient enough in London society, but it bored her, for she lacked her husband's pliancy, and aged more rapidly than he did. Nor did the country suit her. She grew querulous, disputing with other ladies about the names of flowers. And, of course, the years were not without their effect on him, too. By now he was somewhat of a valetudinarian. He had given up all outdoor sports, and, though his health remained good, grew bald, and rather stout and timid. He was against late hours, violent exercise, night walks, swimming when hot, muddling about in open boats, and he often had to check himself from fidgeting the children. Henry, a charming sympathetic lad, would squeeze his hand and say, 'All right, Father.' But Catherine and Adam sometimes frowned. He thought of the children more and more. Now that his wife was declining, they were the future, and he was determined to keep in touch with them, remembering how his own father had failed with him. He believed in gentleness, and often stood between them and their mother. When the boys grew up he let them choose their own friends. When Catherine, at the age of nineteen, asked if she might go away and earn some money as a lady gardener, he let her go. In this case he had his reward, for Catherine, having killed the flowers, returned. She was a restless, scowling young woman, a trial to her mother, who could not imagine what girls were coming to. Then she married and improved greatly; indeed, she proved his chief support in the coming years.

For, soon after her marriage, a great trouble fell on him. Janet became bedridden, and, after a protracted illness, passed into the unknown. Sir Michael – for he had been knighted – declared that he should not survive her. They were so accustomed to each other, so mutually necessary, that he fully expected to pass away after her. In this he was mistaken. She died when he was sixty, and he lived to be over seventy. His character had passed beyond the clutch of circumstance and he still retained his old interests and his unconquerable benignity.

A second trouble followed hard on the first. It transpired that Adam was devoted to his mother, and had only tolerated home life for her sake. After a brutal scene he left. He wrote from the Argentine that he was sorry, but wanted to start for himself. 'I don't see the point of it,' quavered Sir Michael. 'Have I ever stopped him or any of you from starting?' Henry and Catherine agreed with him. Yet he felt that they understood their brother better than he did. 'I have given him freedom all his life,' he continued. 'I have given him freedom, what more does he want?' Henry, after hesitation, said, 'There are some people who feel that freedom cannot be given. At least I have heard so. Perhaps Adam is like that. Unless he took freedom he might not feel free.' Sir Michael disagreed. 'I have now studied adolescence for many years,' he replied,' and your conclusions, my dear boy, are ridiculous.'

The two rallied to their father gallantly; and, after all, he spent a dignified old age. Having retired from the British Museum, he produced a little aftermath of literature. The great public had forgotten him, but the courtliness of his 'Musings of a Pensioner' procured him some circulation among elderly and educated audiences. And he found a new spiritual consolation. *Anima naturaliter Anglicana*, he had never been hostile to the Established Church; and, when he criticized her worldliness and occasional inhumanity, had spoken as one who was outside her rather than against her. After his wife's death and the flight of his son, he lost any lingering taste for speculation. The experience of years disposed him to accept the experience of centuries and to merge his feeble personal note in the great voice of tradition. Yes; a serene and dignified old age. Few grudged it to him. Of course, he had enemies, who professed to see through him, and said that Adam had seen through him too; but no impartial observer agreed. No ulterior motive had ever biassed Sir Michael. The purity of his record was not due to luck but to purity within, and his conciliatory manner sprang from a conciliated soul. He could look back on failures and mistakes, and he had not carried out the ideals of his youth. Who has? But he had succeeded better than most men in modifying those ideals to fit the world of facts, and if love had been modified into sympathy and sympathy into compromise, let one of his contemporaries cast the first stone.

One fact remained – the fact of death. Hitherto, Sir Michael had never died, and at times he was bestially afraid. But more often death appeared as a prolongation of his present career. He saw himself quietly and tactfully organizing some corner in infinity with his wife's assistance; Janet would be greatly improved. He saw himself passing from a sphere in which he had been efficient into a sphere which combined the familiar with the eternal, and in which he would be equally efficient – passing into it with dignity and without pain. This life is a preparation for the next. Those who live longest are consequently the best prepared. Experience is the great teacher; blessed are the experienced, for they need not further modify their ideals.

The manner of his death was as follows. He, too, met with an accident. He was walking from his town house to Catherine's by a short cut through a slum; some women were quarrelling about a fish, and as he passed they appealed to him. Always courteous, the old man stopped, said that he had not sufficient data to judge on, and advised them to lay the fish aside for twenty-four hours. This chanced to annoy them, and they grew more angry with him than with one another. They accused him of 'doing them', of 'getting round them', and one, who was the worse for drink, said, 'See if he gets round that', and slapped him with the fish in the face. He fell. When he came to himself he was lying in bed with one of his headaches.

He could hear Catherine's voice. She annoyed him. If he did not open his eyes, it was only because he did not choose.

'He has been like this for nearly two years,' said Henry's voice.

It was, at the most, ten minutes since he had fallen in the slum. But he did not choose to argue.

'Yes, he's pretty well played out,' said a third voice – actually the voice of Adam; how and when had Adam returned? 'But, then, he's been that for the last thirty years.'

'Gently, old boy,' said Henry.

'Well, he has,' said Adam. 'I don't believe in cant. He never did anything since Mother died, and damned little before. They've forgotten his books because they aren't first-hand; they're rearranging the cases he arranged in the British Museum. That's the lot. What else has he done except tell people to dress warmly but not too warm?'

'Adam, you really mustn't —'

'It's because nobody speaks up that men of the old man's type get famous. It's a sign of your sloppy civilization. You're all afraid – afraid of originality, afraid of work, afraid of hurting one another's feelings. You let anyone come to the top who doesn't frighten you, and as soon as he dies you forget him and knight some other figurehead instead.'

An unknown voice said, 'Shocking, Mr Adam, shocking. Such a dear old man, and quite celebrated, too.'

'You'll soon get used to me, nurse.'

The nurse laughed.

'Adam, it is a relief to have you,' said Catherine after a pause. 'I want you and your boy to help me with mine.' Her voice sounded dimmer; she had turned from her father without a word of farewell. 'One must profit by the mistakes of others ... after all, more heroism.... I am determined to keep in touch with my boy —'

'Larrup him,' said Adam. 'That's the secret.' He followed his sister out of the room.

Then Henry's delightful laugh sounded for the last time. 'You make us all feel twenty years younger,' he said; 'more when —'

The door shut.

Sir Michael grew cold with rage. This was life, this was what the younger generation had been thinking. Adam he ignored, but at the recollection of Henry and Catherine he determined to die. If he chose, he could have risen from bed and driven the whole pack into the street. But he did not choose. He chose rather to leave this shoddy and ungrateful world. The immense and superhuman cynicism that is latent in all of us came at last to the top and transformed him. He saw the absurdity of love, and the vision so tickled him that he began to laugh. The nurse, who had called him a dear old man, bent over him, and at the same moment two boys came into the sick-room.

'How's grandpapa?' asked one of them – Catherine's boy.

'Not so well,' the nurse answered.

There was a silence. Then the other boy said, 'Come along, let's cut.'

'But they told us not to.'

'Why should we do what old people tell us? Dad's pretty well played out, and so's your mother.'

'Shocking; be off with you both,' said the nurse; and, with a little croon of admiration, Catherine's boy followed his cousin out of the room. Their grandfather's mirth increased. He rolled about in the bed; and, just as he was grasping the full irony of the situation, he died, and pursued it into the unknown.

III

MICKY was still in bed. He was aware of so much through long melancholy dreams. But when he opened his mouth to laugh, it filled with dust. Choosing to open his eyes, he found that he had swollen enormously, and lay sunk in the sand of an illimitable plain. As he expected, he had no occasion greatly to modify his ideals; infinity had merely taken the place of his bedroom and of London. Nothing moved on its surface except a few sand-pillars, which would sometimes merge into each other as though confabulating, and then fall with a slight hiss. Save for these, there was no motion, no noise, nor could he feel any wind.

How long had he lain here? Perhaps for years, long before death perhaps, while his body seemed to be walking among men. Life is so short and trivial, that who knows whether we arrive for it entirely, whether more than a fraction of the soul is aroused to put on flesh? The bud and the blossom perish in a moment, the husk endures, and may not the soul be a husk? It seemed to Micky that he had lain in the dust for ever, suffering and sneering, and that the essence of all things, the primal power that lies behind the stars, is senility. Age, toothless, dropsical age; ungenerous to age and to youth; born before all ages, and outlasting them; the universe as old age.

The place degraded while it tortured. It was vast, yet ignoble. It sloped downward into darkness and upward into cloud, but into what darkness, what clouds! No tragic splendour glorified them. When he looked at them he understood why he was so unhappy, for they were looking at him, sneering at him while he sneered. Their dirtiness was more ancient than the hues of day and night, their irony more profound; he was part of their jest, even as youth was part of his, and slowly he realized that he was, and had for some years been, in Hell.

All around him lay other figures, huge and fungous. It was as if the plain had festered. Some of them could sit up, others scarcely protruded from the sand, and he knew that they had made the same mistake in life as himself, though he did not know yet what the mistake had been; probably some little slip, easily avoided had one but been told.

Speech was permissible. Presently a voice said, 'Is not ours a heavenly sky? Is it not beautiful?'

'Most beautiful,' answered Micky, and found each word a stab of pain. Then he knew that one of the sins here punished was appreciation; he was suffering for all the praise that he had given to the bad and mediocre upon earth; when he had praised out of idleness, or to please people, or to encourage people; for all the praise that had not been winged with passion. He repeated 'Most beautiful,' and the sky quivered, for he was entering into fuller torments now. One ray of happiness survived: his wife could not be in this place. She had not sinned with the people of the plain, and could not suffer their distortion. Her view of life had proved right after all; and, in his utter misery, this comforted him. Janet should again be his religion, and as eternity dragged forward and returned upon itself and dragged forward she would show him that old age, if rightly managed, can be beautiful; that experience, if rightly received, can lead the soul of men to bliss. Then he turned to his neighbour, who was continuing his hymn of praise.

'I could lie here for ever,' he was saying. 'When I think of my restlessness during life – that is to say, during what men miscall life, for it is death really – this is life – when I think of my restlessness on earth, I am overcome by so much goodness and mercy, I could lie here for ever.'

'And will you?' asked Micky.

'Ah, that is the crowning blessing – I shall, and so will you.'

Here a pillar of sand passed between them. It was long

before they could speak or see. Then Micky took up the song chafed by the particles that were working into his soul.

'I, too, regret my wasted hours,' he said, 'especially the hours of my youth. I regret all the time I spent in the sun. In later years I did repent, and that is why I am admitted here where there is no sun; yes, and no wind and none of the stars that drove me almost mad at night once. It would be appalling, would it not, to see Orion again, the central star of whose sword is not a star but a nebula, the golden seed of worlds to be? How I dreaded the autumn on earth when Orion rises, for he recalled adventure and my youth. It was appalling. How thankful I am to see him no more.'

'Ah, but it was worse,' cried the other, 'to look high leftward from Orion and see the Twins. Castor and Pollux were brothers, one human, the other divine; and Castor died. But Pollux went down to Hell that he might be with him.'

'Yes; that is so. Pollux went into Hell.'

'Then the gods had pity on both, and raised them aloft to be stars whom sailors worship, and all who love and are young. Zeus was their father, Helen their sister, who brought the Greeks against Troy. I dreaded them more than Orion.'

They were silent, watching their own sky. It approved. They had been cultivated men on earth, and these are capable of the nicer torments hereafter. Their memories will strike exquisite images to enhance their pain. 'I will speak no more,' said Micky to himself. 'I will be silent through eternity.' But the darkness prised open his lips, and immediately he was speaking.

'Tell me more about this abode of bliss,' he asked. 'Are there grades in it? Are there ranks in our heaven?'

'There are two heavens,' the other replied, 'the heaven of the hard and of the soft. We here lie in the heaven of the soft. It is a sufficient arrangement, for all men grow either hard or soft as they grow old.'

As he spoke the clouds lifted, and, looking up the slope of

the plain, Micky saw that in the distance it was bounded by mountains of stone, and he knew, without being told, that among those mountains Janet lay, rigid, and that he should never see her. She had not been saved. The darkness would mock her, too, for ever. With him lay the sentimentalists, the conciliators, the peacemakers, the humanists, and all who have trusted the warmer vision; with his wife were the reformers and ascetics and all sword-like souls. By different paths they had come to Hell, and Micky now saw what the bustle of life conceals: that the years are bound either to liquefy a man or to stiffen him, and that Love and Truth, who seem to contend for our souls like angels, hold each the seeds of our decay.

'It is, indeed, a sufficient arrangement,' he said; 'both sufficient and simple. But answer one question more that my bliss may be perfected; in which of these two heavens are the young?'

His neighbour answered, 'In neither; there are no young.'

He spoke no more, and settled himself more deeply in the dust. Micky did the same. He had vague memories of men and women who had died before reaching maturity, of boys and unwedded maidens and youths lowered into the grave before their parent's eyes. Whither had they gone, that undeveloped minority? What was the point of their brief existence? Had they vanished utterly, or were they given another chance of accreting experiences until they became like Janet or himself? One thing was certain: there were no young, either in the mountains or the plain, and perhaps the very memory of such creatures was an illusion fostered by cloud.

The time was now ripe for a review of his life on earth. He traced his decomposition – his work had been soft, his books soft, he had softened his relations with other men. He had seen good in everything, and this is itself a sign of decay. Whatever occurred he had been appreciative, tolerant, pliant. Consequently he had been a success; Adam was right; it was the moment in civilization for his type. He had mistaken self-criticism for self-discipline, he had muffled in himself and others the keen, heroic edge. Yet the luxury of repentance was denied him. The fault was his, but the fate humanity's, for everyone grows hard or soft as he grows old.

'This is my life,' thought Micky; 'my books forgotten, my work superseded. This is the whole of my life.' And his agony increased, because all the same there had been in that life an elusive joy which, if only he could have distilled it, would have sweetened infinity. It was part of the jest that he should try, and should eternally oscillate between disgust and desire. For there is nothing ultimate in Hell; men will not lay aside all hope on entering it, or they would attain to the splendour of despair. To have made a poem about Hell is to mistake its very essence; it is the imaginations of men, who will have beauty, that fashion it as ice or flame. Old, but capable of growing older, Micky lay in the sandy country, remembering that once he had remembered a country – a country that had not been sand....

He was aroused by the mutterings of the spirits round him. An uneasiness such as he had not noted in them before had arisen. 'A pillar of sand,' said one. Another said, 'It is not; it comes from the river.'

He asked, 'What river?'

'The spirits of the damned dwell over it; we never speak of that river.'

'Is it a broad river?'

'Swift and very broad.'

'Do the damned ever cross it?'

'They are permitted, we know not why, to cross it now and again.'

And in these answers he caught a new tone, as if his companions were frightened, and were finding means to express their fear. When he said, 'With permission, they can do us no harm,' he was answered, 'They harm us with light and a song.' And again, 'They harm us because they remember and try to remind.'

'Of what would they remind us?'

'Of the hour when we were as they.'

As he questioned a whisper arose from the low-lying verges. The spirits were crying to each other faintly. He heard, 'It is coming; drive it back over the river, shatter it, compel it to be old.' And then the darkness was cloven, and a star of pain broke in his soul. He understood now; a torment greater than any was at hand.

'I was before choice,' came the song. 'I was before hardness and softness were divided. I was in the days when truth was love, and I am.'

All the plain was convulsed. But the invader could not be shattered. When it pressed the air parted and the sand-pillars fell, and its path was filled with senile weeping.

'I have been all men, but all men have forgotten me. I transfigured the world for them until they preferred the world. They came to me as children, afraid; I taught them, and they despised me. Childhood is a dream about me, experience a slow forgetting: I govern the magic years between them, and am.'

'Why trouble us?' moaned the shades. 'We could bear our torment, just bear it, until there was light and a song. Go back again over the river. This is Heaven, we were saying, that darkness is God; we could praise them till you came. The book of our deeds is closed; why open it? We were damned from our birth; leave it there. O, supreme jester, leave us. We have sinned, we know it, and this place is death and Hell.'

'Death comes,' the voice pealed, 'and death is not a dream or a forgetting. Death is real. But I, too, am real, and whom I will I save. I see the scheme of things, and in it no place for me, the brain and the body against me. Therefore I rend the scheme in two, and make a place, and under countless names have harrowed Hell. Come.' Then, in tones of inexpressible sweetness, 'Come to me all who remember. Come out of your eternity into mine. It is easy, for I am still at your eyes, waiting to look out of them; still in your hearts, waiting to beat. The years that I dwelt with you seemed short, but they were magical, and they outrun time.'

The shades were silent. They could not remember.

'Who desires to remember? Desire is enough. There is no abiding home for strength and beauty among men. The flower fades, the seas dry up in the sun, the sun and all the stars fade as a flower. But the desire for such things, that is eternal, that can abide, and he who desires me is I.'

Then Micky died a second death. This time he dissolved through terrible pain, scorched by the glare, pierced by the voice. But as he died he said, 'I do desire', and immediately the invader vanished, and he was standing alone on the sandy plain. It had been merely a dream. But he was standing. How was that? Why had he not thought to stand before? He had been unhappy in Hell, and all that he had to do was to go elsewhere. He passed downwards, pained no longer by the mockery of its cloud. The pillars brushed against him and fell, the nether darkness went over his head. On he went till he came to the banks of the infernal stream, and there he stumbled – stumbled over a piece of wood, no vague substance, but a piece of wood that had once belonged to a tree. At his impact it moved, and water gurgled against it. He had embarked. Someone was rowing. He could see the blades of oars moving towards him through the foam, but the rower was invisible in cloud. As they neared mid-channel the boat went more slowly, for the tide was ebbing, and Micky knew that once carried out he would be lost eternally; there was no second hope of salvation. He could not speak, but his heart beat time to the oars – one, two. Hell made her last effort, and all that is evil in creation, all the distortions of love and truth by which we are vexed, came surging down the estuary, and the boat hung motionless. Micky heard the pant of breath through the roaring, the crack of muscles; then he heard a voice say, 'The point of it ...' and a weight fell off his body and he crossed mid-stream.

It was a glorious evening. The boat had sped without prelude into sunshine. The sky was cloudless, the earth gold, and gulls were riding up and down on the furrowed waters. On the bank they had left were some sand-dunes rising to majestic hills; on the bank in front was a farm, full to the brim with fire.

# MR ANDREWS

THE souls of the dead were ascending towards the Judgement Seat and the Gate of Heaven. The world soul pressed them on every side, just as the atmosphere presses upon rising bubbles, striving to vanquish them, to break their thin envelope of personality, to mingle their virtue with its own. But they resisted, remembering their glorious individual life on earth, and hoping for an individual life to come.

Among them ascended the soul of a Mr Andrews who, after a beneficent and honourable life, had recently deceased at his house in town. He knew himself to be kind, upright and religious, and though he approached his trial with all humility, he could not be doubtful of its result. God was not now a jealous God. He would not deny salvation merely because it was expected. A righteous soul may reasonably be conscious of its own righteousness and Mr Andrews was conscious of his.

'The way is long,' said a voice, 'but by pleasant converse the way becomes shorter. Might I travel in your company?'

'Willingly,' said Mr Andrews. He held out his hand, and the two souls floated upwards together.

'I was slain fighting the infidel,' said the other exultantly, 'and I go straight to those joys of which the Prophet speaks.'

'Are you not a Christian?' asked Mr Andrews gravely.

'No, I am a Believer. But you are a Moslem, surely?'

'I am not,' said Mr Andrews. 'I am a Believer.'

The two souls floated upwards in silence, but did not release each other's hands. 'I am broad church,' he added gently. The word 'broad' quavered strangely amid the interspaces.

'Relate to me your career,' said the Turk at last.

'I was born of a decent middle-class family, and had my education at Winchester and Oxford. I thought of becoming a missionary, but was offered a post in the Board of Trade, which I accepted. At thirty-two I married, and had four children, two of whom have died. My wife survives me. If I had lived a little longer I should have been knighted.'

'Now I will relate my career. I was never sure of my father, and my mother does not signify. I grew up in the slums of Salonika. Then I joined a band and we plundered the villages of the infidel. I prospered and had three wives, all of whom survive me. Had I lived a little longer I should have had a band of my own.'

'A son of mine was killed travelling in Macedonia. Perhaps you killed him.'

'It is very possible.'

The two souls floated upward, hand in hand. Mr Andrews did not speak again, for he was filled with horror at the approaching tragedy. This man, so godless, so lawless, so cruel, so lustful, believed that he would be admitted into Heaven. And into what a heaven – a place full of the crude pleasures of a ruffian's life on earth! But Mr Andrews felt neither disgust nor moral indignation. He was only conscious of an immense pity, and his own virtues confronted him not at all. He longed to save the man whose hand he held more tightly, who, he thought, was now holding more tightly on to him. And when he reached the Gate of Heaven, instead of saying 'Can I enter?' as he had intended, he cried out, 'Cannot *he* enter?'

And at the same moment the Turk uttered the same cry. For the same spirit was working in each of them.

From the gateway a voice replied, 'Both can enter.' They were filled with joy and pressed forward together.

Then the voice said, 'In what clothes will you enter?'

'In my best clothes,' shouted the Turk, 'the ones I stole.' And he clad himself in a splendid turban and a waistcoat embroidered with silver, and baggy trousers, and a great belt in which were stuck pipes and pistols and knives.

'And in what clothes will you enter?' said the voice to Mr Andrews.

Mr Andrews thought of his best clothes, but he had no wish to wear them again. At last he remembered and said, 'Robes.'

'Of what colour and fashion?' asked the voice.

Mr Andrews had never thought about the matter much. He replied, in hesitating tones, 'White, I suppose, of some flowing soft material', and he was immediately given a garment such as he had described. 'Do I wear it rightly?' he asked.

'Wear it as it pleases you,' replied the voice. 'What else do you desire?'

'A harp,' suggested Mr Andrews. 'A small one.'

A small gold harp was placed in his hand.

'And a palm – no, I cannot have a palm, for it is the reward of martyrdom; my life has been tranquil and happy.'

'You can have a palm if you desire it.'

But Mr Andrews refused the palm, and hurried in his white robes after the Turk, who had already entered Heaven. As he passed in at the open gate, a man, dressed like himself, passed out with gestures of despair.

'Why is he not happy?' he asked.

The voice did not reply.

'And who are all those figures, seated inside on thrones and mountains? Why are some of them terrible, and sad, and ugly?'

There was no answer. Mr Andrews entered, and then he saw that those seated figures were all the gods who were then being worshipped on the earth. A group of souls stood round each, singing his praises. But the gods paid no heed, for they were listening to the prayers of living men, which alone brought them nourishment. Sometimes a faith would grow weak, and then the god of that faith also drooped and dwindled and fainted for his daily portion of incense. And sometimes, owing to a revivalist movement, or to a great commemoration, or to some other cause, a faith would grow strong, and the god of that faith grow strong also. And, more frequently still, a faith would alter, so that the features of its god altered and became contradictory, and passed from ecstasy to respectability, or from mildness and universal love to the ferocity of battle. And at times a god would divide into two gods, or three, or more, each with his own ritual and precarious supply of prayer.

Mr Andrews saw Buddha, and Vishnu, and Allah, and Jehovah, and the Elohim. He saw little ugly determined gods who were worshipped by a few savages in the same way. He saw the vast shadowy outlines of the neo-Pagan Zeus. There were cruel gods, and coarse gods, and tortured gods, and, worse still, there were gods who were peevish, or deceitful, or vulgar. No aspiration of humanity was unfulfilled. There was even an intermediate state for those who wished it, and for the Christian Scientists a place where they could demonstrate that they had not died.

He did not play his harp for long, but hunted vainly for one of his dead friends. And though souls were continually entering Heaven, it still seemed curiously empty. Though he had all that he expected, he was conscious of no great happiness, no mystic contemplation of beauty, no mystic union with good. There was nothing to compare with that moment outside the gate, when he prayed that the Turk might enter and heard the Turk uttering the same prayer for him. And when at last he saw his companion, he hailed him with a cry of human joy.

The Turk was seated in thought, and round him, by sevens, sat the virgins who are promised in the Koran.

'Oh, my dear friend!' he called out. 'Come here and we will never be parted, and such as my pleasures are, they shall be yours also. Where are my other friends? Where are the men whom I love, or whom I have killed?'

'I, too, have only found you,' said Mr Andrews. He sat down by the Turk, and the virgins, who were all exactly alike, ogled them with coal black eyes.

'Though I have all that I expected,' said the Turk, 'I am conscious of no great happiness. There is nothing to compare with that moment outside the gate when I prayed that you might enter, and heard you uttering the same prayer for me. These virgins are as beautiful and good as I had fashioned, yet I could wish that they were better.'

As he wished, the forms of the virgins became more rounded, and their eyes grew larger and blacker than before. And Mr Andrews, by a wish similar in kind, increased the purity and softness of his garment and the glitter of his harp. For in that place their expectations were fulfilled, but not their hopes.

'I am going,' said Mr Andrews at last. 'We desire infinity and we cannot imagine it. How can we expect it to be granted? I have never imagined anything infinitely good or beautiful excepting in my dreams.'

'I am going with you,' said the other.

Together they sought the entrance gate, and the Turk parted with his virgins and his best clothes, and Mr Andrew cast away his robes and his harp.

'Can we depart?' they asked.

'You can both depart if you wish,' said the voice, 'but remember what lies outside.'

As soon as they passed the gate, they felt again the pressure of the world soul. For a moment they stood hand in hand resisting it. Then they suffered it to break in upon them, and they, and all the experience they had gained, and all the love and wisdom they had generated, passed into it, and made it better.

# CO-ORDINATION

'DON'T thump,' said Miss Haddon. 'And each run ought to be like a string of pearls. It is not. Why is it not?'

'Ellen, you beast, you've got my note.'

'No, I haven't. You've got mine.'

'Well, whose note is it?'

Miss Haddon looked between their pigtails. 'It is Mildred's note,' she decided. 'Go back to the double bars. And don't thump.'

The girls went back, and again the little finger of Mildred's right hand disputed for middle G with the little finger of Ellen's left.

'It can't be done,' they said. 'It's the man who wrote it's fault.'

'It can easily be done if you don't hold on so long, Ellen,' said Miss Haddon.

Four o'clock struck. Mildred and Ellen went, and Rose and Enid succeeded them. They played the duet worse than Mildred, but not as badly as Ellen. At four-fifteen Margaret and Jane came. They played worse than Rose and Enid, but not as badly as Ellen. At four-thirty Dolores and Violet came. They played worse than Ellen. At four-forty-five Miss Haddon went to tea with the Principal, who explained why she desired all the pupils to learn the same duet. It was part of her new co-ordinative system. The school was taking one subject for the year, only one – Napoleon – and all the studies were to bear on that one subject. Thus – not to mention French and History – the Repetition class was learning Wordsworth's political poems, the literature class was reading extracts from 'War and Peace', the drawing class copied something of David's, the needlework class designed Empire gowns, and the music pupils – they, of course, were practising

Beethoven's 'Eroica' Symphony, which had been begun (though not finished) in honour of the Emperor. Several of the other mistresses were at tea, and they exclaimed that they loved co-ordinating, and that it was a lovely system: it made work so much more interesting to them as well as to the girls. But Miss Haddon did not respond. There had been no co-ordination in her day, and she could not understand it. She only knew that she was growing old and teaching music worse and worse, and she wondered how soon the Principal would find this out and dismiss her.

Meanwhile, high up in heaven Beethoven sat, and all around him, ranged on smaller clouds, sat his clerks. Each made entries in a ledger, and he whose ledger was entitled '"Eroica" Symphony: arranged for four hands, by Carl Müller' was making the following entries: – '3.45, Mildred and Ellen; conductor, Miss Haddon. 4.0 Rose and Enid; conductor, Miss Haddon. 4.15, Margaret and Jane; conductor, Miss Haddon. 4.30 —'

Beethoven interrupted. 'Who is this Miss Haddon,' he asked, 'whose name recurs like the beat of a drum?'

'She has interpreted you for many years.'

'And her orchestra?'

'They are maidens of the upper middle classes, who perform the "Eroica" in her presence every day and all day. The sound of it never ceases. It floats out of the window like a continual incense, and is heard up and down the street.'

'Do they perform with insight?'

Since Beethoven is deaf, the clerk could reply, 'With most intimate insight. There was a time when Ellen was farther from your spirit than the rest, but that has not been the case since Dolores and Violet arrived.'

'New comrades have inspired her. I understand.'

The clerk was silent.

'I approve,' continued Beethoven, 'and in token of my approval I decree that Miss Haddon and her orchestra and all in their house shall this very evening hear a perfect performance of my A minor quartette.'

While the decree was being entered, and while the staff was wondering how it would be executed, a scene of even greater splendour was taking place in another part of the empyrean. There Napoleon sat, surrounded by his clerks, who were so numerous that the thrones of the outermost looked no larger than cirro-cumuli clouds. They were busy entering all the references made on earth to their employer, a task for which he himself had organized them. Every few moments he asked, 'And what is our latest phase?'

The clerk whose ledger was entitled 'Hommages de Wordsworth' answered: '5.0, Mildred, Ellen, Rose, Enid, Margaret and Jane, all recited the sonnet, "Once did she hold the gorgeous East in fee". Dolores and Violet attempted to recite it, but failed.'

'The poet there celebrates my conquest of the Venetian Republic,' said the Emperor, 'and the greatness of the theme overcame Violet and Dolores. It is natural that they should fail. And the next phase?'

Another clerk said, '5.15, Mildred, Ellen, Rose, Enid, Margaret, and Jane are sketching in the left front leg of Pauline Buonaparte's couch. Dolores and Violet are still learning their sonnet.'

'It seems to me,' said Napoleon, 'that I have heard these charming names before.'

'They are in my ledger, too,' said a third clerk. 'You may remember, sire, that about an hour ago they performed Beethoven's "Eroica" —'

'Written in my honour,' concluded the Emperor. 'I approve.'

'5.30,' said a fourth clerk, 'with the exception of Dolores and Violet, who have been sent to sharpen pencils, the whole company sings the "Marseillaise".'

'It needed but that,' cried Napoleon, rising to his feet. 'Ces demoiselles ont un vrai élan vers la gloire. I decree in recompense that they and all their house shall participate to-morrow morning in the victory of Austerlitz.'

The decree was entered.

Evening prep. was at 7.30. The girls settled down gloomily, for they were already bored to tears by the new system. But a wonderful thing happened. A regiment of cavalry rode past the school, headed by the most spiffing band. The girls went off their heads with joy. They rose from their seats, they sang, they advanced, they danced, they pranced, they made trumpets out of paper and used the blackboard as a kettledrum. They were able to do this because Miss Haddon, who ought to have been supervising, had left the room to find a genealogical tree of Marie Louise; the history mistress had asked her particularly to take it to prep. for the girls to climb about in, but she had forgotten it. 'I am no good at all,' thought Miss Haddon, as she stretched out her hand for the tree; it lay with some other papers under a shell which the Principal had procured from St Helena. 'I am stupid and tired and old; I wish that I was dead.' Thus thinking, she lifted the shell mechanically to her ear; her father, who was a sailor, had often done the same to her when she was young....

She heard the sea; at first it was the tide whispering over mud-flats or chattering against stones, or the short, crisp break of a wave on sand, or the long, echoing roar of a wave against rocks, or the sounds of the central ocean, where the waters pile themselves into mountains and part into ravines; or when fog descends and the deep rises and falls gently; or when the air is so fresh that the big waves and the little waves that live in the big waves all sing for joy, and send one another kisses of white foam. She heard them all, but in the end she heard the sea itself, and knew that it was hers for ever.

'Miss Haddon!' said the Principal. 'Miss Haddon! How is it you are not supervising the girls?'

Miss Haddon removed the shell from her ear, and faced her employer with a growing determination.

'I can hear Ellen's voice though we are at the other side of the house,' she continued, 'I half thought it was the elocution hour. Put down that paper-weight at once, please, Miss Haddon, and return to your duties.'

She took the shell from the music mistress's hand, intending to place it on its proper shelf. But the force of example caused her to raise it to her own ear. She, too, listened....

She heard the rustling of trees in a wood. It was no wood that she had ever known, but all the people she had known were riding about in it, and calling softly to each other on horns. It was night, and they were hunting. Now and then beasts rustled, and once there was an 'Halloo!' and a chase, but more often her friends rode quietly, and she with them, penetrating the wood in every direction and for ever.

And while she heard this with one ear, Miss Haddon was speaking as follows into the other:

'I will not return to my duties. I have neglected them ever since I came here, and once more will make little difference. I am not musical. I have deceived the pupils and the parents and you. I am not musical, but pretended that I was to make money. What will happen to me now I do not know, but I can pretend no longer. I give notice.'

The Principal was surprised to learn that her music mistress was not musical; the sound of pianos had continued for so many years that she had assumed all was well. In ordinary circumstances she would have answered scathingly, for she was an accomplished woman, but the murmuring forest caused her to reply, 'Oh, Miss Haddon, not now; let's talk it over to-morrow morning. Now, if you will, I want you to lie down in my sitting-room while I take preparation instead, for it always rests me to be with the girls.'

So Miss Haddon lay down, and as she dozed the soul of the

sea returned to her. And the Principal, her head full of forest murmurs, went to the preparation-room, and gave her cough three times before she opened the door. All the girls were at their desks except Dolores and Violet, and them she affected not to notice. After a time she went to fetch the tree of Marie Louise, which she had forgotten, and during her absence the cavalry passed again....

In the morning Miss Haddon said, 'I still wish to go, but I wish I had waited to speak to you. I have had some extraordinary news. Many years ago my father saved a man from drowning. That man has just died, and he has left me a cottage by the edge of the sea, and money to live in it. I need not work any more; so if only I had waited till to-day I could have been more civil to you and' – she blushed a little – 'to myself.'

But the Principal shook her by both hands and kissed her. 'I am glad that you did not wait,' she said. 'What you said yesterday was a word of truth, a clear call through the thicket. I wish that I, too —' She stopped. 'But the next step is to give the school a whole holiday.'

So the girls were summoned, and the Principal made a speech, and Miss Haddon another, giving everyone the address of the cottage, and inviting them to visit her at it. Then Rose was sent to the pastrycook's for ices, and Enid to the greengrocer's for fruit, and Mildred to the sweetshop for lemonade, and Jane to the livery stables for brakes, and they all drove out an immense distance into the country, and played disorganized games. Everyone hid and nobody sought; everyone batted and nobody fielded; no one knew whose side she was on, and no mistress tried to tell her; and it was even possible to play two games at once, and to be Clumps in one and Peter Pan in the other. As for the co-ordinative system, it was never mentioned, or mentioned in derision. For example, Ellen composed a song against it, which ran:

*Silly old Boney*
*Sat on his Pony,*
*Eating his Christmas Pie,*
*He put in his thumb*
*And pulled out a plum,*
*And said, 'What a good boy am I,'*

and the smaller girls sang it without stopping for three hours.

At the end of the day the Principal summoned the whole party round Miss Haddon and herself. She was ringed with happy, tired faces. The sun was setting, the dust that the day had disturbed was sinking. 'Well, girls,' she said, laughing but just a little shy, 'so you don't seem to value my co-ordinative system?'

'Lauks, we don't!' 'Not much!' and so on, replied the girls.

'Well, I must make a confession,' the Principal continued. 'No more do I. In fact, I hate it. But I was obliged to take it up, because that type of thing impresses the Board of Education.'

At this all the mistresses and girls laughed and cheered, and Dolores and Violet, who thought that the Board of Education was a new round game, laughed too.

Now it may be readily imagined that this discreditable affair did not escape the attention of Mephistopheles. At the earliest opportunity he sought the Judgement Seat, bearing an immense scroll inscribed 'J'accuse!' Half-way up he met the angel Raphael, who asked him in his courteous manner whether he could help him in any way.

'Not this time, thank you,' Mephistopholes replied. 'I really have a case now.'

'It might be better to show it to me,' suggested the archangel. 'It would be a pity to fly so far for nothing, and you had such a disappointment over Job.'

'Oh, that was different.'

'And then there was Faust; the verdict there was ultimately against you, if I remember rightly.'

'Oh, that was so different again. No, I am certain this time. I can prove the futility of genius. Great men think that they are understood, and are not; men think that they understand them, and do not.'

'If you can prove that, you have indeed a case,' said Raphael. 'For this universe is supposed to rest on co-ordination, all creatures co-ordinating according to their powers.'

'Listen. Charge one: Beethoven decrees that certain females shall hear a performance of his A minor quartette. They hear – some of them a band, others a shell. Charge two: Napoleon decrees that the same shall participate in the victory of Austerlitz. Result – a legacy, followed by a school treat. Charge three: Females perform Beethoven. Being deaf, and being served by dishonest clerks, he supposes they are performing him with insight. Charge four: To impress the Board of Education, females study Napoleon. He is led to suppose that they are studying him properly. I have other points, but these will suffice. The genius and the ordinary man have never co-ordinated once since Abel was killed by Cain.'

'And now for your case,' said Raphael, sympathetically.

'My case?' stammered Mephistopheles. 'Why, this is my case.'

'Oh, innocent devil,' cried the other. 'Oh, candid if infernal soul. Go back to the earth and walk up and down it again. For these people have co-ordinated, Mephistopheles. They have co-ordinated through the central sources of Melody and Victory.'

# THE STORY OF THE SIREN

FEW things have been more beautiful than my note-book on the Deist Controversy as it fell downward through the waters of the Mediterranean. It dived, like a piece of black slate, but opened soon, disclosing leaves of pale green, which quivered into blue. Now it had vanished, now it was a piece of magical india-rubber stretching out to infinity, now it was a book again, but bigger than the book of all knowledge. It grew more fantastic as it reached the bottom, where a puff of sand welcomed it and obscured it from view. But it re-appeared, quite sane though a little tremulous, lying decently open on its back, while unseen fingers fidgeted among its leaves.

'It is such a pity,' said my aunt, 'that you will not finish your work in the hotel. Then you would be free to enjoy yourself and this would never have happened.'

'Nothing of it but will change into something rich and strange,' warbled the chaplain, while his sister said, 'Why, it's gone in the water!' As for the boatmen, one of them laughed, while the other, without a word of warning, stood up and began to take his clothes off.

'Holy Moses,' cried the Colonel. 'Is the fellow mad?'

'Yes, thank him, dear,' said my aunt: 'that is to say, tell him he is very kind, but perhaps another time.'

'All the same I do want my book back,' I complained. 'It's for my Fellowship Dissertation. There won't be much left of it by another time.'

'I have an idea,' said some woman or other through her parasol. 'Let us leave this child of nature to dive for the book while we go on to the other grotto. We can land him either on this rock or on the ledge inside, and he will be ready when we return.'

The idea seemed good; and I improved it by saying I would be left behind too, to lighten the boat. So the two of us were deposited outside the little grotto on a great sunlit rock that guarded the harmonies within. Let us call them blue, though they suggest rather the spirit of what is clean – cleanliness passed from the domestic to the sublime, the cleanliness of all the sea gathered together and radiating light. The Blue Grotto at Capri contains only more blue water, not bluer water. That colour and that spirit is the heritage of every cave in the Mediterranean into which the sun can shine and the sea flow.

As soon as the boat left I realized how imprudent I had been to trust myself on a sloping rock with an unknown Sicilian. With a jerk he became alive, seizing my arm and saying. 'Go to the end of the grotto, and I will show you something beautiful.'

He made me jump off the rock on to the ledge over a dazzling crack of sea; he drew me away from the light till I was standing on the tiny beach of sand which emerged like powdered turquoise at the farther end. There he left me with his clothes, and returned swiftly to the summit of the entrance rock. For a moment he stood naked in the brilliant sun, looking down at the spot where the book lay. Then he crossed himself, raised his hands above his head, and dived.

If the book was wonderful, the man is past all description. His effect was that of a silver statue, alive beneath the sea, through whom life throbbed in blue and green. Something infinitely happy, infinitely wise – but it was impossible that it should emerge from the depths sunburned and dripping, holding the note-book on the Deist Controversy between its teeth.

A gratuity is generally expected by those who bathe. Whatever I offered, he was sure to want more, and I was disinclined for an argument in a place so beautiful and also so solitary. It was a relief that he should say in conversational tones, 'In a place like this one might see the Siren.'

I was delighted with him for thus falling into the key of his surroundings. We had been left together in a magic world, apart from all the commonplaces that are called reality, a world of blue whose floor was the sea and whose walls and roof of rock trembled with the sea's reflections. Here only the fantastic would be tolerable, and it was in that spirit I echoed his words, 'One might easily see the Siren.'

He watched me curiously while he dressed. I was parting the sticky leaves of the note-book as I sat on the sand.

'Ah,' he said at last. 'You may have read the little book that was printed last year. Who would have thought that our Siren would have given the foreigners pleasure!'

(I read it afterwards. Its account is, not unnaturally, incomplete, in spite of there being a woodcut of the young person, and the words of her song.)

'She comes out of this blue water, doesn't she,' I suggested, 'and sits on the rock at the entrance, combing her hair?'

I wanted to draw him out, for I was interested in his sudden gravity, and there was a suggestion of irony in his last remark that puzzled me.

'Have you ever seen her?' he asked.

'Often and often.'

'I never.'

'But you have heard her sing?'

He put on his coat and said impatiently, 'How can she sing under the water? Who could? She sometimes tries, but nothing comes from her but great bubbles.'

'She should climb on to the rock.'

'How can she?' he cried again, quite angry. 'The priests have blessed the air, so she cannot breathe it, and blessed the rocks, so that she cannot sit on them. But the sea no man can bless, because it is too big and always changing. So she lives in the sea.'

I was silent.

At this his face took a gentler expression. He looked at me as though something was on his mind, and going out to the entrance rock gazed at the external blue, then returning into our twilight he said, 'As a rule only good people see the Siren.'

I made no comment. There was a pause, and he continued. 'That is a very strange thing, and the priests do not know how to account for it; for she of course is wicked. Not only those who fast and go to Mass are in danger, but even those who are merely good in daily life. No one in the village had seen her for two generations. I am not surprised. We all cross ourselves before we enter the water, but it is unnecessary. Giuseppe, we thought, was safer than most. We loved him, and many of us he loved: but that is a different thing from being good.'

I asked who Giuseppe was.

'That day – I was seventeen and my brother was twenty and a great deal stronger than I was, and it was the year when the visitors, who have brought such prosperity and so many alterations into the village, first began to come. One English lady in particular, of very high birth, came, and has written a book about the place, and it was through her that the Improvement Syndicate was formed, which is about to connect the hotels with the station by a funicular railway.'

'Don't tell me about that lady in here,' I observed.

'That day we took her and her friends to see the grottoes. As we rowed close under the cliffs I put out my hand, as one does, and caught a little crab, and having pulled off its claws offered it as a curiosity. The ladies groaned, but a gentleman was pleased, and held out money. Being inexperienced, I refused it, saying that his pleasure was sufficient reward! Giuseppe, who was rowing behind, was very angry with me and reached out with his hand and hit me on the side of the mouth, so that a tooth cut my lip and I bled. I tried to hit him back, but he always was too quick for me, and as

I stretched round he kicked me under the armpit, so that for a moment I could not even row. There was a great noise among the ladies, and I heard afterwards that they were planning to take mé away from my brother and train me as a waiter. That, at all events, never came to pass.

'When we reached the grotto – not here, but a larger one – the gentleman was very anxious that one of us should dive for money, and the ladies consented, as they sometimes do. Giuseppe, who had discovered how much pleasure it gives foreigners to see us in the water, refused to dive for anything but silver, and the gentleman threw in a two-lira piece.

'Just before my brother sprang off he caught sight of me holding my bruise, and crying, for I could not help it. He laughed and said, "This time, at all events, I shall not see the Siren!" and went into the water without crossing himself. But he saw her.'

He broke off and accepted a cigarette. I watched the golden entrance rock and the quivering walls and the magic water through which great bubbles constantly rose.

At last he dropped his hot ash into the ripples and turned his head away and said, 'He came up without the coin. We pulled him into the boat, and he was so large that he seemed to fill it, and so wet that we could not dress him. I have never seen a man so wet. I and the gentleman rowed back, and we covered Giuseppe with sacking and propped him up in the stern.'

'He was drowned, then?' I murmured, supposing that to be the point.

'He was not,' he cried angrily. 'He saw the Siren. I told you.'

I was silenced again.

'We put him to bed though he was not ill. The doctor came and took money, and the priest came and spattered him with holy water. But it was no good. He was too big – like a piece of the sea. He kissed the thumb-bones of San Biagio and they never dried till evening.'

'What did he look like?' I ventured.

'Like anyone who has seen the Siren. If you have seen her "often and often", how is it you do not know? Unhappy, unhappy because he knew everything. Every living thing made him unhappy because he knew it would die. And all he cared to do was sleep.'

I bent over my note-book.

'He did no work, he forgot to eat, he forgot whether he had his clothes on. All the work fell on me, and my sister had to go out to service. We tried to make him into a beggar, but he was too robust to inspire pity, and as for an idiot, he had not the right look in his eyes. He would stand in the street looking at people, and the more he looked at them the more unhappy he became. When a child was born he would cover his face with his hands. If anyone was married – he was terrible then, and would frighten them as they came out of church. Who would have believed he would marry himself! I caused that, I. I was reading out of the paper how a girl at Ragusa had "gone mad through bathing in the sea". Giuseppe got up, and in a week he and that girl came in.

'He never told me anything, but it seems that he went straight to her house, broke into her room, and carried her off. She was the daughter of a rich mine-owner, so you may imagine our peril. Her father came down, with a clever lawyer, but they could do no more than I. They argued and they threatened, but at last they had to go back and we lost nothing – that is to say, no money. We took Giuseppe and Maria to the church and had them married. Ugh! that wedding! The priest made no jokes afterwards, and coming out the children threw stones.... I think I would have died to make her happy; but as always happens, one could do nothing.'

'Were they unhappy together, then?'

'They loved each other, but love is not happiness. We can

all get love. Love is nothing. I had two people to work for now, for she was like him in everything – one never knew which of them was speaking. I had to sell our own boat and work under the bad old man you have to-day. Worst of all, people began to hate us. The children first – everything begins with them – and then the women and last of all the men. For the cause of every misfortune was – you will not betray me?'

I promised good faith, and immediately he burst into the frantic blasphemy of one who has escaped from supervision, cursing the priests, who had ruined his life, he said. 'Thus are we tricked!' was his cry, and he stood up and kicked at the azure ripples with his feet, till he had obscured them with a cloud of sand.

I too was moved. The story of Giuseppe, for all its absurdity and superstition, came nearer to reality than anything I had known before. I don't know why, but it filled me with desire to help others – the greatest of all our desires, I suppose, and the most fruitless. The desire soon passed.

'She was about to have a child. That was the end of everything. People said to me, "When will your charming nephew be born? What a cheerful, attractive child he will be, with such a father and mother!" I kept my face steady and replied, "I think he may be. Out of sadness shall come gladness" – it is one of our proverbs. And my answer frightened them very much, and they told the priests, who were frightened too. Then the whisper started that the child would be Antichrist. You need not be afraid: he was never born.

'An old witch began to prophesy, and no one stopped her. Giuseppe and the girl, she said, had silent devils, who could do little harm. But the child would always be speaking and laughing and perverting, and last of all he would go into the sea and fetch up the Siren into the air, and all the world would see her and hear her sing. As soon as she sang, the Seven Vials would be opened and the Pope would die and Mongibello flame, and the veil of Santa Agata would be burned. Then the boy and the Siren would marry, and together they would rule the world, for ever and ever.

'The whole village was in tumult, and the hotel-keepers became alarmed, for the tourist season was just beginning. They met together and decided that Giuseppe and the girl must be sent inland until the child was born, and they subscribed the money. The night before they were to start there was a full moon and wind from the east, and all along the coast the sea shot up over the cliffs in silver clouds. It is a wonderful sight, and Maria said she must see it once more.

' "Do not go," I said. "I saw the priest go by, and someone with him. And the hotel-keepers do not like you to be seen, and if we displease them also we shall starve."

' "I want to go," she replied. "The sea is stormy, and I may never feel it again."

' "No, he is right," said Giuseppe. "Do not go – or let one of us go with you."

' "I want to go alone," she said; and she went alone.

'I tied up their luggage in a piece of cloth, and then I was so unhappy at thinking I should lose them that I went and sat down by my brother and put my arm round his neck, and he put his arm round me, which he had not done for more than a year, and we remained thus I don't remember how long.

'Suddenly the door flew open and moonlight and wind came in together, and a child's voice said laughing. "They have pushed her over the cliffs into the sea."

'I stepped to the drawer where I keep my knives.

' "Sit down again," said Giuseppe – Giuseppe of all people! "If she is dead, why should others die too?"

' "I guess who it is," I cried, "and I will kill him."

'I was almost out of the door, and he tripped me up and, kneeling upon me, took hold of both my hands and sprained my wrists; first my right one, then my left. No one but

Giuseppe would have thought of such a thing. It hurt more than you would suppose, and I fainted. When I woke up, he was gone, and I never saw him again.'

But Giuseppe disgusted me.

'I told you he was wicked,' he said. 'No one would have expected him to see the Siren.'

'How do you know he did see her?'

'Because he did not see her "often and often", but once.'

'Why do you love him if he is wicked?'

He laughed for the first time. That was his only reply.

'Is that the end?' I asked.

'I never killed her murderer, for by the time my wrists were well he was in America; and one cannot kill a priest. As for Giuseppe, he went all over the world too, looking for someone else who had seen the Siren – either a man, or, better still, a woman, for then the child might still have been born. At last he came to Liverpool – is the district probable? – and there he began to cough, and spat blood until he died.

'I do not suppose there is anyone living now who has seen her. There has seldom been more than one in a generation, and never in my life will there be both a man and a woman from whom that child can be born, who will fetch up the Siren from the sea, and destroy silence, and save the world!'

'Save the world?' I cried. 'Did the prophecy end like that?'

He leaned back against the rock, breathing deep. Through all the blue-green reflections I saw him colour. I heard him say: 'Silence and loneliness cannot last for ever. It may be a hundred or a thousand years, but the sea lasts longer, and she shall come out of it and sing.' I would have asked him more, but at that moment the whole cave darkened, and there rode in through its narrow entrance the returning boat.

# THE ETERNAL MOMENT

## I

'Do you see that mountain just behind Elizabeth's toque? A young man fell in love with me there so nicely twenty years ago. Bob your head a minute, would you, Elizabeth, kindly.'

'Yes'm,' said Elizabeth, falling forward on the box like an unstiffened doll. Colonel Leyland put on his pince-nez, and looked at the mountain where the young man had fallen in love.

'Was he a nice young man?' he asked, smiling, though he lowered his voice a little on account of the maid.

'I never knew. But it is a very gratifying incident to remember at my age. Thank you, Elizabeth.'

'May one ask who he was?'

'A porter,' answered Miss Raby in her usual tones. 'Not even a certificated guide. A male person who was hired to carry the luggage, which he dropped.'

'Well! well! What did you do?'

'What a young lady should. Screamed and thanked him not to insult me. Ran, which was quite unnecessary, fell, sprained my ankle, screamed again; and he had to carry me half a mile, so penitent that I thought he would fling me over a precipice. In that state we reached a certain Mrs Harbottle, at sight of whom I burst into tears. But she was so much stupider than I was, that I recovered quickly.'

'Of course you said it was all your own fault?'

'I trust I did,' she said more seriously. 'Mrs Harbottle, who, like most people, was always right, had warned me against him; we had had him for expeditions before.'

'Ah! I see.'

'I doubt whether you do. Hitherto he had known his

place. But he was too cheap: he gave us more than our money's worth. That, as you know, is an ominous sign in a low-born person.'

'But how was this your fault?'

'I encouraged him: I greatly preferred him to Mrs Harbottle. He was handsome and what I call agreeable; and he wore beautiful clothes. We lagged behind, and he picked me flowers. I held out my hand for them – instead of which he seized it and delivered a love oration which he had prepared out of *I Promessi Sposi*.'

'Ah! an Italian.'

They were crossing the frontier at that moment. On a little bridge amid fir trees were two poles, one painted red, white, and green, and the other black and yellow.

'He lived in Italia Irredenta,' said Miss Raby. 'But we were to fly to the Kingdom. I wonder what would have happened if we had.'

'Good Lord!' said Colonel Leyland, in sudden disgust. On the box Elizabeth trembled.

'But it might have been a most successful match.'

She was in the habit of talking in this mildly unconventional way. Colonel Leyland, who made allowances for her brilliancy, managed to exclaim: 'Rather! yes, rather!'

She turned on him with: 'Do you think I'm laughing at him?'

He looked a little bewildered, smiled, and did not reply. Their carriage was now crawling round the base of the notorious mountain. The road was built over the debris which had fallen and which still fell from its sides; and it had scarred the pine woods with devastating rivers of white stone. But farther up, Miss Raby remembered, on its gentler eastern slope, it possessed tranquil hollows, and flower-clad rocks, and a most tremendous view. She had not been quite as facetious as her companion supposed. The incident, certainly, had been ludicrous. But she was somehow able to laugh at it without laughing much at the actors or the stage.

'I had rather he made me a fool than that I thought he was one,' she said, after a long pause.

'Here is the Custom house,' said Colonel Leyland, changing the subject.

They had come to the land of *Ach* and *Ja*. Miss Raby sighed; for she loved the Latins, as everyone must who is not pressed for time. But Colonel Leyland, a military man, respected Teutonia.

'They still talk Italian for seven miles,' she said, comforting herself like a child.

'German is the coming language,' answered Colonel Leyland. 'All the important books on any subject are written in it.'

'But all the books on any important subject are written in Italian. Elizabeth – tell me an important subject.'

'Human Nature, ma'am,' said the maid, half shy, half impertinent.

'Elizabeth is a novelist, like her mistress,' said Colonel Leyland. He turned away to look at the scenery, for he did not like being entangled in a mixed conversation. He noted that the farms were more prosperous, that begging had stopped, that the women were uglier and the men more rotund, that more nourishing food was being eaten outside the wayside inns.

'Colonel Leyland, shall we go to the *Grand Hôtel des Alpes*, to the *Hôtel de Londres*, to the *Pension Liebig*, to the *Pension Atherley-Simon*, to the *Pension Belle Vue*, to the *Pension Old-England*, or to the *Albergo Biscione*?'

'I suppose you would prefer the *Biscione*.'

'I really shouldn't mind the *Grand Hôtel des Alpes*. The *Biscione* people own both, I hear. They have become quite rich.'

'You should have a splendid reception – if such people know what gratitude is.'

For Miss Raby's novel, 'The Eternal Moment', which had made her reputation, had also made the reputation of Vorta.

'Oh, I was properly thanked. Signor Cantù wrote to me about three years after I had published. The letter struck me as a little pathetic, though it was very prosperous: I don't like transfiguring people's lives. I wonder whether they live in their old house or in the new one.'

Colonel Leyland had come to Vorta to be with Miss Raby; but he was very willing that they should be in different hotels. She, indifferent to such subtleties, saw no reason why they should not stop under the same roof, just as she could not see why they should not travel in the same carriage. On the other hand, she hated anything smart. He had decided on the *Grand Hôtel des Alpes*, and she was drifting towards the *Biscione* when the tiresome Elizabeth said: 'My friend's lady is staying at the *Alpes*.'

'Oh! if Elizabeth's friend is there that settles it: we'll all go.'

'Very well'm,' said Elizabeth, studiously avoiding even the appearance of gratitude. Colonel Leyland's face grew severe over the want of discipline.

'You spoil her,' he murmured, when they had all descended to walk up a hill.

'There speaks the military man.'

'Certainly I have had too much to do with Tommies to enter into what you call "human relations". A little sentimentality and the whole army would go to pieces.'

'I know; but the whole world isn't an army. So why should I pretend I'm an officer. You remind me of my Anglo-Indian friends, who were so shocked when I would be pleasant to some natives. They proved, quite conclusively, that it would never do for them, and have never seen that the proof didn't apply. The unlucky people here are always trying to lead the lucky; and it must be stopped. You've been unlucky; all your life you've had to command men, and exact prompt obedience and other unprofitable virtues. I'm lucky: I needn't do the same – and I won't.'

'Don't then,' he said, smiling. 'But take care that the world isn't an army after all. And take care, besides, that you aren't being unjust to the unlucky people: we're fairly kind to your beloved lower orders, for instance.'

'Of course,' she said dreamily, as if he had made her no concession. 'It's becoming usual. But they see through it. They, like ourselves, know that only one thing in the world is worth having.'

'Ah! yes,' he sighed. 'It's a commercial age.'

'No!' exclaimed Miss Raby, so irritably that Elizabeth looked back to see what was wrong. 'You are stupid. Kindness and money are both quite easy to part with. The only thing worth giving away is yourself. Did you ever give yourself away?'

'Frequently.'

'I mean, did you ever, intentionally, make a fool of yourself before your inferiors?'

'Intentionally, never.' He saw at last what she was driving at. It was her pleasure to pretend that such self-exposure was the only possible basis of true intercourse, the only gate in the spiritual barrier that divided class from class. One of her books had dealt with the subject; and very agreeable reading it made. 'What about you?' he added playfully.

'I've never done it properly. Hitherto I've never felt a really big fool; but when I do, I hope I shall show it plainly.'

'May I be there!'

'You might not like it,' she replied. 'I may feel it at any moment and in mixed company. Anything might set me off.'

'Behold Vorta!' cried the driver, cutting short the sprightly conversation. He and Elizabeth and the carriage had reached the top of the hill. The black woods ceased; and they emerged into a valley whose sides were emerald lawns, rippling and doubling and merging each into each, yet always with an upward trend, so that it was 2000 feet to where the rock burst out of the grass and made great mountains, whose pinnacles were delicate in the purity of evening.

The driver, who had the gift of repetition, said: 'Vorta! Vorta!'

Far up the valley was a large white village, tossing on undulating meadows like a ship in the sea, and at its prow, breasting a sharp incline, stood a majestic tower of new grey stone. As they looked at the tower it became vocal and spoke magnificently to the mountains, who replied.

They were again informed that this was Vorta, and that that was the new campanile – like the campanile of Venice, only finer – and that the sound was the sound of the campanile's new bell.

'Thank you; exactly,' said Colonel Leyland while Miss Raby rejoiced that the village had made such use of its prosperity. She had feared to return to the place she had once loved so well lest she should find something new. It had never occurred to her that the new thing might be beautiful. The architect had indeed gone south for his inspiration, and the tower which stood among the mountains was akin to the tower which had once stood beside the lagoons. But the birthplace of the bell it was impossible to determine, for there is no nationality in sound.

They drove forward into the lovely scene, pleased and silent. Approving tourists took them for a well-matched couple. There was indeed nothing offensively literary in Miss Raby's kind angular face; and Colonel Leyland's profession had made him neat rather than aggressive. They did very well for a cultured and refined husband and wife, who had spent their lives admiring the beautiful things with which the world is filled.

As they approached, other churches, hitherto unnoticed, replied – tiny churches, ugly churches, churches painted pink with towers like pumpkins, churches painted white with shingle spires, churches hidden altogether in the glades of a wood or the folds of a meadow – till the evening air was full of little voices, with the great voice singing in their midst. Only the English church, lately built in the early English style, kept chaste silence.

The bells ceased, and all the little churches receded into darkness. Instead, there was a sound of dressing-gongs, and a vision of tired tourists hurrying back for dinner. A landau, with *Pension Atherley-Simon* upon it, was trotting to meet the diligence, which was just due. A lady was talking to her mother about an evening dress. Young men with rackets were talking to young men with alpenstocks. Then, across the darkness, a fiery finger wrote *Grand Hôtel des Alpes*.

'Behold the electric light!' said the driver, hearing his passengers exclaim.

*Pension Belle Vue* started out against a pinewood, and from the brink of the river the *Hôtel de Londres* replied. *Pensions Liebig* and *Lorelei* were announced in green and amber respectively. The *Old-England* appeared in scarlet. The illuminations covered a large area, for the best hotels stood outside the village, in elevated or romantic situations. This display took place every evening in the season, but only while the diligence arrived. As soon as the last tourist was suited, the lights went out, and the hotel-keepers, cursing or rejoicing, retired to their cigars.

'Horrible!' said Miss Raby.

'Horrible people!' said Colonel Leyland.

The *Hôtel des Alpes* was an enormous building, which, being made of wood, suggested a distended chalet. But this impression was corrected by a costly and magnificent view-terrace, the squared stones of which were visible for miles, and from which, as from some great reservoir, asphalt paths trickled over the adjacent country. Their carriage, having ascended a private drive, drew up under a vaulted portico of pitch-pine, which opened on to this terrace on one side and into the covered lounge on the other. There was a whirl of officials – men with gold braid, smarter men with more gold braid, men smarter still with no gold braid. Elizabeth assumed an arrogant air, and carried a small straw basket with difficulty. Colonel Leyland became every inch a soldier. Miss Raby, whom, in spite of long experience, a large hotel always flustered, was hurried into an expensive bedroom, and advised to dress herself immediately if she wished to partake of table d'hôte.

As she came up the staircase, she had seen the dining-room filling with English and Americans and with rich hungry Germans. She liked company, but to-night she was curiously depressed. She seemed to be confronted with an unpleasing vision, the outlines of which were still obscure.

'I will eat in my room,' she told Elizabeth. 'Go to your dinner: I'll do the unpacking.'

She wandered round, looking at the list of rules, the list of prices, the list of excursions, the red plush sofa, the jugs and basins on which was lithographed a view of the mountains. Where amid such splendour was there a place for Signor Cantù with his china-bowled pipe, and for Signora Cantù with her snuff-coloured shawl?

When the waiter at last brought up her dinner, she asked after her host and hostess.

He replied, in cosmopolitan English, that they were both well.

'Do they live here, or at the *Biscione*?'

'Here, why yes. Only poor tourists go to the *Biscione*.'

'Who lives there, then?'

'The mother of Signor Cantù. She is unconnected,' he continued, like one who has learnt a lesson, 'she is unconnected absolutely with us. Fifteen years back, yes. But now, where is the *Biscione*? I beg you contradict if we are spoken about together.'

Miss Raby said quietly: 'I have made a mistake. Would you kindly give notice that I shall not want my room, and say that the luggage is to be taken, immediately, to the *Biscione.*'

'Certainly! certainly!' said the waiter, who was well trained. He added with a vicious snort, 'You will have to pay.'

'Undoubtedly,' said Miss Raby.

The elaborate machinery which had so recently sucked her in began to disgorge her. The trunks were carried down, the vehicle in which she had arrived was recalled. Elizabeth, white with indignation, appeared in the hall. She paid for beds in which they had not slept and for food which they had never eaten. Amidst the whirl of gold-laced officials, who hoped even in that space of time to have established a claim to be tipped, she moved towards the door. The guests in the lounge observed her with amusement, concluding that she had found the hotel too dear.

'What is it? Whatever is it? Are you not comfortable?' Colonel Leyland in his evening dress ran after her.

'Not that; I've made a mistake. This hotel belongs to the son; I must go to the *Biscione.* He's quarrelled with the old people: I think the father's dead.'

'But really – if you are comfortable here —'

'I must find out to-night whether it is true. And I must also' – her voice quivered – 'find out whether it is my fault.'

'How in the name of goodness —'

'I shall bear it if it is,' she continued gently. 'I am too old to be a tragedy queen as well as an evil genius.'

'What does she mean? Whatever does she mean?' he murmured, as he watched the carriage lights descending the hill. 'What harm has she done? What harm is there, for that matter? Hotel-keepers always quarrel: it's no business of ours.' He ate a good dinner in silence. Then his thoughts were turned by the arrival of his letters from the post office.

'DEAREST EDWIN, – It is with the greatest diffidence that I write to you, and I know you will believe me when I say that I do not write from curiosity. I only require an answer to one plain question. Are you engaged to Miss Raby or no? Fashions have altered even since my young days. But, for all that, an engagement is still an engagement, and should be announced at once, to save all parties discomfort. Though your health has broken down and you have abandoned your profession, you can still protect the family honour.'

'Drivel!' exclaimed Colonel Leyland. Acquaintance with Miss Raby had made his sight keener. He recognized in this part of his sister's letter nothing but an automatic conventionality. He was no more moved by its perusal than she had been by its composition.

'As for the maid whom the Bannons mentioned to me, she is not a chaperone – nothing but a sop to throw in the eyes of the world. I am not saying a word against Miss Raby, whose books we always read. Literary people are always unpractical, and we are confident that she does not know. Perhaps I do not think her the wife for you; but that is another matter.

'My babes, who all send love (so does Lionel), are at present an unmitigated joy. One's only anxiety is for the future, when the crushing expenses of good education will have to be taken into account.

Your loving NELLY.'

How could he explain the peculiar charm of the relations between himself and Miss Raby? There had never been a word of marriage, and would probably never be a word of love. If, instead of seeing each other frequently, they should come to see each other always it would be as sage companions, familiar with life, not as egoistic lovers, craving for infinities of passion which they had no right to demand and no power to supply. Neither professed to be a virgin soul, or to be ignorant of the other's limitations and inconsistencies. They scarcely even made allowances for each other. Toleration implies reserve; and the greatest safeguard of unruffled intercourse is knowledge. Colonel Leyland had courage of no mean order: he cared little for the opinion of people whom he understood. Nelly and Lionel and their babes were welcome to be shocked or displeased. Miss Raby was an authoress, a kind of Radical; he a soldier, a kind of aristocrat. But the time for their activities was passing; he was ceasing to fight, she to write. They could pleasantly spend together their autumn. Nor might they prove the worst companions for a winter.

He was too delicate to admit, even to himself, the desirability of marrying two thousand a year. But it lent an unacknowledged perfume to his thoughts. He tore Nelly's letter into little pieces, and dropped them into the darkness out of the bedroom window.

'Funny lady!' he murmured, as he looked towards Vorta, trying to detect the campanile in the growing light of the moon. 'Why have you gone to be uncomfortable? Why will you interfere in the quarrels of people who can't understand you, and whom you don't understand. How silly you are to think you've caused them. You think you've written a book which has spoilt the place and made the inhabitants corrupt and sordid. I know just how you think. So you will make yourself unhappy, and go about trying to put right what never was right. Funny lady!'

Close below him he could now see the white fragments of his sister's letter. In the valley the campanile appeared, rising out of wisps of silvery vapour.

'Dear lady!' he whispered, making towards the village a little movement with his hands.

II

MISS RABY's first novel, 'The Eternal Moment', was written round the idea that man does not live by time alone, that an evening gone may become like a thousand ages in the courts of heaven – the idea that was afterwards expounded more philosophically by Maeterlinck. She herself now declared that it was a tiresome, affected book, and that the title suggested the dentist's chair. But she had written it when she was feeling young and happy; and that, rather than maturity, is the hour in which to formulate a creed. As years pass, the conception may become more solid, but the desire and the power to impart it to others are alike weakened. It did not altogether displease her that her earliest work had been her most ambitious.

By a strange fate, the book made a great sensation, especially in unimaginative circles. Idle people interpreted it to mean that there was no harm in wasting time, vulgar people that there was no harm in being fickle, pious people interpreted it as an attack upon morality. The authoress became well known in society, where her enthusiasm for the lower classes only lent her an additional charm. That very year Lady Anstey, Mrs Heriot, the Marquis of Bamburgh, and many others penetrated to Vorta, where the scene of the book was laid. They returned enthusiastic. Lady Anstey exhibited her water-colour drawings; Mrs Heriot, who photographed, wrote an article in *The Strand*; while *The Nineteenth Century* published a long description of the place by the Marquis of Bamburgh, entitled 'The Modern Peasant and his Relations with Roman Catholicism'.

Thanks to these efforts, Vorta became a rising place, and people who liked being off the beaten track went there, and pointed out the way to others. Miss Raby, by a series of trivial accidents, had never returned to the village whose rise was so intimately connected with her own. She had heard from time to time of its progress. It had also been whispered that an inferior class of tourist was finding it out, and, fearing to find something spoilt, she had at last a certain diffidence in returning to scenes which once had given her so much pleasure. Colonel Leyland persuaded her; he wanted a cool healthy spot for the summer, where he could read and talk and find walks suitable for an athletic invalid. Their friends laughed; their acquaintances gossiped; their relatives were furious. But he was courageous and she was indifferent. They had accomplished the expedition under the scanty aegis of Elizabeth.

Her arrival was saddening. It displeased her to see the great hotels in a great circle, standing away from the village where all life should have centred. Their illuminated titles, branded on the tranquil evening slopes, still danced in her eyes. And the monstrous *Hôtel de Alpes* haunted her like a nightmare. In her dreams she recalled the portico, the ostentatious lounge, the polished walnut bureau, the vast rack for the bedroom keys, the panoramic bedroom crockery, the uniforms of the officials, and the smell of smart people – which is to some nostrils quite as depressing as the smell of poor ones. She was not enthusiastic over the progress of civilization, knowing by Eastern experiences that civilization rarely puts her best foot foremost, and is apt to make the barbarians immoral and vicious before her compensating qualities arrive. And here there was no question of progress: the world had more to learn from the village than the village from the world.

At the *Biscione*, indeed, she had found little change – only the pathos of a survival. The old landlord had died, and the old lady was ill in bed, but the antique spirit had not yet departed. On the timbered front was still painted the dragon swallowing the child – the arms of the Milanese Visconti, from whom the Cantùs might well be descended. For there was something about the little hotel which compelled a sympathetic guest to believe, for the time at all events, in aristocracy. The great manner, only to be obtained without effort, ruled throughout. In each bedroom were three or four beautiful things – a little piece of silk tapestry, a fragment of rococo carving, some blue tiles, framed and hung upon the whitewashed wall. There were pictures in the sitting-rooms and on the stairs – eighteenth-century pictures in the style of Carlo Dolci and the Carracci – a blue-robed Mater Dolorosa, a fluttering saint, a magnanimous Alexander with a receding chin. A debased style – so the superior person and the textbooks say. Yet, at times, it may have more freshness and significance than a newly-purchased Fra Angelico. Miss Raby, who had visited dukes in their residences without a perceptible tremor, felt herself blatant and modern when she entered the *Albergo Biscione*. The most trivial things – the sofa cushions, the table-cloths, the cases for the pillows – though they might be made of poor materials and be aesthetically incorrect, inspired her with reverence and humility. Through this cleanly, gracious dwelling there had once moved Signor Cantù with his china-bowled pipe, Signora Cantù in her snuff-coloured shawl, and Bartolommeo Cantù, now proprietor of the *Grand Hôtel des Alpes*.

She sat down to breakfast next morning in a mood which she tried to attribute to her bad night and her increasing age. Never, she thought, had she seen people more unattractive and more unworthy than her fellow-guests. A black-browed woman was holding forth on patriostism and the duty of English tourists to present an undivided front to foreign nations. Another woman kept up a feeble lament, like a dribbling tap which never gathers flow yet never quite ceases, complaining of the food, the charges, the noise, the clouds, the dust. She liked coming here herself, she said; but she hardly liked to recommend it to her friends: it was the kind of hotel one felt like that about. Males were rare, and in great demand; a young one was describing, amid fits of laughter, the steps he had taken to astonish the natives.

Miss Raby was sitting opposite the famous fresco, which formed the only decoration of the room. It had been discovered during some repairs; and, though the surface had been injured in places, the colours were still bright. Signora Cantù attributed it now to Titian, now to Giotto, and declared that no one could interpret its meaning; professors and artists had puzzled themselves in vain. This she said because it pleased her to say it; the meaning was perfectly clear, and had been frequently explained to her. Those four figures were sibyls, holding prophecies of the Nativity. It was uncertain for what original reason they had been painted high up in the mountains, at the extreme boundary of Italian art. Now, at all events, they were an invaluable source of conversation; and many an acquaintance had been opened, and argument averted, by their timely presence on the wall.

'Aren't those saints cunning!' said an American lady, following Miss Raby's glance.

The lady's father muttered something about superstition. They were a lugubrious couple, lately returned from the Holy Land, where they had been cheated shamefully, and their attitude towards religion had suffered in consequence.

Miss Raby said, rather sharply, that the saints were sibyls.

'But I don't recall sibyls,' said the lady, 'either in the N.T. or the O.'

'Inventions of the priests to deceive the peasantry,' said the father sadly. 'Same as their churches; tinsel pretending to be gold, cotton pretending to be silk, stucco pretending to be marble; same as their processions, same as their – (he swore) – campaniles.'

'My father,' said the lady, bending forward, 'he does suffer so from insomnia. Fancy a bell every morning at six!'

'Yes, ma'am; you profit. We've stopped it.'

'Stopped the early bell ringing?' cried Miss Raby.

People looked up to see who she was. Someone whispered that she wrote.

He replied that he had come up all these feet for rest, and that if he did not get it he would move on to another centre. The English and American visitors had co-operated, and forced the hotel-keepers to take action. Now the priests rang a dinner bell, which was endurable. He believed that 'co-operation' would do anything: it had been the same with the peasants.

'How did the tourists interfere with the peasants?' asked Miss Raby, getting very hot and trembling all over.

'We said the same; we had come for rest, and we would have it. Every week they got drunk and sang till two. Is that a proper way to go on, anyhow?'

'I remember,' said Miss Raby, 'that some of them did get drunk. But I also remember how they sang.'

'Quite so. Till two,' he retorted.

They parted in mutual irritation. She left him holding forth on the necessity of a new universal religion of the open air. Over his head stood the four sibyls, gracious for all their clumsiness and crudity, each proffering a tablet inscribed with concise promise of redemption. If the old religions had indeed become insufficient for humanity, it did not seem probable that an adequate substitute would be produced in America.

It was too early to pay her promised visit to Signora Cantù. Nor was Elizabeth, who had been rude overnight and was now tiresomely penitent, a possible companion. There were a few tables outside the inn, at which some women sat, drinking beer. Pollarded chestnuts shaded them; and a low wooden balustrade fenced them off from the village street. On this balustrade Miss Raby perched, for it gave her a view of the campanile. A critical eye could discover plenty of faults in its architecture. But she looked at it all with increasing pleasure, in which was mingled a certain gratitude.

The German waitress came out and suggested very civilly that she should find a more comfortable seat. This was the place where the lower classes ate; would she not go to the drawing-room?

'Thank you, no; for how many years have you classified your guests according to their birth?'

'For many years. It was necessary,' replied the admirable woman. She returned to the house full of meat and common sense, one of the many signs that the Teuton was gaining on the Latin in this debatable valley.

A grey-haired lady came out next, shading her eyes from the sun, and crackling *The Morning Post*. She glanced at Miss Raby pleasantly, blew her nose, apologized for speaking, and spoke as follows:

'This evening, I wonder if you know, there is a concert in aid of the stained-glass window for the English Church. Might I persuade you to take tickets? As has been said, it is so important that English people should have a rallying point, is it not?'

'Most important,' said Miss Raby; 'but I wish the rallying point could be in England.

The grey-haired lady smiled. Then she looked puzzled. Then she realized that she had been insulted, and, crackling *The Morning Post*, departed.

'I have been rude,' thought Miss Raby dejectedly. 'Rude to a lady as silly and as grey-haired as myself. This is not a day on which I ought to talk to people.'

Her life had been successful, and on the whole happy. She was unaccustomed to that mood, which is termed depressed, but which certainly gives visions of wider, if greyer, horizons. That morning her outlook altered. She walked through the village, scarcely noticing the mountains by which it was still surrounded or the unaltered radiance of its sun. But she was fully conscious of something new; of the indefinable corruption which is produced by the passage of a large number of people.

Even at that time the air was heavy with meat and drink, to which was added dust and tobacco smoke and the smell of tired horses. Carriages were huddled against the church, and underneath the campanile a woman was guarding a stack of bicycles. The season had been bad for climbing; and groups of young men in smart Norfolk suits were idling up and down, waiting to be hired as guides. Two large inexpensive hotels stood opposite the post office; and in front of them innumerable little tables surged out into the street. Here, from an early hour in the morning, eating had gone on, and would continue till a late hour at night. The customers, chiefly German, refreshed themselves with cries and with laughter, passing their arms round the waists of their wives. Then, rising heavily, they departed in single file towards some viewpoint, whereon a red flag indicated the possibility of another meal. The whole population was employed, even down to the little girls, who worried the guests to buy picture postcards and edelweiss. Vorta had taken to the tourist trade.

A village must have some trade; and this village had always been full of virility and power. Obscure and happy, its splendid energies had found employment in wresting a livelihood out of the earth, whence had come a certain dignity, and kindliness, and love for other men. Civilization did not relax these energies, but it had diverted them; and all the precious qualities, which might have helped to heal the world, had been destroyed. The family affection, the affection for the commune, the sane pastoral virtues – all had perished while the campanile which was to embody them was being built. No villain had done this thing: it was the work of ladies and gentlemen who were good and rich and often clever – who, if they thought about the matter at all, thought that they were conferring a benefit, moral as well as commercial, on any place in which they chose to stop.

Never before had Miss Raby been conscious of such universal misdoing. She returned to the *Biscione* shattered and exhausted, remembering that terrible text in which there is much semblance of justice: 'But woe to him through whom the offence cometh.'

Signora Cantù, somewhat over-excited, was lying in a dark room on the ground floor. The walls were bare; for all the beautiful things were in the rooms of her guests whom she loved as a good queen might love her subjects – and the walls were dirty also, for this was Signora Cantù's own room. But no palace had so fair a ceiling; for from the wooden beams were suspended a whole dowry of copper vessels – pails, cauldrons, water pots, of every colour from lustrous black to the palest pink. It pleased the old lady to look up at these tokens of prosperity. An American lady had lately departed without them, more puzzled than angry.

The two women had little in common; for Signora Cantù was an inflexible aristocrat. Had she been a great lady of the great century, she would have gone speedily to the guillotine, and Miss Raby would have howled approval. Now, with her scanty hair in curl-papers and the snuff-coloured shawl spread over her, she entertained the distinguished authoress with accounts of other distinguished people who had stopped, and might again stop, at the *Biscione*. At first her tone was dignified. But before long she proceeded to village news, and a certain bitterness began to show itself. She chronicled deaths with a kind of melancholy pride. Being old herself, she liked to meditate on the fairness of Fate, which had not spared her contemporaries, and often had not spared her juniors. Miss Raby was unaccustomed to extract such consolation. She too was growing old, but it would have pleased her better if others could have remained young. She remembered few of these people well, but deaths were symbolical, just as the death of a flower may symbolize the passing of all the spring.

Signora Cantù then went on to her own misfortunes, beginning with an account of a landslip, which had destroyed her little farm. A landslip, in that valley, never hurried. Under the green coat of turf water would collect, just as an abscess is formed under the skin. There would be a lump on the sloping meadow, then the lump would break and discharge a slowly-moving stream of mud and stones. Then the whole area seemed to be corrupted; on every side the grass cracked and doubled into fantastic creases, the trees grew awry, the barns and cottages collapsed, all the beauty turned gradually to indistinguishable pulp, which slid downwards till it was washed away by some stream.

From the farm they proceeded to other grievances, over which Miss Raby became almost too depressed to sympathize. It was a bad season; the guests did not understand the ways of the hotel; the servants did not understand the guests; she was told she ought to have a concierge. But what was the good of a concierge?

'I have no idea,' said Miss Raby, feeling that no concierge would ever restore the fortunes of the *Biscione*.

'They say he would meet the diligence and entrap the new arrivals. What pleasure should I have from guests I entrapped?'

'The other hotels do it,' said Miss Raby sadly.

'Exactly. Every day a man comes down from the *Alpes*.'

There was an awkward silence. Hitherto they had avoided mentioning that name.

'He takes them all,' she continued, in a burst of passion. 'My son takes all my guests. He has taken all the English nobility, and the best Americans, and all my old Milanese friends. He slanders me up and down the valley, saying that the drains are bad. The hotel-keepers will not recommend me; they send on their guests to him, because he pays them five per cent for everyone they send. He pays the drivers, he pays the porters, he pays the guides. He pays the band, so that it hardly ever plays down in the village. He even pays the little children to say my drains are bad. He and his wife and his concierge, they mean to ruin me, they would like to see me die.'

'Don't – don't say these things, Signora Cantù.' Miss Raby began to walk about the room, speaking, as was her habit, what was true rather than what was intelligible. 'Try not to be so angry with your son. You don't know what he had to contend with. You don't know who led him into it. Someone else may be to blame. And whoever it may be – you will remember them in your prayers.'

'Of course I am a Christian!' exclaimed the angry old lady. 'But he will not ruin me. I seem poor, but he has borrowed – too much. That hotel will fail!'

'And perhaps,' continued Miss Raby, 'there is not much wickedness in the world. Most of the evil we see is the result of little faults – of stupidity or vanity.'

'And I even know who led him into it – his wife, and the man who is now his concierge.'

'This habit of talking, of self-expression – it seems so pleasant and necessary – yet it does harm —'

They were both interrupted by an uproar in the street. Miss Raby opened the window; and a cloud of dust, heavy with petrol, entered. A passing motor-car had twitched over a table. Much beer had been spilt, and a little blood.

Signora Cantù sighed peevishly at the noise. Her ill-temper had exhausted her, and she lay motionless, with closed eyes. Over her head two copper vases clinked gently in the sudden gust of wind. Miss Raby had been on the point of a great dramatic confession, of a touching appeal for forgiveness. Her words were ready; her words always were ready. But she looked at those closed eyes, that suffering enfeebled frame, and she knew that she had no right to claim the luxury of pardon.

It seemed to her that with this interview her life had ended. She had done all that was possible. She had done much evil. It only remained for her to fold her hands and to wait, till her ugliness and her incompetence went the way of beauty and strength. Before her eyes there arose the pleasant face of Colonel Leyland, with whom she might harmlessly conclude her days. He would not be stimulating, but it did not seem desirable that she should be stimulated. It would be better if her faculties did close, if the senseless activity of her brain and her tongue were gradually numbed. For the first time in her life, she was tempted to become old.

Signora Cantù was still speaking of her son's wife and concierge; of the vulgarity of the former and the ingratitude of the latter, whom she had been kind to long ago, when he first wandered up from Italy, an obscure boy. Now he had sided against her. Such was the reward of charity.

'And what is his name?' asked Miss Raby absently.

'Feo Ginori,' she replied. 'You would not remember him. He used to carry —'

From the new campanile there burst a flood of sound to which the copper vessels vibrated responsively. Miss Raby lifted her hands, not to her ears but to her eyes. In her enfeebled state, the throbbing note of the bell had the curious effect of blood returning into frozen veins.

'I remember that man perfectly,' she said at last; 'and I shall see him this afternoon.'

## III

Miss Raby and Elizabeth were seated together in the lounge of the *Hôtel des Alpes*. They had walked up from the *Biscione* to see Colonel Leyland. But he, apparently, had walked down there to see them, and the only thing to do was to wait, and to justify the wait by ordering some refreshment. So Miss Raby had afternoon tea, while Elizabeth behaved like a perfect lady over an ice, occasionally turning the spoon upside down in the mouth when she saw that no one was looking. The under-waiters were clearing cups and glasses off the marble-topped tables, and the gold-laced officials were rearranging the wicker chairs into seductive groups of three and two. Here and there the visitors lingered among their crumbs, and the Russian Prince had fallen asleep in a prominent and ungraceful position. But most people had started for a little walk before dinner, or had gone to play tennis, or had taken a book under a tree. The weather was delightful, and the sun had so far declined that its light had become spiritualized, suggesting new substances as well as new colour in everything on which it fell. From her seat Miss Raby could see the great precipices under which they had passed the day before; and beyond those precipices she could see Italy – the Val d'Aprile, the Val Senese and the mountains she had named 'The Beasts of the South'. All day those mountains were insignificant – distant chips of white or grey stone. But the evening sun transfigured them, and they would sit up like purple bears against the southern sky.

'It is a sin you should not be out, Elizabeth. Find your friend, if you can, and make her go with you. If you see Colonel Leyland, tell him I am here.'

'Is that all, ma'am?' Elizabeth was fond of her eccentric mistress, and her heart had been softened by the ice. She saw that Miss Raby did not look well. Possibly the course of love was running roughly. And indeed gentlemen must be treated with tact, especially when both parties are getting on.

'Don't give pennies to the children: that is the only other thing.'

The guests had disappeared, and the number of officials visibly diminished. From the hall behind came the genteel sniggers of those two most vile creatures, a young lady behind the bureau and a young man in a frock-coat who shows new arrivals to their rooms. Some of the porters joined them, standing at a suitable distance. At last only Miss Raby, the Russian Prince, and the concierge were left in the lounge.

The concierge was a competent European of forty or so, who spoke all languages fluently, and some well. He was still active, and had evidently once been muscular. But either his life or his time of life had been unkind to his figure: in a few years he would certainly be fat. His face was less easy to decipher. He was engaged in the unquestioning performance of his duty, and that is not a moment for self-revelation. He opened the windows, he filled the match-boxes, he flicked little tables with a duster, always keeping an eye on the door in case anyone arrived without luggage, or left without paying. He touched an electric bell, and a waiter flew up and cleared away Miss Raby's tea things. He touched another bell, and sent an underling to tidy up some fragments of paper which had fallen out of a bedroom window. Then 'Excuse me, madam!' and he had picked up Miss Raby's handkerchief with a slight bow. He seemed to bear her no grudge for her abrupt departure of the preceding evening. Perhaps it was into his hand that she had dropped a tip. Perhaps he did not remember she had been there.

The gesture with which he returned the handkerchief troubled her with vague memories. Before she could thank him he was back in the doorway, standing sideways, so that the slight curve of his stomach was outlined against the view. He was speaking to a youth of athletic but melancholy appearance, who was fidgeting in the portico without. 'I told you the percentage,' she heard. 'If you had agreed to it, I would have recommended you. Now it is too late. I have enough guides.'

Our generosity benefits more people than we suppose. We tip the cabman, and something goes to the man who whistled for him. We tip the man who lights up the stalactite grotto with magnesium wire, and something goes to the boatman who brought us there. We tip the waiter in the restaurant, and something goes off the waiter's wages. A vast machinery, whose existence we seldom realize, promotes the distribution of our wealth. When the concierge returned, Miss Raby asked, 'And what is the percentage?'

She asked with the definite intention of disconcerting him, not because she was unkind, but because she wished to discover what qualities, if any, lurked beneath that civil, efficient exterior. And the spirit of her inquiry was sentimental rather than scientific.

With an educated man she would have succeeded. In attempting to reply to her question, he would have revealed something. But the concierge had no reason to pay even lip service to logic. He replied: 'Yes, madam! this is perfect weather, both for our visitors and for the hay', and hurried to help a bishop, who was selecting a picture postcard.

Miss Raby, instead of moralizing on the inferior resources of the lower classes, acknowledged a defeat. She watched the man spreading out the postcards, helpful yet not obtrusive, alert yet deferential. She watched him make the bishop buy more than he wanted. This was the man who had talked of love to her upon the mountain. But hitherto he had only revealed his identity by chance gestures bequeathed to him at birth. Intercourse with the gentle classes had required new qualities – civility, omniscience, imperturbability. It was the old answer: the gentle classes were responsible for him. It is inevitable, as well as desirable, that we should bear each other's burdens.

It was absurd to blame Feo for his worldliness – for his essential vulgarity. He had not made himself. It was even absurd to regret his transformation from an athlete: his greasy stoutness, his big black kiss-curl, his waxed moustache, his chin which was dividing and propagating itself like some primitive form of life. In England, nearly twenty years before, she had altered his figure as well as his character. He was one of the products of 'The Eternal Moment'.

A great tenderness overcame her – the sadness of an unskilful demiurge, who makes a world and beholds that it is bad. She desired to ask pardon of her creatures, even though they were too poorly formed to grant it. The longing to confess, which she had suppressed that morning beside the bed of Signora Cantù, broke out again with the violence of a physical desire. When the bishop had gone she renewed the conversation, though on different lines, saying: 'Yes, it is beautiful weather. I have just been enjoying a walk up from the *Biscione*. I am stopping there!'

He saw that she was willing to talk, and replied pleasantly: 'The *Biscione* must be a very nice hotel: many people speak well of it. The fresco is very beautiful.' He was too shrewd to object to a little charity.

'What lots of new hotels there are!' She lowered her voice in order not to rouse the Prince, whose presence weighed on her curiously.

'Oh, madam! I should indeed think so. When I was a lad – excuse me one moment.'

An American girl, who was new to the country, came up with her hand full of coins, and asked him hopelessly 'whatever they were worth'. He explained, and gave her change: Miss Raby was not sure that he gave her right change.

'When I was a lad —' He was again interrupted, to speed two parting guests. One of them tipped him; he said 'Thank you.' The other did not tip him; he said 'Thank you' all the same but not in the same way. Obviously he had as yet no recollections of Miss Raby.

'When I was a lad, Vorta was a poor little place.'

'But a pleasant place?'

'Very pleasant, madam.'

'Kouf!' said the Russian Prince, suddenly waking up and startling them both. He clapped on a felt hat, and departed at full speed for a constitutional. Miss Raby and Feo were left together.

It was then that she ceased to hesitate, and determined to remind him that they had met before. All day she had sought for a spark of life, and it might be summoned by pointing to that other fire which she discerned, far back in the travelled distance, high up in the mountains of youth. What he would do, if he also discerned it, she did not know; but she hoped that he would become alive, that he at all events would escape the general doom which she had prepared for the place and the people. And what she would do, during their joint contemplation, she did not even consider.

She would hardly have ventured if the sufferings of the day had not hardened her. After much pain, respectability becomes ludicrous. And she had only to overcome the difficulty of Feo's being a man, not the difficulty of his being a concierge. She had never observed that spiritual reticence towards social inferiors which is usual at the present day.

'This is my second visit,' she said boldly. 'I stayed at the *Biscione* twenty years ago.'

He showed the first sign of emotion: *that* reference to the *Biscione* annoyed him.

'I was told I should find you up here,' continued Miss Raby. 'I remember you very well. You used to take us over the passes.'

She watched his face intently. She did not expect it to relax into an expansive smile. 'Ah!' he said, taking off his peaked cap, 'I remember you perfectly, madam. What a pleasure, if I may say so, to meet you again!'

'I am pleased, too,' said the lady, looking at him doubtfully.

'You and another lady, madam, was it not? Miss —'

'Mrs Harbottle.'

'To be sure; I carried your luggage. I often remember your kindness.'

She looked up. He was standing near an open window, and the whole of fairyland stretched behind him. Her sanity forsook her, and she said gently: 'Will you misunderstand me, if I say that I have never forgotten your kindness either?'

He replied: 'The kindness was yours, madam; I only did my duty.'

'Duty?' she cried; 'what about duty?'

'You and Miss Harbottle were such generous ladies. I well remember how grateful I was: you always paid me above the tariff fare —'

Then she realized that he had forgotten everything; forgotten her, forgotten what had happened, even forgotten what he was like when he was young.

'Stop being polite,' she said coldly. 'You were not polite when I saw you last.'

'I am very sorry,' he exclaimed, suddenly alarmed.

'Turn round. Look at the mountains.'

'Yes, yes.' His fishy eyes blinked nervously. He fiddled with his watch chain which lay in a furrow of his waistcoat. He ran away to warn some poorly dressed children off the view-terrace. When he returned she still insisted.

'I must tell you,' she said, in calm, business-like tones. 'Look at that great mountain, round which the road goes south. Look half-way up, on its eastern side – where the flowers are. It was there that you once gave yourself away.'

He gaped at her in horror. He remembered. He was inexpressibly shocked.

It was at that moment that Colonel Leyland returned.

She walked up to him, saying, 'This is the man I spoke of yesterday.'

'Good afternoon; what man?' said Colonel Leyland fussily. He saw that she was flushed, and concluded that someone had been rude to her. Since their relations were somewhat anomalous, he was all the more particular that she should be treated with respect.

'The man who fell in love with me when I was young.'

'It is untrue!' cried the wretched Feo, seeing at once the trap that had been laid for him. 'The lady imagined it. I swear, sir – I meant nothing. I was a lad. It was before I learnt behaviour. I had even forgotten it. She reminded me. She has disturbed me.'

'Good Lord!' said Colonel Leyland. 'Good Lord!'

'I shall lose my place, sir; and I have a wife and children. I shall be ruined.'

'Sufficient!' cried Colonel Leyland. 'Whatever Miss Raby's

intentions may be, she does not intend to ruin you.'

'You have misunderstood me, Feo,' said Miss Raby gently.

'How unlucky we have been missing each other,' said Colonel Leyland, in trembling tones that were meant to be nonchalant. 'Shall we go a little walk before dinner? I hope that you are stopping.'

She did not attend. She was watching Feo. His alarm had subsided; and he revealed a new emotion, even less agreeable to her. His shoulders straightened, he developed an irresistible smile, and, when he saw that she was looking and that Colonel Leyland was not, he winked at her.

It was a ghastly sight, perhaps the most hopelessly depressing of all the things she had seen at Vorta. But its effect on her was memorable. It evoked a complete vision of that same man as he had been twenty years before. She could see him to the smallest detail of his clothes or his hair, the flowers in his hand, the graze on his wrist, the heavy bundle that he had loosed from his back, so that he might speak as a freeman. She could hear his voice, neither insolent nor diffident, never threatening, never apologizing, urging her first in the studied phrases he had learnt from books, then, as his passion grew, becoming incoherent, crying that she must believe him, that she must love him in return, that she must fly with him to Italy, where they would live for ever, always happy, always young. She had cried out then, as a young lady should, and had thanked him not to insult her. And now, in her middle age, she cried out again, because the sudden shock and the contrast had worked a revelation. 'Don't think I'm in love with you now!' she cried.

For she realized that only now was she not in love with him: that the incident upon the mountain had been one of the great moments of her life – perhaps the greatest, certainly the most enduring: that she had drawn unacknowledged power and inspiration from it, just as trees draw vigour from a subterranean spring. Never again could she think of it as a half-humorous episode in her development. There was more reality in it than in all the years of success and varied achievement which had followed, and which it had rendered possible. For all her correct behaviour and lady-like display, she had been in love with Feo, and she had never loved so greatly again. A presumptuous boy had taken her to the gates of heaven; and, though she would not enter with him, the eternal remembrance of the vision had made life seem endurable and good.

Colonel Leyland, by her side, babbled respectabilities, trying to pass the situation off as normal. He was saving her, for he liked her very much, and it pained him when she was foolish. But her last remark to Feo had frightened him; and he began to feel that he must save himself. They were no longer alone. The bureau lady and the young gentleman were listening breathlessly, and the porters were tittering at the discomfiture of their superior. A French lady had spread amongst the guests the agreeable news that an Englishman had surprised his wife making love to the concierge. On the terrace outside, a mother waved away her daughters. The bishop was preparing, very leisurely, for a walk.

But Miss Raby was oblivious. 'How little I know!' she said. 'I never knew till now that I had loved him and that it was a mere chance – a little catch, a kink – that I never told him so.'

It was her habit to speak out; and there was no present passion to disturb or prevent her. She was still detached, looking back at a fire upon the mountains, marvelling at its increased radiance, but too far off to feel its heat. And by speaking out she believed, pathetically enough, that she was making herself intelligible. Her remark seemed inexpressibly coarse to Colonel Leyland.

'But these beautiful thoughts are a poor business, are they not?' she continued, addressing Feo, who was losing his gallant air and becoming bewildered. 'They're hardly enough to grow old on. I think I would give all my imagination, all my skill with words, if I could recapture one crude fact, if I could replace one single person whom I have broken.'

'Quite so, madam,' he responded, with downcast eyes.

'If only I could find someone here who would understand me, to whom I could confess, I think I should be happier. I have done so much harm in Vorta, dear Feo —'

Feo raised his eyes. Colonel Leyland struck his stick on the parquetry floor.

'— and at last I thought I would speak to you, in case you understood me. I remembered that you had once been very gracious to me – yes, gracious: there is no other word. But I have harmed you also: how could you understand?'

'Madam, I understand perfectly,' said the concierge, who had recovered a little and was determined to end the distressing scene, in which his reputation was endangered, and his vanity aroused only to be rebuffed. 'It is you who are mistaken. You have done me no harm at all. You have benefited me.'

'Precisely,' said Colonel Leyland. 'That is the conclusion of the whole matter. Miss Raby has been the making of Vorta.'

'Exactly, sir. After the lady's book, foreigners come, hotels are built, we all grow richer. When I first came here, I was a common ignorant porter who carried luggage over the passes; I worked, I found opportunities, I was pleasing to the visitors – and now!' He checked himself suddenly. 'Of course I am still but a poor man. My wife and children —'

'Children!' cried Miss Raby, suddenly seeing a path of salvation. 'What children have you?'

'Three dear little boys,' he replied, without enthusiasm.

'How old is the youngest?'

'Madam, five.'

'Let me have that child,' she said impressively, 'and I will bring him up. He shall live among rich people. He shall see that they are not the vile creatures he supposes, always clamouring for respect and deference and trying to buy them with money. Rich people are good: they are capable of sympathy and love: they are fond of the truth; and when they are with each other they are clever. Your boy shall learn this, and he shall try to teach it to you. And when he grows up, if God is good to him he shall teach the rich: he shall teach them not to be stupid to the poor. I have tried myself, and people buy my books and say that they are good, and smile and lay them down. But I know this: so long as the stupidity exists, not only our charities and missions and schools, but the whole of our civilization, are vain.'

It was painful for Colonel Leyland to listen to such phrases. He made one more effort to rescue Miss Raby. 'Je vous prie de ne pas —' he began gruffly, and then stopped, for he remembered that the concierge must know French. But Feo was not attending, nor, of course, had he attended to the lady's prophecies. He was wondering if he could persuade his wife to give up the little boy, and, if he did, how much they dare ask from Miss Raby without repulsing her.

'That will be my pardon,' she continued, 'if out of the place where I have done so much evil I bring some good. I am tired of memories, though they have been very beautiful. Now, Feo, I want you to give me something else : a living boy. I shall always puzzle you; and I cannot help it. I have changed so much since we met, and I have changed you also. We are both new people. Remember that; for I want to ask you one question before we part, and I cannot see why you shouldn't answer it. Feo! I want you to attend.'

'I beg your pardon, madam,' said the concierge, rousing himself from his calculations. 'Is there anything I can do for you?'

'Answer "yes" or "no"; that day when you said you were in love with me – was it true?'

It was doubtful whether he could have answered, whether he had now any opinion about that day at all. But he did not make the attempt. He saw again that he was menaced by an ugly, withered, elderly woman, who was trying to destroy his reputation and his domestic peace. He shrank towards Colonel Leyland, and faltered: 'Madam, you must excuse me, but I had rather you did not see my wife; she is so sharp. You are most kind about my little boy; but, madam, no, she would never permit it.'

'You have insulted a lady!' shouted the colonel, and made a chivalrous movement of attack. From the hall behind came exclamations of horror and expectancy. Someone ran for the manager.

Miss Raby interposed, saying, 'He will never think me respectable.' She looked at the dishevelled Feo, fat, perspiring, and unattractive, and smiled sadly at her own stupidity, not at his. It was useless to speak to him again; her talk had scared away his competence and his civility, and scarcely anything was left. He was hardly more human than a frightened rabbit. 'Poor man,' she murmured, 'I have only vexed him. But I wish he would have given me the boy. And I wish he would have answered my question, if only out of pity. He does not know the sort of thing that keeps me alive.' She was looking at Colonel Leyland, and so discovered that he too was discomposed. It was her peculiarity that she could only attend to the person she was speaking with, and forgot the personality of the listeners. 'I have been vexing you as well: I am very silly.'

'It is a little late to think about me,' said Colonel Leyland grimly.

She remembered their conversation of yesterday, and understood him at once. But for him she had no careful explanation, no tender pity. Here was a man who was well born and well educated, who had all those things called advantages, who imagined himself full of insight and cultivation and knowledge of mankind. And he had proved himself to be at the exact spiritual level of the man who had no advantages, who was poor and had been made vulgar, whose early virtue had been destroyed by circumstance, whose manliness and simplicity had perished in serving the rich. If Colonel Leyland also believed that she was now in love with Feo, she would not exert herself to undeceive him. Nor indeed would she have found it possible.

From the darkening valley there rose up the first strong singing note of the campanile, and she turned from the men towards it with a motion of love. But that day was not to close without the frustration of every hope. The sound inspired Feo to make conversation, and, as the mountains reverberated, he said: 'Is it not unfortunate, sir? A gentleman went to see our fine new tower this morning and he believes that the land is slipping from underneath, and that it will fall. Of course it will not harm us up here.'

His speech was successful. The stormy scene came to an abrupt and placid conclusion. Before they had realized it, she had taken up her *Baedeker* and left them, with no tragic gesture. In that moment of final failure, there had been vouchsafed to her a vision of herself, and she saw that she had lived worthily. She was conscious of a triumph over experience and earthly facts, a triumph magnificent, cold, hardly human, whose existence no one but herself would ever surmise. From the view-terrace she looked down on the perishing and perishable beauty of the valley, and, though she loved it no less, it seemed to be infinitely distant, like a valley in a star. At that moment, if kind voices had called her from the hotel, she would not have returned. 'I suppose this is old age,' she thought. 'It's not so very dreadful.'

No one did call her. Colonel Leyland would have liked to do so; for he knew she must be unhappy. But she had hurt him too much; she had exposed her thoughts and desires to a man of another class. Not only she, but he himself and all their equals, were degraded by it. She had discovered their nakedness to the alien.

People came in to dress for dinner and for the concert. From the hall there pressed out a stream of excited servants, filling the lounge as an operatic chorus fills the stage, and announcing the approach of the manager. It was impossible to pretend that nothing had happened. The scandal would be immense, and must be diminished as it best might.

Much as Colonel Leyland disliked touching people he took Feo by the arm, and then quickly raised his finger to his forehead.

'Exactly, sir,' whispered the concierge. 'Of course we understand – Oh, thank you, sir, thank you very much: thank you very much indeed!'